Of Tails, Curses and Kings

CIP - Kataložni zapis o publikaciji
Narodna in univerzitetna knjižnica, Ljubljana

821.163.6-31

POLIČAR, Justin Luka
    Of Tails, Curses and Kings: roman / Justin L. Poličar. - Brezje
: samozal., 2024

ISBN 978-961-07-1899-4
COBISS.SI-ID 177947907

Dedicated to my delightful family and friends.

Chapter 1

1

After a time, the villagers would eventually come to agree that the two must have been about as confused as the rest of them had been.

They appeared out of nowhere, in a flash of light in the middle of the village square, right next to a market stall. Many had missed it, as they had chosen that precise moment to blink, but in the next instant, they were there. Just standing there, looking around, confused.

That was when the screaming started. It ended only a moment later, when half of the people in the market turned to stone.

Most of those who had managed not to look at them ran as fast as they could towards any sort of shelter. Others hid in whatever spot they could find at a moment's notice.

"They started talking," one of them would later report. The man, he called her an idiot, and then told her to put on her mask. He said that she was making trouble for him again, in many harsh words.

"But then she got angry. She told him she was sick of wearing it. That she wanted to feel the sun on her face. I was so scared. I thought for sure I was going to die when they came over to me. What happened instead, though, was… strange. I turned to stone the moment I looked her in the eyes, I know, and after that, I was trapped in my own body, unable to move even my eyes. But I still heard everything."

After a time, the villagers started growing nervous. They began peeking out of their hiding spots, trying to find out where the two were, and how best to avoid them. They ran around, shouting for help and informing other villagers of the danger. One of them ran to the nearby army encampment to get help.

During that time, either oblivious or indifferent to the terror they inspired, the two made their way to the local tavern.

The old barkeep hadn't been warned of their appearance, and even if he had been, he wouldn't have believed a word of it. But upon seeing them, he found himself dropping his mug and taking a step back into the wooden counter, tipping over the jars of lukewarm beer behind him.

Instantly, the patrons of the bar went stiff.

The first of the two appeared normal enough, he had the human visage of a young man, though one could tell from a glance that he was no stranger to violence.

The woman, however, was another matter. Concealing her face then was a rusty golden mask that depicted a fanged, shouting woman's face, with black crystals covering her eyes and jeweled snakes peering over her forehead and hair. Only she had no real hair. In its place were real, live snakes, unlike those sculpted onto the mask, that hissed at everyone in the tavern, revealing fangs that dripped with poison.

And it was not only her hair that was inhuman. Far more noticeable than that, in retrospect, was her lower body, from the stomach down, where in the place of legs the girl had nothing but a long, green and black diamond patterned snake's tail.

She was a lamia, a monster thought to have been brought to extinction decades ago.

While everyone stared at her golden mask, paralyzed in fear, she and her companion simply looked around, puzzled, and made their way towards the barkeep. As soon as their backs were turned, the patrons ran off out of the tavern.

The apparently human man, shrugging, walked over and sat on one of the stools opposite the barkeep, while the half-snake slithering beside him did the same. She wriggled around uncomfortably on the small stool and wrapped her tail in loops around it.

"I hate drinking from under the veil," she complained with a strange accent. "It's impossible to do it without spilling. Hey, barkeep – what's up with everyone? The smell of fear is everywhere. Even you – you'll need a change of trousers."

The man looked towards the trembling barkeep. "He's not the only one, I imagine. Seriously, have you lost your mind? We're not in Aeliah anymore. Server, please get us some drinks, would you? I'm being plagued by a long parade of disappointments today; I'll need some assistance if I am to cope."

The lamia seemed to make a face at her companion, though it was hidden by her mask.

"Server, are you there?" she then asked, the snakes on her head coiling, ready to strike, while she waved a delicate hand in front of the barkeep's face. With stiff movements, he quickly turned around to create distance between them and shoved towards each of them a mug of ale that had not spilled.

"I don't understand why they're so scared of us," the lamia spoke to the young man. "Last time we were in Evaria, people were aware of mythics."

"Evidently, things have changed," the man said, downing his mug and handing it back to the barkeep for more. "I hope we really are in Evaria, at least. If that damned witch brought us to the wrong end of the world…"

"They probably think we're monsters," the lamia murmured.

"People will do that if you turn them to stone. Do you want to keep going, by the way? You could probably beat your score at Westmire if we continue like this. You're off to a great start. Hey! Don't hit me. Oh, you, relax, barkeep, I'm only joking. We're not looking to kill anyone right now. Except Lenah."

"Are we really back to that?" the lamia asked.

"Yes. Why do I need to keep telling you this? The fastest way to break a curse—"

"Is to kill the one who cast it, yeah, yeah. You're still not going to kill your friend."

"Friend? You clearly haven't been paying attention. What kind of friend would force such nonsense on me?"

"One with a sense of humor," the lamia laughed.

The barkeep, still shaking and frightened to breathe, handed him the refilled mug of ale without a word. The man, grimacing, tried to meet his gaze, but he avoided it.

"Where are we?" the man asked.

A moment passed in deathly silence.

"I'd rather not ask everything twice," he continued.

"The… the Garland, sir. In Coldbarrow, the kingdom of Evaria."

"The Garland being the name of the tavern, I take it. Thank the divines, we're in Evaria. Is Coldbarrow the right place?"

The lamia turned to him, stroking the vipers writhing on her head. "I think so. At the very least, we are in the north."

"Idiot, that's obvious. We were supposed to go north. But is this the right village? Any more brilliant insights?"

"Well… no."

The man snorted. "You're entirely unhelpful. Urgh. At this rate, we'll have to ask these damned humans our questions, once they're capable of answering us. Make them breathe again soon, will you?"

"I'll need some ravenwood for that."

"Yeah, yeah. And I'll have to be the one to get it. No way. It's your turn this time."

A small army of soldiers suddenly bounded into the tavern, then, their steel boots loudly thudding on the wooden floor. The man who'd run off from the market to get them had been quick. They wore steel plate armor and drew their swords in unison the moment they entered. The lamia gasped in surprise from behind her golden mask at the sight of them.

One more man, the soldiers' commander, walked into the tavern from behind the others.

"Remove your weapons and come quietly!" he shouted at the two with an authoritative voice.

Hearing that, the young man at the bar quietly chuckled.

"You're coming with us!" the knight yelled again. "And if I smell even a whiff of magic, I'll have my men cut you down like dogs!"

At that, the lamia leaned over to the man. "Like dogs, Emony," she said, apparently holding back a chuckle.

"Shut up," the man said.

One of the footmen roughly kicked aside a stool that was in the way between him and them. "Are you two deaf? Do as you're told!"

A moment of peace hung on a razer's edge.

"We have more men coming," said the commander from behind the other soldiers. "They'll be here in minutes."

The man and snake glanced at each other, shrugged, and downed their drinks. The lamia really did spill a lot of the ale. Upon seeing that, the man instantly jumped away from her so as not to get wet before quickly composing himself again.

"We don't have any weapons," he said, turning to the soldiers. "And you won't be needing yours. We'd be glad to come with you."

After a moment, the commander nodded and tapped one of the men in front of him on the shoulder. One by one, they stepped out of the tavern until they surrounded the door from the outside. The two strangers followed.

2

Yperian

Fear and paranoia filled the tent almost as quickly as the snakes on the lamia's head. That was just one of the things that bothered Yperian, the knight commander of the locally stationed field army and militia.

He was staring up at the golden mask beneath the writhing vipers, feeling himself growing nervous at the sight of them, when he noticed his men standing around in the background, clutching their sword handles in shaky readiness. He judged that he couldn't have them cut short the fragile peace.

"Leave us," he sordidly ordered them and looked away from the snakes. "All of you. Do your duties, I'm sure your captains have something for you."

He turned towards the two newcomers.

"Man, lamia, come closer and sit down. I hear you've been brought to me from the Garland. Would you like another drink?"

The pair walked and slithered towards him, barely making a sound as they did so.

"Please," the man answered, "We weren't finished yet at the tavern when your men came to get us."

Yperian filled up two silver chalices and placed them on the wooden desk in front of them before getting one himself and sitting down across from them.

"I apologize for that. You must understand that they were shocked after seeing human beings turn into statues. They must have thought the men of the lake were attacking us again, thus the haste. I'm glad they were wrong. But anyway – I am Yperian, knight commander of this field legion. Talk to me. Who are you, why did you come here and why shouldn't I have you executed?"

With one hand, he raised the silver chalice towards his lips, and put his other hand on the hilt of his sheathed dagger. The man before him was eyeing him like a piece of meat. He wondered what kind of monster the latter was, to be found accompanying a being as obviously cursed as this lamia.

"Thirteen men and women lost their lives today," he continued. "And it's clear you were the cause. You have the Eyes, don't you, snake? That must be why this happened."

"You know of my curse?" she asked.

"I'm somewhat well-versed in the old legends. Of course, it's entirely something else to bear witness to them – but as it turns out, I'm also aware that the effects of a curse may be reversed if its source is killed. "Kill the caster, break the curse," and all that. It's possible to save the villagers."

"Not that way," the man interrupted. "The Eyes are no lesser knot of black magic. If you kill her, those villagers remain pretty rocks until the end of time. Anyway, my name is Emony, and this is Tiphaine. You know what she is. I'm human."

The lamia, Tiphaine, turned her jeweled gaze curiously towards the man, but said nothing. It was obvious that his description didn't match up – and he was probably also lying about the lamia's legendary curse. Unfortunately, Yperian couldn't challenge him about it.

"It's a pleasure to make your acquaintance," he said.

The man continued: "We were teleported here by an unreliable, idiotic witch named Lenah. She forgot to mention we would be appearing right in the middle of a village, thus the unfortunate accident. We were told by the barkeep in the tavern that we are in the kingdom of Evaria, though."

"We're northeast of the capital, Terrena. You say a witch brought you here? Where from? For what purpose?"

The man took a few careful sips of his wine. Yperian was sure he was trying to see if the drink was poisoned. It wasn't. He also noticed the man did not let the silver touch his skin, covering it with his sleeve. A peculiar action, one that got him thinking.

"We've come from Aeliah. It's an island a few days sail from the continent, if you believe it exists. We're here to break a curse, we were told there may be an expert on them somewhere nearby – if we are in the right place, that is."

"I've never heard of Aeliah."

"But you have heard of curses, clearly. Have you perhaps recently noted anything strange about the water?"

"Actually, yes, now that you mention it. Something has been defiling this place of late. Unnatural powers are stirring in the lake."

Yperian noticed the man's pupils expand for a moment, betraying surprise. He downed his chalice quickly.

"Haha. You know, that's the first promising news I've heard all day. Tell me about it."

"I really don't see how anyone could describe the situation as "promising". Rotting corpses are walking out of the lake about two miles from here and attacking people. My field legion was dispatched from Terrena to help the militia protect the locals. This started about two months ago. Could it be the reason you've decided to come here?"

"Perhaps," the man said, provoking another look from the snake.

"So, you mean to help us break the curse that defiles the lake?" he asked. "Is that what I am to believe?"

"We have indeed come to break a curse. Do the dead have some sort of ruler? A mermaid, perhaps?"

Yperian scratched his chin. "Hm… Interesting you mention rulers and mermaids. I've received reports of both. The locals mentioned an old legend about this place being home to mermaids. Something about the village not ending on the shore.

They say that before the arrival of the men of the lake, they could hear singing every night that seemed to come from the water. Apparently, a mermaid was to blame. Since then, they seem to have ceased, though, and all of the militiamen have been telling me of some "king" terrorizing the place instead, which would be a strange coincidence, except that the last king of Evaria, the late Aulduyen, really did die here."

The snake sitting beside the man whispered something to him. Upon hearing that, his lips stretched into a tight smile.

"Then we may be in the right place. I believe we can help each other."

"Is that so? You seem to be hiding quite a lot. Though honestly, despite your uncommon, mythic nature, I wouldn't be opposed to cooperation, if we could all benefit from it. But, of course, that can only begin with trust."

The man exchanged glances with the snake.

"Trust and cooperation are beautiful things. In the name of building them, we'll correct the mistake my companion made. We'll unpetrify the villagers."

"You can do that?"

"Of course," the lamia said. Yperian hid the sudden rise of nervousness from his face upon glancing again at her coiling hair of serpents. "I just need some—"

"Trade secrets," the man interrupted. "But we will do it. There is more than one way to break a curse."

Yperian leaned back in his chair, considering what to say next. He knew far too little about mythics and the dark arts. What if there was a catch? But the curse of the Eyes the lamia possessed was a legend. Only one unfortunate snake in the whole world possessed it at any given time. Who knew if his small force could defeat her in battle? And what the consequences of killing her would really be?

"If you are successful, you will have my gratitude," he said, opting to gain some more time to plan any potential course of action. "Along with that of many others. What about the witch that brought you here? Should we prepare for any more unexpected arrivals?"

"I couldn't tell you," the man said. "This witch is unpredictable. At any rate, we need to go on an errand. Gather the statues in one place, if you please. We'll make them breathe again soon."

Chapter 2

1

Emony

Afterwards, that same afternoon, Emony was lounging on a tree branch high above a small stream, watching Tiphaine gather ravenwood bark from the darkened trees, avoiding both her petrifying eyes and doing the work himself. She had put off her mask; she had been complaining that she wanted to feel the sun on her skin again.

"Don't you know that I'm cold-blooded? How many times do I have to tell you? You keep forgetting and making me go to cold places!"

I didn't ask you to come, he thought.

Unfortunately, he couldn't say anything, for he knew perfectly well that if she turned him into a rock on that tree, she wouldn't be capable or willing to climb up it and revive him. Still, his position high above her did have its perks. Specifically, it was fairly comfortable up on the branch, and its view let him avoid his companion's eyes while peeping at her best assets from an alluringly revealing angle.

She really isn't dressed for the cold, he thought to himself.

Anyway, as long as he could stare in peace, he could convince himself that she was a pretty good person to get teleported to another continent with to break the newest annoying curse Lenah *accidentally* put on him. Not to mention, after he murdered that witch, she would be the only friend he had left.

And she certainly was pretty… But nothing could last.

The vipers on top of her head noticed his gaze and began hissing in his direction. Quickly committing to memory what he saw, he looked straight ahead before he could get caught.

"You could help me, you know!" Tiphaine shouted in some random direction.

He considered it for a brief second before once again surveying the surrounding area instead. The ten soldiers secretly sent to follow them were hiding behind trees and bushes about fifty feet away.

He wondered what their orders were. Probably nothing dangerous to them just yet. They apparently harbored hope that the two of them would help them destroy the "men of the lake", whatever those were, and hadn't realized how easily Tiphaine and her legendary curse could be defeated.

Still, it'd be best if he watched out for her and warned her of any reflective surfaces. Speaking of which…

"Careful about the stream. The water's pretty still, you might see your reflection."

"Hm? Where are you? Ohhh. Haha, I thought dogs couldn't climb trees. Maybe Lenah's curse is actually an upgrade? But anyway, do you really think I'm that stupid? I'm not like you—"

Abrupt silence. That could only mean one thing.

Emony looked down. Sure enough, the idiot had petrified herself again. Sighing, he leisurely jumped off the tree and landed a few feet away from her on a bed of fallen leaves.

"You were saying?" he asked, poking her rock-solid forehead. He could look at her face safely when she was a rock without fear of becoming one himself, so he took advantage of the opportunity. It was a beautiful sight, even if she was all gray – he almost lost his train of thought.

"I must have misheard," he continued, "did you call me a dog again? You stupid, unobservant, cold-blooded—"

At that moment, his senses detected something strange. His finger, still poking her stone forehead, was vibrating. *Oh, no.*

It was happening again. The vibration was spreading – just like it would before he'd transform into a wolf on a full moon, though Lenah's curse had changed everything else. Though the sun had yet to go down, he was powerless and couldn't resist what was coming. The vibration was darting towards his heart from the finger that had touched Tiphaine.

"You devious, irredeemable little snake…"

That was the last thought he had before he abruptly lost the fight to resist the change.

It happened instantaneously. Irritated as he was, he flopped down to the ground within the second, losing the balance he normally would have had on four legs. But that was because he didn't have four legs. He didn't even have two anymore. His aberrating mind only registered one, and it certainly wasn't that of a wolf.

With only the slightest sliver of hope that it would be different this time, he tried lifting his torso off the ground.

The hope died. It was difficult – once again, he had those humanlike arms that were not his own. They were slim and frail, even more so than Tiphaine's, barely more than soft skin and bone.

Grimacing, he rolled onto his side so that he was lying on his back. Seeing the rest, he was forced to accept what he'd become again.

Instead of the limbs and dark fur of a giant and menacing werewolf, he witnessed bare female breasts on a chest that didn't look at all like his own, and that long, scaly, golden fish's tail.

Emony's pants had been ripped apart and were lying uselessly atop her widened hips… *wait, what? Her? Her?!* By the divines, she wasn't just imagining it, there really was magic strangling her mind! *That damned witch!*

"Tiphaine, if you did that on purpose," Emony hissed, before *her* embarrassment defeated her anger. Her voice had been changed, too. It was a high-pitched, girly squeak that perfectly matched her disgustingly cute new appearance. Sitting up straight, Emony saw that the fin at the end of her tail was touching the water of the stream. She'd have to dry herself off to change back, and that wouldn't be so easy, given how weak her new body was. At least for the near future, she was stuck as a mermaid. And her mind was poisoned.

"Tiphaine, what kind of idiot petrifies herself to do this to me?" Emony asked herself.

She let her upper body drop back to the ground with a thud, hoping to escape reality for a moment, just lying on the fallen leaves and letting the dread envelop her.

"So Lenah puts a horrible curse on me, and you delight in triggering it. I don't have any real friends at all, do I?"

Emony's emotions were spiraling in all directions. Eventually, after a long period of shock and contemplation, one emerged victorious. She turned her stare away from her newfound breasts and gazed at the sky.

"I'm going to murder you, Tiphaine," she said with that cute tone. "Not just Lenah, but you too. And everyone else that was even remotely involved in making me like this. I'm going to slaughter you all."

Suddenly, embracing the thought, Emony could hear a high-pitched, downright adorable giggle escape her small lips. She could feel tears in her own eyes, it was such a profoundly beautiful thing that she was imagining, Tiphaine squirming underneath her while she got her revenge.

It was enough even to make Emony forget for a moment that, years ago, she'd orphaned the both of them.

Wait, what? I didn't—

...

A moment later, she lost the thought.

She heard leaves rustling behind her. Quickly, pushing herself with her tail, Emony rolled back onto her stomach and found herself facing one of the soldiers who had been following her and Tiphaine. Emony was being stared at in shock. At first, the human looked over her tail, then her eyes, but his gaze eventually settled on her altered chest. At that, an atypical, disturbing shyness overcame her.

"Back off, human," Emony spat at the man. "Or I'll feed you your own guts!"

A frown appeared on her face as soon as she heard her own words. She truly did hate how unthreatening, and in fact, endearing her voice had sounded while issuing the threat, but she quickly realized she had more to worry about than just the strings of magic messing with her brain. She couldn't move, let alone fight, in this form, and Tiphaine was a statue. How had things gotten so bad so quickly?!

But the human obeyed her without question or delay, taking a step away from her. "What's going on?" he asked, unnerved. "Why are my legs moving without my…"

Oh, yeah, that's right.

"I'm a siren, according to the damned witch, so I can control your mind with my song. And I'm not even singing, my voice is just that damned pretty. Divines, I really want to kill something. But no, leave, and forget what you saw here," Emony said grimly. "Go report to your commander or something."

The man's pupils dilated to an unnatural size, covering nearly his whole irises. "Yes," he murmured, seemingly in a trance, and ran away.

Emony, shaking her head – oh no… she had to hurry. Rolling her eyes, Emony grabbed some of the ravenwood bark Tiphaine had gathered on the ground before realizing she couldn't get up to feed it to her. After a moment of thought, Emony raised her hand and began the necessary deed.

She missed about twenty times before she succeeded in throwing the wood into Tiphaine's mouth. Now, with a little luck, the damned snake could finally help her dry off.

When the bark touched Tiphaine's lips, the color slowly began to return to them. The magic was absorbed. But, damn it, she needed more. Emony kept throwing.

For some reason, though, every time the color reached Tiphaine's eyes, the stone enveloped her again. A whole minute had gone by before Emony realized she was an idiot too, and she understood why. Then she started to wonder how she could cover her eyes, which were stuck gazing into the water.

The idea that eventually came to her was glorious.

"Haha! This is your own fault, Tiphaine," Emony laughed, smiling again despite being stuck as a mermaid, as she gathered some dirt in her hand and turned it to mud with the help of the stream. "Remember that!"

Then, with a rare spark of glee, she threw the mud.

2

"Emony!" Tiphaine shrieked a few minutes later. She hadn't seen the color come back to her face, covered with mud as it was. At least it looked like her solution had worked.

"Emony, why in undeath did you do that?!" she shouted, wiping it from her eyes.

"Tiphaine, look away! I understand that you're upset, but – I said look away! Before you wipe it off! You're going to become a rock again!"

At least Tiphaine still listened to her.

"You stupid dog! Where are you?! You didn't have to go that far! I was just having a little fun!" shouted Tiphaine.

"Don't move, Tiphaine, you're going to hit your head on a tree! Stop going forward! Thank you. Now, then… Are you dumb?! You petrified yourself and did this to me for fun?! Do you have any idea of the kind of crisis I am having in my mind right now?! Hey! Don't look in that direction! Stupid snake, you deserved it and you know it! I said, don't look in that direction! Don't you dare petrify yourself again, or I'll have to do it all over again!"

"Don't you dare!" Tiphaine sobbed.

Slowly, Emony's *friend* removed the mud from her eyes and flicked it away from her fingers before carefully peeking through them and looking at her.

"Come here," Emony said, beckoning towards her whilst avoiding her gaze. "You missed a bit. But close your eyes, don't make me a statue now."

While Tiphaine slithered over and laid down next to her, Emony wet her hands in the stream and helped her clean up her face. It was difficult for Tiphaine to do it all herself, since she couldn't risk looking at it. Once Emony was done, Tiphaine slithered away to grab her mask and put it back on.

"You're pretty cute again, though. It was worth the trouble," the damned snake said.

"Shut up."

Again, the cuteness of her new voice disturbed Emony. Not to mention the magic she could acutely feel tying itself in knots in her mind.

"Oh, don't worry, Emony, you still look really threatening! Yes, that's the expression! You're so adorable – I mean scary! Definitely scary! Here, fishy doggy!"

"By the divines, Tiphaine, as soon as this curse is lifted and I'm a werewolf again, I will eat your living hair-vipers while you watch. Shut up!"

Though Tiphaine was laughing, her mouth slammed shut in an instant. Emony noticed her pupils dilate for a moment, just like the soldier's had.

She hadn't meant to do that.

"I'm sorry! Divines, are you okay? You can speak again," Emony said. "You didn't bite off your tongue, did you?"

Tiphaine opened her mouth and started checking up on her jaw.

"Are you okay?" Emony asked again.

"Yeah. I'm fine. You're pretty mean today, Emony."

Emony looked away. "Yeah, I know. I'm sorry, I've had a stressful week. I'll make it up to you."

Tiphaine stared at her suspiciously from behind her mask for a moment before gazing to the side, lost in thought.

"I'll help you dry off."

A few minutes later, with immeasurable relief, Emony felt her body begin to vibrate again, and powerful legs once again replaced her golden-scaled tail. As soon as she dared risk it, she patted herself … himself down and looked down under his tunic. The breasts were gone. *He* was a man again.

With immense relief Emony noticed the strings of magic begin losing their grip on his mind. He was becoming himself again.

"Praise all that is divine," he said, gazing up at the sky.

"Your pants are a little… gone," Tiphaine said beside him, looking in another direction while the vipers on her head stared at him curiously. "It wasn't me."

"Technically it was, since you tricked me into transforming. But whatever. So much for Lenah's magical unrippable clothing. I knew she was a useless, stupid little witch. Where's my backpack?"

His companion slithered over to a nearby tree and threw the thing over to him. Luckily, he managed to find his pair of backup pants in it. He'd need to get a new backup, though.

"So, do you want to go check out the lake later? You think your friend is in there?" he asked.

"Well, I can smell a lot of magic in the air, so there's definitely something," Tiphaine responded. He missed his own empowered sense of smell. "But I don't know if it's her. She doesn't do dark magic. And the most potent smell is… death.

Look how many ravenwood trees there are around here."

"You're right, there are a lot of them. Lucky for the petrified villagers, I suppose, but something pretty bad must have happened here in the past. Perhaps those "men of the lake" the humans mentioned are connected to it. You know, I don't remember Lenah saying anything about any black magic in the area. I thought we were just going to have a nice, friendly little chat with your mermaid friend."

"Yeah, me too. But if Verena's really in the lake with those undead and some king... Emony... I'm worried. Can we check up on her?"

Emony scratched his chin. "'I wonder... I can't exactly fight off an army of the undead as a fish, so should we side with the humans? That'd leave a bad taste in my mouth – but at the very least, we need more information. For now, let's play nice. Let's get back to camp."

Chapter 3

1

Yperian

"The villagers are still afraid of you. The soldiers are, too, so I'm sure you understand my hesitation."

They were sitting in the knight commander's tent again, just minutes after depetrifying fifty-six people.

"I understand perfectly, but we have things to do."

Yperian turned his gaze back towards the pair.

The masked snake, Tiphaine, was still struggling to sit comfortably in her chair, which was poorly suited to a member of her species. He wondered what she looked like under her mask. The unpetrified villagers said she had a human-looking, enchantingly beautiful face. Green eyes. Still, he'd rather not see it if it meant he would become a statue.

Yperian shook his head and took a sip of his drink, weighing his options. Mythics of any kind were not to be tolerated in Evaria, by order of the king. That decree was made years ago. Still, attempting to have these two killed could very likely turn out to be a bad decision – He still didn't know for sure if they were friend or foe, and, more importantly, he didn't know if they could be beaten. His men couldn't even look at the snake. How could they win a battle with their eyes closed?

Lorick, one of the men sent after them into the forest, had come to report back to him ahead of the group, witless and confused, saying he saw nothing at all. It was unnervingly strange… They had obviously done something to him. Perhaps the man was a sorcerer. He did claim to be friendly with a witch…

A soldier carrying a jug of wine and some clothes entered the tent. Yperian noticed that the man, Emony, flinched at the sight of the liquid and subtly leaned away. He beckoned the soldier to put the things on the table and leave.

"You requested a pair of pants, along with these furs," he said, taking the jug and pouring himself some more wine. "You seem to have changed already, though, so you clearly have two pairs already. Why do you need a third?"

"One can never have enough," Emony responded, giving the warmest of the offered clothing to his companion. "This is for you, Tiphaine."

"Thanks."

Yperian shrugged. "No matter. Would you like another drink?"

"No, thank you. I haven't finished the previous one. Anyway, since you'd prefer us not to go to the village, where would you have us sleep?"

"I've arranged for a tent on the far end of the encampment. You will be given suitable lodgings."

"I hope it's in the sun," said Tiphaine from behind her mask, stretching her arms and putting on the offered furs. "It's freezing around here."

Especially for the cold-blooded, Yperian thought. He noticed the man shift in his seat closer towards her.

"Unfortunately, the days are getting shorter," he said. "It will get colder before it gets warmer, though snow likely won't fall for another month or two. That said, if you are to be our allies, you'll be welcome by our fire."

The lamia's vipers ceased their quiet hissing for a moment. "Thank you," she said.

"On that note, I'd like to thank you for reviving the villagers. Many of my men had family among them, and they are very happy to have them back."

"I'm sure they have enough to deal with already, with those undead," she responded.

"Tell us what you think of us," Emony said suddenly, interrupting them. His tone had completely changed. It was as though he were attempting to sing.

"What do you mean?" asked Yperian.

Emony blinked, seemingly unnerved for a moment, before exchanging a glance with Tiphaine and regaining his composure. "Nothing in particular. I'd simply like to know what you would like our relationship to look like in the near future."

Is he actually trying to sing? Yperian thought. He must have drunk more than he'd thought.

"Well," Yperian said honestly, "I don't know what to think of you. You appeared here out of the blue, turning half the villagers to stone. We thought you might be connected with the men of the lake, the other hostile mythics in the area, but then, upon our request, you revived everyone. So, neither of you are mindless aggressors, as the men of the lake seem to be. In fact, your friend Tiphaine really does seem to be cursed with the legendary. Eyes, which, as unfortunate as it is, would explain some of today's nonsense. I would wager you may really not be connected with the men of the lake. Most of us are afraid of you regardless, of course, given your nature and capabilities, and none of us know just about anything about you, other than that you claim to be willing to aid us."

The lamia turned her head towards her partner again, while he simply offered Yperian a smile that didn't reach his eyes.

He still wasn't entirely sure which of the two would pose a greater threat if it came to violence.

"At any rate, despite the law, we'd appreciate your help, and we would be happy to reward you for it. However, as mythics and magic have been officially forbidden from entering Evaria under the penalty of death, we cannot exactly let you two roam freely."

"Do you really think you can prevent us from doing so?" Emony asked.

Gazing towards the two, Yperian honestly pondered the question in his mind. How many lives would it take to end theirs? Perhaps simply having them followed would suffice.

"Well, I suppose it would be unnecessary to move against you right at this moment. The law states exceptions can be made for mythics that prove themselves allies of humanity. I would have you do so, so that the king in Terrena won't come for my head."

"You would have us abide by your human laws?" Emony said, sipping his drink while staring at him.

"Earlier, you claimed to be human yourself," Yperian said in turn. "I speak only to the lamia. What say you, Tiphaine?"

In response, the man gave him a particularly venomous smile.

"Come on, Emony," Tiphaine said. "We have stuff to do here anyway. Let's not make enemies for no reason. Besides, how dangerous can those men of the lake be? I mean, even if they're undead, they're just human. No offense, sir."

"None taken, but I believe you may be underestimating them. Those cadavers are formidable foes. What do you know of necromancy?"

"Not a thing," Emony said.

"I take it you, lady Tiphaine, cannot simply turn them to stone with a glance? Your curse is legend."

"Thoroughly impossible," Emony interrupted. "Her power doesn't work on magical beings or dead people. Only on the living."

If that was to be believed, it would seem that they were natural enemies, Yperian thought. Still, if they could help them push back the men of the lake… That was an impossibly enticing prospect. And it wasn't the lamia's fault she was cursed with the Eyes. The divines were often cruel to the least deserving. She seemed to be the friendlier of the two.

"Alright, then. I will allow you to leave our encampment, to go about your business. I'd advise you to stay in camp until tomorrow, though, and especially, to stay away from the lake. It's only a matter of time until the corpses attack again. So far, they've always come during rain, and we are expecting some tonight."

2

Emony

The knight commander personally led the pair to their tent after their conversation, with assurances that they would not be disturbed in the night unless it were necessary. Their place of sleep was somewhat distant from the rest of the soldiers' tents. Emony couldn't really complain about that – only that he was expected to share a space with Tiphaine. Sleeping next to her was always a dreadful experience. Whether she only wrapped herself around him to get warm and ended up breaking his bones or also turned him into a rock, he just couldn't win.

Her sleeping face was stupidly cute, though. And after some initial panic, he could sleep just fine while being a statue.

A trio of torches illuminated the area surrounding the tent, apparently for her benefit, but likely to actually make it easier for the soldiers watching them to track their movements. The soldiers were sitting around fires all around the encampment, keeping warm with their weapons in their scabbards. Some were staring at him and Tiphaine, while others gazed nervously into the darkness under the trees surrounding the camp.

Though he couldn't smell their fear, not being a werewolf at the moment, he could tell they were all very anxious. Perhaps the men of the lake were really more dangerous than he'd thought.

He and Tiphaine entered their medium-sized tent. It was a simple one, with a big pile of straw and blankets in the center of it and a small table at the side. A waterskin lay on the table, beside a silver chalice that would normally burn Emony if he touched it. The stale air was illuminated somewhat by the light of the torches outside.

I miss being a werewolf, he thought, poking at the silver and feeling nothing.

"I trust you haven't really put your faith in that man?" he asked Tiphaine. It was nice that she was appeasing him and letting him do most of the talking, but he couldn't have her thinking anything foolish. In this situation, he wasn't sure how well he could protect the two of them what with his supernatural strength, speed and ferocity being replaced by the unreliable powers of a half-fish. After his embarrassing experiment back in the commander's tent, he'd surmised he could only use his siren power when he had a tail. When he was a female.

His body shook at the thought.

"Tiphaine, how about we go meet your friend? he asked.

"What?" she asked, "What do you mean? We have to stay in here, didn't you hear the commander? The men of the lake may come tonight."

"Do you mean to take orders from the humans? We don't even know for sure that those undead are our enemies if your friend is in the lake among them. I think we should leave, Tiphaine. Either that, or you stay up all night, turning anyone that comes too close into a rock. We can't trust these people not to murder us in our sleep."

"You're always far too paranoid about humans, Emony. You just want to do the opposite of what they say. Look, the knight commander said the men of the lake swarm the whole forest when they attack."

"It's not paranoia if they are actually out to get you, Tiphaine. Anyway, you're right, the human did say that, but there is also something he failed to explain. Did you notice? Don't you find it strange that all of the soldiers are still here? The village they're supposed to protect, right next to the lake, has been left defenseless, while all these soldiers are just sitting around on top of this hill. Don't you find that weird? It's just a guess but... what if the men of the lake, if they really do exist, are going to come straight here? That would explain why they've built up all these nice walls and left the people they're supposed to be protecting to fend for themselves, don't you think?"

"I'm not so sure…"

"Neither am I. But I think it's either that, or there are no men of the lake, and after spinning that web of lies, they're grouping up because they plan on killing us tonight, so it makes sense that they should all be present. Either way, I think we should leave."

"I don't know, Emony. I don't think that man was lying. The magic in the air is getting really thick, and it's all black. No, really, I'm serious. All of it is black."

"Is it that bad? I wish I could still smell it, myself. Then… do you think we should run away? Not to the lake, in the opposite direction?"

Tiphaine nodded. "That might be a good idea. I'd rather not leave all these people to die, but… but if we do, then let's leave now, before it starts raining. I don't want to have to drag a mermaid around a forest while it rains."

Emony stuck his head out of the tent and looked at the sky.

"Then we don't have long. Let's go."

3

"It's cold out here," Tiphaine shuddered, covering her shoulders with the humans' blanket only a minute after they had left the tent. "I wish we could just stay by the fire…"

"I mentioned the necessity of being quiet thirty seconds ago!" Emony whispered, holding out his hand. "I thought you agreed we should leave?

Come on. Quickly. I think the lake is that way. Your plan – we're going in the opposite direction."

Tiphaine took his hand, likely appreciating the warmth, and nodded.

They silently made their way to the nearby tree line, keeping their distance from the light of the torches surrounding the encampment. Soldiers were standing around, keeping watch, but they didn't seem to notice them leave. Over the years, the two of them had gotten very good at sneaking around. They passed beyond their perimeter without incident. Honestly, it was child's play.

In fact, Emony thought it might have gone too smoothly, and he became anxious that they might have been followed. His senses had been dulled by his becoming a mermaid a few weeks ago – his werewolf hearing and sense of smell, as well as his ability to see in the dark, were nothing compared to how they had been before. He was practically as limited as one of the humans he scorned.

Which is why he made sure to take extra precautions, stopping in the shadows and listening for a few moments every now and then before moving on. Tiphaine, too, remained quieter than the wind.

Just as they started to move again from one of the trees, thunder began to roll across the sky. Dark clouds covered the rising moon, promising rain that would take away his legs. Looking back, Emony noticed the camp sentries begin groaning and covering themselves with long cloaks, while others ran around with torches preparing fires.

Should we turn back? he wondered. If there really was an army of undead roaming about, he could use the humans as a meat shield for him and Tiphaine if they chose to remain with them.

"We're running out of time," whispered Tiphaine next to him, pulling him out of his thoughts. "The magic is getting even thicker. I'm sure something is going to happen once the rain comes – and then you won't be able to move. We have to hurry."

"Agreed. Let's go."

"Okay. Wait, what—"

As soon as he turned to look at her, Emony saw the sword being held to his neck. Holding it was a man in steel plate armor and a helmet. This human he somehow recognized, it was one of those that had ordered them out of the tavern hours earlier.

"I knew you were traitors," the knight growled. "You monsters always stick together. You scum have friends in that lake?"

Emony sighed. His senses really must have dulled more than he'd thought, since a human managed to sneak up on them. Though Tiphaine hadn't noticed him either.

The blade suddenly cut three inches forward, reaching his skin and drawing a small trickle of blood.

"Not a move, snake! Or I slit his throat!" the human shouted. "You won't manage to turn me to stone before I do. What are you, anyway, vagabond? Her wretchedness is visible, at least, but you are clearly a beast as well, since you are with her. So, what are you? And what are you up to? Answer me!"

Emony weighed up the situation and his options. Considering his dulled senses and lack of supernatural strength, aggressive resistance could well lead to his death, though he doubted it.

"Answer me, I said!"

He subtly glanced past the human's blade, over at Tiphaine. She was terrified by this human.

That made him irritated. He noticed the skin on his neck starting to vibrate in a familiar way, though it hadn't started to rain yet.

The blood, he realized. The transformation was coming, slowly, from where the blood the human had drawn was leaking onto his skin. It was a weak vibration – but it was an option. Focusing his mind, he leaned into it, giving himself over to the change and signaling Tiphaine with a wink.

"So, what is more important to you?" he asked the human, buying time for the transformation to surge through his body. "Killing me, or saving everyone in that camp? Because the men of the lake are coming. I know exactly how it's going to happen."

"I have no problem killing every last one of you monsters," the knight responded menacingly. "Well? Where are the drowned going to attack from tonight? How many are coming? Hm? What is – don't move!"

The change happened in no more than an instant, as he forced the magic to wash over him. The human jumped back for a split second, thinking it was a form of attack, before leaping forward again and bringing his sword down towards him. He was too late.

The same moment the magic tied itself around her tongue, before she lost her balance and flopped onto the ground, Emony laced her voice with magic:

"Stop."

The man became stiff in an instant, ceasing his movements halfway, not stirring a muscle. The sword stopped an inch from Emony's head.

Tiphaine caught Emony in her arms. "My turn?" she asked. "We don't know how long that magic lasts."

"No. They know your petrification can be reversed. You, human. Die."

Hearing the last word, the knight's eyes widened in sudden panic. Moments later, he began wheezing, struggling for breath, flailing around with his entire body and losing his footing.

"Help!" the human cried, losing his voice. "Men, aid me! The beasts! The beasts, stop them!"

"Urgh," Emony said, grimacing. The magic hadn't worked as quickly as she'd hoped. The man was making a racket. *She* should have told him to die quietly. Urgh, and that *she* nonsense was back, too.

"What do we do?" asked Tiphaine, panicking.

"Wipe the blood off my neck! I need legs!" Emony hissed.

Tiphaine did so quickly while the dying man screamed, and right after Emony's twin limbs returned to him, he picked up the human's sword and finished the deed more quickly.

But likely not quickly enough. Lightning was already flashing through the sky, accompanying the roaring thunder. It was only a matter of time before he lost his legs and mind again, just as he had lost his pants.

"We need to leave, now!"

Tiphaine didn't need any encouragement. As quickly as she could, she nodded and grabbed his hand before speeding away through the undergrowth of the forest, leading the way through the darkness.

"Sir Meheyn!" they heard the shouting a minute later. "Sir Meheyn – he's... He's dead! There are enemies in the area!"

"Sound the alarm! The men of the lake must be here!"

"It's not even raining yet! How?! The scouts haven't reported anything! What if it's the newcomers?!"

They ran. The dark shadows of the forest were now being constantly illuminated by lightning. Emony swore, hearing the shouts of the humans continue behind them, and the thudding of their metal boots running across the tree roots and stones on their trail. That was when the rain began to pour from the sky.

"Patrols, out! Be on your guard!"

Shouting was coming from all around them. It seemed there were even more human soldiers guarding the forest than he had thought.

"I'm starting to transform, Tiphaine," he hissed while he ran, vibrations spreading from every spot the rain touched his skin. "I can't hold it off for long!"

"Let me know when it happens! I've got you!" she shouted back to him.

Emony saw shadows moving in front of them as a flash of lightning illuminated the forest. *But the humans are behind us!*

His confusion didn't last longer than a moment. Through the rain, he heard an inhuman gurgling. A second streak of white in the sky revealed the monsters that were suddenly racing towards them. And they really were monsters. Just as the knight commander had described them, they were corpses in varying stages of decay, racing through the undergrowth on whatever limbs they had left, wielding rusted, bloodied swords with their broken fingers.

"Duck!" he shouted to Tiphaine. She swerved at the last moment, dodging a blackened blade belonging to one of the monsters. Furious, he slashed forward with his own, with the sword he'd just stolen from the human, and cut into the thing's ribcage before slamming it upwards and slicing open the rotting flesh from stomach to forehead.

The undead monster only stared at him with empty eye sockets. Then it raised its sword again.

"Emony!" shrieked Tiphaine, just ahead of him.

Well, she's worried, he thought in that moment, smiling despite it all while watching the blade come down. Then he dodged it with a lithe sidestep and threw his sword spinning toward the corpse's neck, slamming the monster into a nearby tree and decapitating it.

Then, seeing more of the things approaching, he quickly darted over to Tiphaine, grabbed her hand and yanked her after him.

"This way! Don't stop!" he shouted to make sure she heard him over the thunder. Discretion was pointless now. "Men of the lake! We come in peace, to speak to Verena! We are not your enemies!"

"What was that?! The men of the lake are coming! Here, men! They're here! I can see them! We need reinforcements!" a human voice shouted behind them.

He could hear others' panicked voices too, throwing around orders even while the dead were hurtling towards him and Tiphaine in a deranged charge. The sound of the thudding of hooves quickly enveloped the dark forest.

"They're here! To battle! For Evaria! For the king!"

Unable to avoid both the humans and the undead, he led Tiphaine and bolted between the trees and undergrowth along the line of the living, avoiding the men charging forward on horses, ducking low and trying to escape the place where the two armies would collide at any moment.

The vibrating of his entire body was becoming unbearable, the rain was already soaking through what remained of his clothes and dripping off his skin, demanding a change he couldn't refuse.

"Tiphaine, I—"

It came suddenly. His legs were forced together against his will for the third time that day, and he fell over himself during the mad dash away from the coming battle.

Tiphaine, still clinging to his hand as he collapsed, caught him quickly enough to betray that she was expecting it. Just as quickly, she let go of his hand as he fell and coiled the end of her tail around his shrunken waist. Then, she dragged *him/her*, immobile, through the hundreds of thorned bushes that lined the ground.

"Don't look at me," she hissed, "I'm taking my veil off! It might work!"

Even if it was unlikely to, it was worth a chance. And if Emony was to be a weight to be dragged around, she would have to make use of her own power, too.

"Whoever can hear us, protect us!" she shrieked as loud as she could, magic surging off her tongue. "Protect the lamia and the mermaid!"

They suddenly changed direction, Tiphaine doing her best to avoid the jaws of death. Emony's head hit a tree, stunning her momentarily and turning her around so that she saw what they were leaving as opposed to where they were going.

Behind them, the two armies were explosively clashing, the horsemen reaching the undead and cutting through their ranks before being stopped and stranded within the army of corpses. Their pained cries were honestly horrible to listen to, even for her.

They slithered away from them as quickly as they could.

Many minutes later, Tiphaine began to slow down, breathing hard. She couldn't carry her much further, Emony knew it.

"You were right, the Eyes don't work on corpses," she panted.

"Damn. I was just making things up back at the knight commander's. I was hoping I'd be wrong – but I don't think my voice works, either."

The battle in the forest behind them raged on in the dark rain, thunder and lightning crackling overhead, drowning out only most of the screams.

"We have to get further away," Tiphaine muttered, exhausted, convincing herself to move forward.

"Keep us safe, humans!" Emony shouted again with magic dripping off her voice, not knowing if she would be heard or obeyed. "Keep them away from us!"

The screams and the neighing of horses seemed to grow louder and louder, even as their distance from the battle slowly increased. Emony then decided to be quiet, opting instead for stealth again as Tiphaine carried her away.

The rain kept falling from the dark sky.

4

"Fine, I'll admit it, I'm an idiot. I should've trusted the humans. We never should have left the camp," Enomy said, still thoroughly aware of and annoyed by the magic poisoning *her... her – his – no, her, no... urgh... whatever...* mind.

"Did you see how many there were?" asked Tiphaine, unaware of her mental battle, still slowly dragging Emony limply behind her with the back of her tail. "That was no small skirmish! I hope the humans win – those dead people really are crazed monsters!"

"Makes you question who you make friends with, I hope. By the divines, what has that Verena gotten involved with? Also, are you sure we are going in the right direction? We've been going downwards for a while now."

She/*no, definitely he – no, wait... she?... Which one was it? She* should have definitely been feeling emasculated by then, she thought, after being carried around by Tiphaine for so long, but, disturbingly, she didn't.

"You still don't trust me?" Tiphaine inquired. "I think I've proved myself both smarter and more capable than you tonight. Urgh, I'm sorry, I have to stop for a moment. I'm going to throw up. I'm exhausted… you're heavy."

"Rude. You should never say that to a woman."

"Haha, have you accepted that you are one right now, then?" Tiphaine laughed before spitting a couple of times on the ground. "Lenah did say it would affect your mind, too. Feeling girly?"

"That's not happening," Emony lied. "It's just hard to deny it, what with me being forced to watch my very own tits bounce around on the ground. Hey, Tiphaine. Mine are bigger than yours."

"No, they're not. Pervert. We'll have to find you a bra after this."

"Yeah, sure. I'll just ask the knight commander to give me one, that's a conversation I'll look forward to. I'll need a new tunic too, actually. This one's ripped in so many places it's a miracle it's still on. Won't be for long, though, since you were so rough with me. And I need pants again. I blame Lenah for all of this. Say, what's that over there? Something looks shiny. I think we're reaching the end of the forest."

"Thank the divines," Tiphaine said.

A moment later, however, they realized their mistake.

Emony simply smiled. "You're an idiot, Tiphaine," she laughed, feeling a perverse resignation cloud her mind, momentarily filling her with glee even as she noticed again how cute she sounded. "You brought us straight to the lake." She looked into the jeweled eye sockets of her mask. "Ha! And you're too tired to carry me any further! We're dead!"

Still breathing hard, Tiphaine reached under her mask and wiped off the rain and sweat from her forehead while Emony laughed.

"No, we're not. Not yet. I was lying, you're actually really light. I can easily keep going, I won't leave you. But look – the rain is starting to stop. Maybe you can grow legs again if we dry you off quickly."

"I'd have to be completely dry, Tiphaine. That's not going to happen. Oh, and… The human said the undead return to the lake when it stops raining. We're screwed."

"No... Verena might be able to help us! If only we could find her…"

Emony quickly glanced over at her surroundings. The only mermaid she could see was herself.

"Hey, do you think the men of the lake are better swimmers than a mermaid? Maybe I could carry you now."

Tiphaine slithered nervously back and forth, looking in the direction of the lake. "Even if you're a fish now, you don't have much experience swimming, doggy."

"Stop calling me that. Well then… we really are down to screaming for help. I can hear them coming."

It was true, the quiet rustling of the forest's undergrowth was slowly getting louder behind them. The dead were returning to the lake, and the two of them were in their way.

"Verena!" Tiphaine shouted at the top of her lungs. "Verena, we're here to see you! Are you there?!"

"Mermaid, king of the lake! We come in peace! We are friends!" Emony joined in.

The army of the undead had reached the edge of the woods and was already stepping onto the pebble beach the two of them were stranded on. A hundred rotting faces stared at them with lifeless eyes, a hundred swords clutched in what remained of their bony hands. They walked towards them in unison, as though a single entity.

"Stop moving!" Emony hissed, lacing her voice with magic. It worked – but on Tiphaine. Not on the men of the lake. "Don't get any closer!"

As the undead moved unrelentingly closer, a trickle of water sounded right behind her. Turning around quickly, she saw something resembling a human walking out of the lake.

He was a gaunt, tall and pale man, with majestic clothing that had been ripped apart by age and murky water, and long grey-white hair tied in knots over his middle-aged face. There was a long, broad sword on his back, and he wore an expression of undiluted contempt. He stalked out of the water towards them, completely unimpeded by it, and looked down at them from the wet ground.

Emony noticed out of the corner of her eyes that the undead had stopped moving towards them.

"King of the lake," she proclaimed quickly, unable to show much respect as she was already laid low on the ground without her legs, "We come in peace."

"You can move again," Emony whispered to Tiphaine, noticing her companion's affliction.

I should have made her leave me while I had the chance! she realized in horror, though by then it was too late.

Tiphaine quickly bowed. The snakes on her head were dead quiet. Even those things were afraid.

The king glared at the two of them, as if disgusted. Emony looked down from her face towards the ground, signaling submission. She noticed his chest was moving, so he must have been breathing. He was alive – if only sort of. Tiphaine was struggling for breath. He must have been the source of all the black magic in the air. Even Emony could feel it.

"Who are you?" the king asked calmly, seemingly putting away his anger for a moment.

"I am Emony, and this is Tiphaine," she said. "We've come here because we were told our friend lives in this lake. Her name is Verena."

"You know the lady Verena?"

The lady? Are you friends? If not, we're dead.

"Tiphaine used to be close to the lady Verena. We don't mean to interfere with anything happening here. We only want to speak to her, but if you wish it, we will leave immediately," Emony said, daring for merely a moment to look up from the ground.

The king's murderous stare was pointed straight at her eyes. He left it there for many moments before turning it to her golden tail and studying it for a few long, quiet seconds.

"Men!" he suddenly boomed. Emony flinched. "Return to your stations."

Upon hearing the command, the entire army of corpses surrounding them started walking towards the lake and disappearing, one after the other, under its surface. Emony saw, from the corner of her field of vision, that some were carrying soldiers that he'd seen in the camp that very day.

More fodder for the army, she thought. *The volume of black magic this king must possess... There is too much.*

Even the one she'd decapitated earlier was walking into the water, apparently unimpeded, holding its severed head in its hands.

Only once the entire army, a thousand men at least, had left, did the king speak again.

"I believe I may have heard of you, snake, from the lady Verena. You two will find her in the depths. Should you be friends, I will refrain from making you join the ranks of the dead. If you are not, you will become tools, like the rest."

"Understood," Emony and Tiphaine said in unison.

"Come, then. I take it the water will welcome you, snake?"

Tiphaine glanced over at Emony in fear, shaking her head. "I... I can't breathe underwater."

The king, despite his showing a smile, seemed ever more ready to grasp his sword. "Is that so? You claim to have been close with Verena, yet she hasn't given you the gift? That is strange. Well, perhaps your friend can give it to you, then."

"I don't know how. I've never done it before," said Emony, who knew next to nothing about the powers of mermaids. She wasn't a real one, anyway.

"You don't know... how?"

"It's a long story."

The king seemed to contemplate something, his suspicious demeanor abating for a moment. "Are you from the seas of Aeliah? Your accents betray you. Verena told me of those ignorant few that never left the waters there, that taught her of magic… They were opposed to my love… Alas, it matters not if it is merely your family that is wretched. We are at an impasse. You need to kiss."

"K-kiss?" Tiphaine stuttered.

"As I said. A mermaid's kiss allows a being of the land a life underwater."

Emony glanced over at Tiphaine nervously. "Maybe... if you don't want to, you could stay out here. I could talk to Verena alone."

"No. You will both go – and enough delays. I will not be made to wait," growled the king. "Are you friends or foes?"

"It's okay," said Tiphaine fearfully, shakily taking off her mask, her eyes closed.

It'd be impossible to miss the blush on Emony's face. But under these circumstances… she'd have to accept that their first would be with her in this form. "Then… come closer," she said, lacing magic into her voice.

Both Tiphaine and the king did so immediately, startling all three of them. A moment later, the confusion that'd spread across the king's face turned to rage. The air swirled, tendrils of black magic becoming visible and spreading all around them. With unbridled fury, the king brought his wicked sword down within an inch of Emony's eyes.

"Do not enchant your words to me! Nobody will sing to me but my queen!" he bellowed.

"I'm sorry, I didn't mean to!" Emony cried, her voice reaching a fever pitch.

The tendrils of black magic spread angrily through the air.

"No more delays," the king snarled.

Emony hastily nodded.

"Tiphaine, I can't reach you. Lean in," she said quietly. This time, the magic worked only on her.

As soon as her companion got close enough, Emony raised herself off the ground on thin arms and reached for her lips.

Tiphaine's expression tightened when they touched, her face becoming a crimson shade of red. But then her expression abruptly changed.

All of a sudden, she lurched away from Emony, convulsing on the pebbly ground, clutching her stomach with an expression of pure agony written all over her.

She was writhing right in front of her. Forgetting everything else, Emony grabbed Tiphaine's shoulders, quickly trying to find a way to help. She didn't know where to start.

"Tiphaine!" she squeaked. The king only looked on with indifference. "Tiphaine, don't feel pain! It doesn't hurt!" she shouted, over and over again. It didn't work. "You're okay!"

A minute later, after Emony had failed to help her in any way, Tiphaine stopped shaking and opened her eyes. Emony quickly avoided them.

"I'm okay," she whispered, and put her golden mask back on, her hands trembling, before gently leaning on Emony's shoulder.

The king gave them a moment to compose themselves before he spoke again: "Come. I have no more time to waste on your nonsense. Follow me and meet your fates. If you spoke the truth regarding your relationship with the lady Verena, I will apologize for causing you this pain. If you lied, you will die horrible deaths."

The king turned towards the lake, giving them no more of his attention, and walked into the water.

Emony and Tiphaine glanced at each other for a moment, unsure, then nodded. Tiphaine wrapped her tail around Emony and dragged her across the pebbles to the edge of the water. There, she saw steps leading down into the lake. Real, stone steps, carved into the ground, without a trace of dirt or seaweed on them.

Emony likely couldn't use them, though the king was somehow doing so just ahead of them. In any case, she hoped swimming would come naturally to her – along with breathing underwater. She'd never tried either.

Still nervous, she and Tiphaine shared one last look before they each took a deep breath and held it for as long as they could while they pulled themselves under the surface.

Chapter 4

1

But they had to let them go eventually. And then… Then they could feel water in their lungs. It was impossibly unnerving, letting it pour down their throats. Every instinct and sense they had was screaming at them to get back to the surface, that they couldn't live breathing in water no matter how much of it they pushed into themselves. That it was killing them.

But they hung there, forever suspended in that last moment before they'd drown, their bodies expecting a death that wouldn't come. In the beginning, the panic grasped them tightly. Only time would make it weaken.

The first to recover was Emony, who kept nervously glancing at Tiphaine, ready to intervene at the first sign that something was wrong.

Was Tiphaine feeling the same way she was? she wondered. The magic keeping her alive at the bottom of the lake was clearly different. Like the king, she did not swim – she moved unperturbed through the water, exactly as she would on land. She slithered down the steps cut into the seabed. As she kept to the ground, Emony swam through the water, seemingly free of gravity, kicking her tail and trying to stay on Tiphaine's level.

As they made their way behind the king along the polished stone steps that split the seabed, she saw countless schools of fish in every direction, stretching far above them, too, while crabs and snails crawled along the ground, seaweed like tall grass making its way past the pebbles. Eventually, as they reached the bottom of the lake, the steps they followed became a path, before becoming a long bridge where the fields of seaweed abruptly stopped and the seabed was cut short by a pitch-black, bottomless abyss.

"Do not fall," the king warned Tiphaine once they made it to the edge, before turning back around and moving on. "You would not make it back."

Emony gulped, awkwardly swimming over to Tiphaine with her golden tail, getting ready to catch her companion if anything happened. The bridge had no railings, and it wasn't very wide. But to Emony's immeasurable relief, her companion stayed on it.

"None of this is possible," whispered Tiphaine as she floated beside her. Her voice sounded different in the water. "There's no way such a small lake could be this deep. It's like another world. And can you feel it? The sheer volume of magic?"

"Yes," she whispered back. "Even I can, at this point. My bones are shaking. It really is all black, isn't it? It must be hard for you. Let's just focus on getting through this, okay?"

She nodded. "Yeah. Hey, um, on another note, you'd just as easily kiss the king as you would me? You literally just met him – way to make me feel special… Even after I saw you staring at me all those times. Like today, while you were on the tree…"

She was only trying to lighten the tense mood, Emony knew it, but she could practically feel the blood rushing to her cheeks.

"You saw...? Ha… Well… My bad," Emony stammered.

Tiphaine gazed at her curiously.

"I'm sorry, okay?"

"I didn't say anything," Tiphaine said.

"Then… stop looking at me like that!"

"Like what?"

She was obviously smirking. Emony, on the other hand, was quickly finding that her cute new face was far more prone to blushing than her usual one. She looked away, covering up her unfamiliarly rosy and hairless cheeks with her hands.

"…I hate you," Emony said.

"Oh? Is that why you didn't want to kiss me?"

"That must be it…"

"Ouch."

Emony shook her head. "No, that wasn't it. I just wanted our first time to be different. Like… like not because we were forced to do it by some all-powerful undead king, and… not when I was wearing this face… I'm glad it worked, though. Are you breathing alright?"

Emony could have sworn that she saw Tiphaine smile, even though she had her mask on.

"I happen to like both your faces, so I wonder if I should lie, and apply some force myself," she said.

Emony flicked her lightly on the shoulder. "Very funny."

A while later, swimming over the path beside her, she saw the far edge marking the end of the abyss. A bed of seaweed was climbing over the cliff out of the darkness to reach their level. But beyond that, through the clear, dark water, she saw castle walls.

It was another impossible sight. For over a minute, Emony thought her eyes were deceiving her. There was no reason for such a structure to exist at the bottom of a lake. Stone walls and towers, covered in seaweed, grime and sand, stood before them like a human castle on the surface, dirty red banners lined with seashells swaying gently in the current. The stone path led them directly towards open, rotting wooden gates in the center, where a drawbridge was laid down for them.

Once past the walls, Emony stared in awe at the many towers standing tall over the seabed and the palace from which they rose. They made their way towards the building, moving between beautiful statues lined up symmetrically on either side of the marble path, each depicting the most alluring of mermaids. Behind them, she suddenly noticed, stood the undead, the men of the lake. They were completely still, staring at nothing, unmoving despite the tide that was gently shifting the seabed. They stood in groups of twenty, seemingly surrounding the palace.

She, Tiphaine and the king swam, slithered and walked past them, straight towards the doors of the gilded marble palace. The king stopped in front of them, at the door, turning around and speaking to her and Tiphaine for the first in a long time.

"This is the sunken palace of Acu'enah. A place mostly forgotten by the world outside these waters."

He lifted a hand and gently touched the stone archway leading into the castle. "This is my wife's home. My queen's. You will not disrespect it."

Emony and Tiphaine nodded in unison. "We won't disrespect it."

After a long, appraising stare, the king nodded back.

"Then I invite you in. Verena will come to see you shortly, and after hearing what she has to say, you may or may not leave this place alive."

"Understood," they breathed.

"And you, siren," the king continued, "You will not sing while in my presence. In addition, you will beg the lady Verena for some clothing, which you will wear. I will not be brought to lust anyone but my queen."

The sudden realization hit Emony rather quickly. She'd lost her ripped tunic somewhere in the water quite a while ago. She quickly concealed her bare chest with her hands, again made acutely aware of the magic that was tying itself around her/*no, his* brain.

But with those words, the king turned around again, grasped the twin mermaid handles of the huge, ornately gilded marble door of the palace, and pushed it open.

About an hour later, in the palace's dining hall, except for the occasional grunt and nod in their direction, the king ignored them all as he sat at the end of the long banquet table, letting Verena, Tiphaine's mermaid friend, explain the current situation to them. His expression was one of utter indifference – he clearly didn't believe they could be trusted with anything. He'd rather simply kill them and have them join the corpses, though luckily, it seemed he would stay his hand due to Verena's wishes.

The table they were sat or floating at in the cavernous palace dining hall was huge, it could easily seat a hundred men. Emony briefly wondered about its purpose, given the four of them were the only ones there, sitting at one of its ends, while fish of every variety swam under the beautifully ornamented domed ceiling.

"It's not necromancy," Verena was explaining in answer to one of Tiphaine's questions.

"They're not undead – just puppets controlled with strings of magic. The same spell could be used on a wooden doll, it's just that skeletons and corpses are better suited for the task."

"What task is that?" Emony asked. She had been avoiding the question for a few minutes now, speaking around the issue instead.

The real mermaid uneasily glanced over at her and sighed. "I suppose I should tell you… We want to find my sister. She's… missing. She was taken by the humans, over ten years ago."

"I heard the men of the lake started attacking about two months ago," she thought out loud, privately wondering about which exit would most likely get her and Tiphaine out of the palace alive if things went sour. There were no good options.

"That's what they call them on the surface, isn't it? Yes, you're right. Aulduyen only recently managed to climb up out of the abyss, gaining these strange powers. But this whole tragic story started much earlier. Did they tell you anything about the rebellion? About the coup?"

"Not really," Tiphaine said, "But we've only been here a day, and we spent it gathering things to unpetrify the villagers."

"A poor excuse," the king murmured, mostly to himself. "Nothing is more important than my queen."

Verena glanced at him for a moment before continuing. "Aulduyen's taken her loss poorly, as have I. We just want her back… But, Tiphaine, I hope my veil is serving you well. Are you still on your quest to cure yourself of the Eyes?"

"Yes, I am. I'm… not having much luck. It doesn't seem like the curse can be broken. But the veil is great."

"I'm sorry to hear that. I must confess that I've found nothing, either, and I have spent some time searching. Even the sea witch couldn't find a solution. The Eyes are truly a terrible curse, and for you to be the one unfortunate lamia in the whole world that must bear it… It must be difficult for you, no? I'm so glad you've found a companion. But how did you come to meet another mermaid?"

"About that… I first met Emony before I did you, actually. And he's been great, though I wonder how long he'll stay with me, considering the things I get him into—"

"You're admitting they're your fault?"

"I'm sorry, *him*?" Verena asked.

The king, sitting on his throne, threw them a bemused look, removing himself from his thoughts for a quick moment.

"Emony is… a guy," Tiphaine stammered, "Though me and Lenah complicated things slightly a few weeks ago."

"I'm still a guy," Emony corrected.

A quiet chuckle escaped Verena. "Lenah? That hedonist? You're still in touch with her?"

"Yeah. And she is the one who brought us here, actually. We thought you might know something about how to help Emony. You're the only mermaid any of us know."

"What happened, precisely?"

"Let's just say Lenah's tinkering didn't work properly. Emony used to be a werewolf, but now… he seems to be human on land, but whenever he touches water, he becomes a mermaid."

"I'm no human."

"That's… some tinkering. Could it really be possible?"

"You can see my tail, can't you?" Emony asked.

The real mermaid turned to her. "Yes, but to create something like this out of lycanthropy… And for you to be able to leave the water freely and walk the surface, regrowing legs at will… That makes you one of a kind. No mermaid could do such a thing – and Aulduyen tells me you are even able to sing as a siren? Lenah must have seriously improved her craft. The last time I saw her, she was still abusing love potions. I don't know if I can help you… But… but Aulduyen might be able to."

The king turned his gaze upon them again. "The only thing that is important is the return of my queen," he said quietly, before becoming lost in thought again.

Verena turned to face Emony again with a look of uncertainty. "I think… Maybe if you could help us, we could help you."

Emony exchanged a glance with Tiphaine. She really made the worst kinds of friends.

"Actually, if there is a solution in this world for your curse, too, Tiphaine, it may be here. Aulduyen possesses magic the likes of which has never been seen," Verena said. "The measure of it is unbelievable. I've never seen something so dark, but perhaps it could erode even the Eyes. He may be able to cure you! We just… we need your help first. Emony, your song could prove useful if you could deploy it on land, along with Tiphaine's Eyes, as long as she has them."

"Do you really think…?" Tiphaine exclaimed. "I've… I never thought… Do you really think I can be cured?"

Emony hoped Tiphaine wasn't getting her hopes up too high again. Hers was truly a vicious cycle of dreams and disappointment. After being thoroughly manipulated by every sage, mystic and witch they could find, they'd always been told the same thing – that only her death could make it move on, and that nothing could break it. Not the Eyes.

"You want us to help you find your sister – the queen?" she interrupted.

"Yes, that's right. The villagers avoid the lake, and they always run at the first sight of our soldiers, but you could go ashore and make them speak the truth. If you find Imarah… I can see your doubt. No, you're right, Emony, we don't know if she's alive. It's been ten years, and while Aulduyen has been in the abyss, I have done next to nothing, as I cannot leave these waters. The last we saw her… well, it was… Aulduyen, it was when you died."

The king lifted his head and glanced over at them, pulled away from his thoughts once again.

"Yes… It was the day of my greatest mistake. When the bastard usurper came for my head…"

Sickly grief flashed through the king's gaunt face for a few moments before rapidly turning into a homicidal rage. "Raynardt… He took our kingdom from us! He terrorized my love! She was so scared… I will rip him apart, limb from limb! Oh, my love… Where is she…? Oh, you are wrong, my lady Verena, she is alive out there somewhere. I can still see the strings of magic and love connecting the two of us, I can still hear her songs in my ears. "Aulduyen, save me!" she cries. Oh, my love…"

Verena swam over to the king and laid a hand gently upon his shoulder. The king laid his own hand, trembling, atop it, black tears leaving his eyes and staining the water.

"The villagers will speak of it as *the rebellion*," Verena said. "That much I have heard. Who knows what they might say, they may be afraid of the usurper's wrath. But Aulduyen died that day, ten years ago. He was thrown into this lake, bleeding, tied to an anchor falling into the abyss, while I tried in vain to untie him. I couldn't help him. But… my sister did not share his fate. She's not in these waters. They took her off that boat, so she may be alive."

The king suddenly arose from his throne, staring madly at the mermaid.

"As I said, lady Verena, Imarah *is* alive! Death has not claimed my queen, I know it hasn't! Do not look at me now as though I am a fool! It was her song that pulled me off that anchor and lifted me from the depths of the blackened abyss! She cries to me, even now that I must find her and save her! We must do so without delay! Without her…! Without her… there is only darkness."

"We will, Aulduyen. We'll find her. We will bring her home, I promise," Verena murmured.

The king quietly sobbed onto the mermaid's shoulder. Caressing him gently, she turned back towards Emony and Tiphaine.

"Tiphaine, Emony, Imarah was a siren. Her mouth may have been bound, but she might have gotten a chance to escape. The shortest of songs could have brought her freedom if only a single human had made a mistake. Please… I won't lie to you, I do not know for sure that we can free you of your curses, especially not you, Tiphaine. But we could really use your help."

Emony, though likely only due to her altered mind, found even herself slightly moved. She turned to Tiphaine. No doubt she wanted to help her friend, perhaps she even pitied the king… But still. The two were in league with magic so dark even she was disgusted by it. And they were certainly killing a lot of humans…

What if there was a chance, though? She knew full well that she was being a fool, too, but…

What if they really could free Tiphaine from the curse of the Eyes? What if their magic was even darker than her legendary curse? There was nothing she had wanted more.

Emony sighed, noticing Tiphaine shake nervously.

Despite it all, she made her choice stupidly easily.

"We'll help you. Tell us what you need."

"Thank you. Thank you so, so much," sighed Verena. "Please, we just need you to talk to the villagers. They might know something. I cannot leave the lake with my tail, and Aulduyen inspires far too much terror. We've tried making contact with them before, but they were always so fearful. So… sing to them, make them tell you the truth. And those knights and the soldiers that came, could they be from that city? What was it called, where you were born, Aulduyen, was it Terrena? If so, those men may know something too. Could you talk to them?"

"Yes. We'll do it, we'll make them help. What about the men of the lake?"

"You have nothing to fear. They're Aulduyen's puppets, he controls them. We can probably even offer you some if you come to fear for your safety, surrounded by those humans – but know that they cannot touch dry ground. Aulduyen's magic is tied to water, were they to lose contact with it, they would crumble to dust. That is why we are limited by rain – until the snow begins to fall."

"Understood. I'm sure Tiphaine will be able to keep me safe."
Emony glanced over at the king, who was merely looking through him, lost in thought.

"The trail leads south," the king said quietly. "I cannot reach far enough yet, but the trail of magic…"

"We'll follow it," Emony said. "We can't see it, but we will find it. To do so… I think… as much as I hate it, I think that we will need to work with the humans. But if we want to continue dealing with them, at the very least, before we return to them... We cannot rely on our powers alone. We'll need to employ deception."

The king stared blankly into her eyes.

"The humans will have seen that we disobeyed them and escaped their camp before the battle began. But we need them to think we are on their side."

She was understood quite quickly. The king got up from his chair without a word, taking up the hilt of his long sword.

2

The two of them were found by the soldiers just before noon the next day, lying on the pebbly beach, battered, bruised and wounded, in the middle of a large pile of body parts ripped off of men of the lake.

The humans had clearly been expecting to find them dead. Instead, upon hearing Emony's threats to kill them all if they did not comply, they tossed them bandages from afar, which Emony quickly deployed on Tiphaine's bloody gash.

"We're on your side," he snapped at the soldiers. "Come help! I can't tie this myself with one hand, and my left is broken!"

"Let me do it," said Tiphaine, helping him tie the bandage with one hand whilst putting pressure on the bleeding slash that seemed to cut through a fourth of her waist with the other.

The king had been merciless. Lamias healed quickly, so she would be fine in a couple of days – but he took the job of making the wounds look grave very seriously, especially with her. He couldn't hurt Emony too much, as too much blood would hinder his ability to keep his legs, but with Tiphaine, despite Verena's protests, he had been downright cruel. It was all for his queen, he'd said. The man was insane. Also, as mermaids were not blessed with the same regenerative powers as lamias and werewolves, Emony would remain unfit for combat for quite a while – though it was his left arm he'd had broken, so he could likely still defeat a couple of ordinary humans.

"Those damned corpses just didn't stop," he groaned loudly. "Is that normal? No matter how many limbs we removed, they just kept coming! I swear, taking their heads didn't even slow them down!"

After exchanging glances with the others, one of the men finally came closer, taking off his helmet and nodding understandingly. "A rookie mistake, going for the head. It's their arms you need. They can't swing their swords after you remove those," he said.

"I guess I'll have to remember that," Emony replied, wincing in only half-faked pain as Tiphaine, finished with her own wound, tied up his broken arm and hung a sling around his neck to keep it in place.

"We're surprised you're alive," the human said. "We heard you'd gone missing. Sir Meheyn was found dead – he was supposed to be following you."

Emony nodded, playing up his display of discomfort. "He was. She and I had gone to relieve ourselves, and the damned pervert was watching us. He served some purpose, though. His scream warned us to finish up quickly. Then we ran."

"Seems you ran the wrong way, though. Why stray so far from the camp simply to pee? And did it at all occur to you that the *men of the lake* may have been coming *from the lake*?"

Emony shrugged, giving Tiphaine a pointed stare.

"You run faster downhill than uphill," she defended herself.

The human laughed. "Idiots, the both of you. Well, maybe you're not so bad. My name is Aylard."

"Emony. This is Tiphaine."

"Nice to meet you both. It looks like you destroyed quite a few of those things, so let's get you back to camp. We can use finding you as an excuse to have lunch early."

After they had made the trek up the hill with the humans to the encampment and had been welcomed back, with obvious suspicion, the two found themselves sitting in the commander's tent again.

"It seems you had quite the night," their commander, Yperian, said, after pouring wine into their silver chalices. "I must have made a horrible mistake, not informing you about the location of the pit latrines. It's good to see you're still alive."

"Just barely," Emony responded. Too bad your man wasn't so lucky."

"Thirty-three died last night, by our latest count, which one are you referring to? Bah, forget it. It's clear you know I had you followed. Yes, Sir Meheyn really must have had a stroke of… bad luck. Some of our men say he was the first to fall. One even claims that he died before the men of the lake arrived… strange… But I'm sure that's untrue. In any case, Sir Meheyn was a good soldier, an honorable knight. He did his duty, warning the rest of us before he died."

He lifted his chalice. "To Meheyn."

"To Meheyn."

"And all the others," murmured Tiphaine.

"Yes. So, you were found this morning next to the lake?"

"Yes."

"What were you doing there?"

He shrugged. "That's where we ran. It's hard to avoid two battling armies and go whichever direction you want. I was following her."

Tiphaine turned her head in his direction. He knew she was glaring at him, from behind her mask. He just smiled at her.

"You must understand why I would find this suspicious. Even though you are wounded, and were apparently found surrounded by defeated foes, how did you manage to survive after running directly into the lion's den with no weapons? And find yet another change of clothes, while you were at it? Though in poor condition, those seem fit for a king. Did you take them from one of the men of the lake?"

Emony considered what to say for a few moments, tugging on the sleeves of his new tunic. Of course it was fit for a king. It'd belonged to one. He gave the human a wide smile.

"Well… I could spin a lie, I'm sure I could somehow fool you, clever as you are. But why waste the effort? Oops, it seems I've spilled my drink."

"What are you saying? Hm? Magic? Guard—"

The human turned to stone before he could finish uttering the word. Emony somehow managed to remain in her seat, despite the tail replacing her legs. So that was a win.

"Thank you, Tiphaine," Emony squeaked in that cute voice of hers she hated . "Now, I'm ready. Bring him back. And watch out for anyone who might want to disturb us. Oh, damn it, I forgot to take my pants off. I really should learn how to sew."

"And quickly," Tiphaine said, flashing him a smile with her eyes closed. "I think the king might kill you if he sees that. Weren't those his?"

Urk. That meant trouble.

Tiphaine put her mask back on and slithered over to the petrified knight commander before sticking some ravenwood bark onto his stone lips. Color began to return to him quickly, since he'd only spent a few seconds as a stone.

"You will not make a sound unless directed to do so. You will not try to escape," Emony said. "Nod if you understand what I'm saying, as soon as you are able."

After a time, once the color had spread down to his neck, the human did so. It seemed he was struggling against Emony's magic, his face was contorting into an expression of fear and anger.

"From now on, you will be our obedient servant," she said, continuing her spelled tune.

"That's going a little far, isn't it?" Tiphaine asked.

"Shush. Ah, damn it. I'm sorry, again. You can do whatever you please, Tiphaine. I only command you, human."

"Ouch," Emony's companion moaned, again having to check up on her teeth.

"Now, human. You're not going to remember that you are our servant, but you will be all the same. You will help us, but not allow anyone to find out that this conversation of ours is the reason why. Now, as soon as I grow legs again, you will regain full control of your body, be under our command, and forget that this latest startling event took place. Nod if you understand."

Head shaking, with pupils dilated to cover his entire irises, the human did as he was told. Emony took a washcloth from the table and wiped off the wine that she'd spilled onto her hand.

A minute later, the human began blinking wildly, looking around in immense confusion as Emony regained his male form. He needed over a minute to calm down.

"Hm? What happened? I must have dozed off for a minute," he finally said, bewildered. "I feel like time has gone by without me."

Emony made a brief expression of bemusement. "Well, we are drinking wine."

"Oh, yes. I suppose that must be it. So, as I was saying… Hm? … What was I saying?" he asked. "And… I'm sorry, what happened to your pants again? Weren't they fine just a second ago?"

"It's not important, though I am going to need some new ones. For now, though, please answer one of my questions. Do you know anything of the rebellion that happened here a decade ago?"

"The rebellion? Everyone knows about it. Oh, that's right, I suppose you may not, you are foreigners. Basically, the last king of Evaria was deposed about ten years ago. A contentious issue, to be sure, a bastard ascending the throne in his place, but the old king was a brute. I think the land is better off for it."

"What do you mean?"

"Well, Raynardt, the current king of Evaria, is a naturalized bastard. Ten years ago, after all his older brothers save one died, the appointed king was a man named Aulduyen, the seventh son of the late king Ovesen. Perhaps a year or so into his reign, Raynardt staged a coup, right here in Coldbarrow. The late Aulduyen was deposed by his bastard half-brother, who is now the new king."

Interesting.

"The man killed his half-brother, and became king?" exclaimed Tiphaine, "That's horrible! Why do you stand for it?!"

"Because the former king, Aulduyen, was a horrible one," Yperian said calmly. "A pompous, elitist snob, with no regard for the common man, if memory serves. Well, he was a seventh son, himself, so he was never supposed to amount to much more. He was certainly never expected to ascend the throne – and he didn't want to, in the first place. But then all six of his older brothers grew ill and died. He had fallen ill, too, but he survived and so became king, as the rightful heir. In any case, Evaria is better off with him dead, too. This is where King Raynardt had him killed. But why the interest? Do you think he might be the king of the lake?"

"Yes, and we're conspiring with the undead madman to kill you all."

"Fascinating. Let me know if there is anything I can do to help," the human replied.

"This is too weird," Tiphaine said.

"Interesting that he's letting you go to the village," said Aylard, their new human minder, the next day. "Only yesterday he was groaning about how terrified the villagers were that you would return. Did you threaten him?"

"Wouldn't you personally find it more interesting that he only ordered one person to follow us around? I think it's clear he doesn't think even a group of you could defeat us. Better only one human die than many if we turn out to be enemies."

Aylard shrugged. "Yeah, you're probably right. Lucky me... We can't exactly fight with our eyes closed, can we? The lady snake is unbeatable. And what are you? An elf? A vampire? A werewolf?"

"Why would you possibly think to ask me that? I'm clearly just like you. I'm human."

"Very funny."

The road was a poorly maintained one, with loose stones threatening to twist Emony's legs the wrong way if he stepped on them carelessly. He had to be careful, given his reduced powers of regeneration. He really did feel like a human at this point, he was so uncomfortably vulnerable. He hated it. Tiphaine was lucky not to have such problems, whether she was cursed or not.

"It's cold," she went and grumbled, despite her luck. "I want to lie in the sun – why is it cloudy again today?

"It will be for a while yet, my lady. Summer has long gone," responded Aylard.

"You know I'm not a lady, right?" she responded.

"I know you could turn me to stone with one look, my lady," the human replied. Tiphaine chuckled.

Emony glanced around at their surroundings. The forest was to their left, made up of countless pine trees, hornbeams and ravenwood oaks. Far more ravenwood oaks than were in most places. Even if, currently being half-mermaid, he couldn't smell it, he could see that the place must reek of dark magic.

He also noticed that the forest's thorny bushes, nettles and small flowers were all trampled into the dirt.

The reason why was obvious. Just on the other side of the road was the lake.

3

Aulduyen

He cursed his imperfect memories every time he thought of her.

Sitting at his throne at the end of the empty dining hall, at the bottom of the lake that had been their home, Aulduyen was perfectly aware of the terrible truth – that his mind had never truly captured her perfection, had never even really come close.

Sometimes, when he envisioned her in his flawed mind, she stood before him, smiling, yet the smile was not the same. Other times he heard her voice calling to him, "Aulduyen, Aulduyen," as she had a decade ago before he'd died – yet the tone was never exactly as hers had been.

She was always there, haunting the edge of his field of vision, just out of reach. The moment he turned to look at her, she disappeared.

And he only had himself to blame. He'd abandoned her ten years ago, when death dropped him into that abyss with an opened and bleeding heart. He should have returned more quickly. He should have never let himself sink into the abyss in the first place. Even if she'd forgive him once he'd find her, he'd never be able to do so himself.

He got up from the marble throne, leaving the palace that was rightfully hers and walking through the courtyard. The army of puppets stood around there, by the grimy stone walls, awaiting orders. They were a hideous sight to behold. He would never let Imarah see it.

"Begone!" he bellowed, suddenly enraged. "Leave this place, filth, I command you! Stain a different part of these waters!"

The corpses turned away in an instant, then jumped and swam upwards, away from Acu'enah.

"Do not defile our home a moment longer!"

Through the magic connecting them to him, they would hear and obey his orders no matter how far away he was from them.

He lowered his eyes from their repulsiveness and returned to walking through the tranquil garden.

He stopped by a gilded marble statue of a mermaid to the side of the path. It was covered, somewhat, by seaweed and grime, but it remained a magnificent sight to behold, mostly unravaged by time and the water. It was made in the likeness of Imarah's grandmother. She had *her* nose, he thought. The eyes were too close together, and the cheekbones were not as high as his love's. Yet the statue was one of the closest things he had left of her.

It wasn't fair.

Suddenly possessed with rage again, cursing madly, Aulduyen grabbed the kingly blade on his back and slammed it into the stone path, cracking the bedrock underneath and sending a vicious tremor all across the lake.

"Where is she?!" he shouted through the water, furious at the divines that she had believed in. "Why do you keep her from me?! Answer me! Where is she?! Where does this magic wrapped around my heart lead?!"

Seething, he looked up through the water straight at the dull blue sky, utilizing the eyes of his puppets.

"Continue to defy me, then. It matters not. I demand her return – until she is back in my embrace, all before me will die."

He violently ripped his sword out of the stone, determined to bring forth rain and death again.

"I hope that does not include me, Aulduyen?" said a quiet, gentle voice behind him.

The lady Verena. Imarah's sister. He hadn't noticed her approach.

He turned around to look at her, quickly putting away the blade. Her face was so unlike Imarah's… But the scales on her tail were the same shape, the same color. Though their voices were different, they shared a similar accent, one that had otherwise been lost to the world.

He had shamed himself before her. It was nowhere near the first time.

"Lady Verena. I apologize for my outburst. I misspoke. You will never be endangered, I swear this upon my unlife."

She gave him a small smile and swam over to his side with her golden tail. That smile was closer to Imarah's than her grandmother's was.

"I was only jesting," she said. "I know you didn't mean it that way."

"Do you have any news from your friends?" he asked after a moment of silence. "I'd like to go to the surface again and scour it myself for any trace of my queen."

"It hasn't been much more than a day, Aulduyen. Give them time – they might need a lot of it, considering the wounds you gave them. Please do nothing, at least for a little while."

Aulduyen frowned. He'd had to be meticulous in creating the wounds. He would take no chances in the deception being noticed, and his queen being parted from him for longer than necessary due to it... But had he perhaps made a mistake, and delayed her return with his own blade? Should he have been gentler with the two creatures?

"I'm sorry," he breathed, the horror closing in.

He felt Verena's arms pull him into a gentle embrace as he held his eyes closed. She was warm, alive, unlike himself. Just as Imarah was sure to be.

Once again seeing the shadow of his love for a hint of a moment, before she instantly disappeared from his sight again, he cried upon her sister's shoulder, falling to his knees on the sandy seabed. "Verena… I must have her back. I cannot begin to describe how much I miss her. My heart… My blackened heart…! It hurts so much!"

Chapter 5

1

Emony

The three entered the Garland quietly with pouches full of silver tied to their waists and Aylard up in front, talking to the villagers calmly to lessen the fear Tiphaine's appearance inspired in the humans.

Out of the corner of his eye, Emony saw the children being ushered away towards a backdoor as they approached the bar. That was fine. It wasn't them that they needed to talk to. Thankfully, a good number of villagers were still gathered around the tables and bar, likely afraid to leave, as according to Aylard's words, doing so might anger Tiphaine.

Perhaps he was a somewhat useful human to keep around.

They made their way to the small wooden stools, paying the patron who was still deathly afraid of them handsomely and asking for ale.

"Come on, are you really going to make me drink from under the veil again?" Tiphaine complained like an idiot.

"We've only come to ask you some questions," Emony said loudly to the humans, ignoring her and repeating Aylard's words. "We will not hurt you in the slightest, and we will pay you well for anything you tell us. Nobody will be petrified."

"We want to help you with the men of the lake," Tiphaine continued after a moment. The men were still desperately avoiding looking at her, even though she was wearing her jeweled mask. "Don't you want to be rid of them?"

"Very much!" shouted Aylard, of all people, to their audience. "Please, help us get rid of the undead scourge! What information could you possibly need?"

"We just need to know about the rebellion that happened here ten years ago."

The villagers began looking over amongst themselves, casting nervous glances and whispering too quietly for Emony's newly insensitive half-mermaid ears to hear.

"Right! The rebellion!" responded Aylard. "The time our esteemed bastard king Raynardt went and murdered the rightful one, and took his place! Hey, why don't you help, old man? I've no doubt you've been here all your life. You must have seen it."

"The insolence… to call him a bastard…"

"The rightful king…"

As people murmured amongst themselves, Emony and Tiphaine turned to look at the old human Aylard had pushed their way. He was shaking slightly, staring in any direction other than theirs. He sensed Tiphaine wanted to comfort him somehow. As if that would work.

"Well?" Emony asked. "Do you know anything? I'll give you a silver if you tell me one thing I don't."

"Um… The coup… It was years ago, maybe ten… It wasn't very big, it was quite peaceful, considering what it was… I took no part in it…"

"Really!?" said Emony loudly, annoyed, yet trying to hide it. "I didn't know that! Here, take a silver! Do you know anything more?"

"Well… Sir Raynardt became king after that. He proclaimed that he'd been naturalized, that he was Ovesen's true heir. And he'd just killed the last trueborn heir anyway, so…"

"That's interesting. Anything else? No? Well, thank you. Anyone else? Who knows anything more about the old king? Does anyone know anything about his wife? It doesn't matter how trivial the information; I've got plenty of silver."

"It's not cursed, the money," Aylard added. "The knight commander gave it to these two only an hour ago, there's nothing to fear. He trusts them, and you know what he's like. You should, too."

The villagers looked amongst themselves distrustfully. The old man stepped away from Emony in some haste.

"The last king, he came here while surveying the lands he was to rule," said a woman's voice from one of the tables. Emony and Tiphaine looked over towards her. She was a grubby human approaching old age, with the distinct smell that that entailed.

So, my nose does work, after all, Emony thought.

Tiphaine slithered over closer to the woman, stopping when she showed the first sign of discomfort.

"He came from Terrena, right?" she asked.

"Yes. From the capital. Though he probably went elsewhere before making it to Coldbarrow," responded the woman. "Anyway, he… he was cruel. That was one of the reasons why people accepted the new king so quickly."

"Cruel?"

"To us. To the lowborn."

"Unlucky for us," said a man sitting quietly behind the old woman. He dared to look at Tiphaine's jeweled-covered eyes for a moment. "After King Aulduyen arrived, he spent all his days crossing swords with and making fools of the youth. Peasants, he called us. Never bothered with names."

Emony put another two silvers on the table.

"So, not very kingly."

"No. He was unrivaled with his sword, though."

"How did the rebellion happen, then? How did it begin?"

"He… fell in love," the old woman interjected.

"Hm. That's right. He fell in love with a girl here. I remember all the girls were gossiping about it. It was the strangest thing – for days, he'd been calling us peasants, lowborn scum and the like – and then, all of a sudden, he fell madly in love with the very lowest among us. This strange girl that used to live on the shore by the lake with her sister. The two kept to themselves, we never really saw them, but their parents were gone, so we used to give them soup. I think… My memories are somewhat muddled when it comes to them."

Emony placed another silver on the table. The man's eyes flitted over to it. Things were progressing well. Emony smiled – perhaps he wouldn't have to turn into a female.

"Do you remember their names?" he asked.

"They were strange ones, I recall."

"One of them was Imarah," said a voice from another table. "And her sister was Verena. Come to think of it, my memories are all fuzzy, too… They used to splash water on me from the lake when we were little, though. They were playful, but… shy."

Probably because they were a different species, and you humans would hunt them down and kill them if they gave you the chance, Emony thought, a dark memory surfacing for a moment.

"Yes, they were. I liked them. It's a shame," said another voice.

"What is?" asked Tiphaine.

"What happened to them. The king back then, Aulduyen, fell in love with the younger one. Nobody knows how or why. She had nothing to her name – not even the roof of the little shack, which was falling apart over her head. Yet the king suddenly became obsessed with her, and afterward, he… well, first, he started making an effort."

"He became a better person?"

"I don't think so," the man replied. "Not in his heart. But in his actions, yes. He tried to remember our names and to be good to us. He was polite, even to the women. And this one time, he went fishing with the other men, instead of thrashing them around in a sparring match. He had materials imported from Terrena to repair our boats, bought us new nets… It was unnerving."

"It must have been true love," said Tiphaine.

"Strange, to tell you the truth. It happened so suddenly. One day he was… well…"

"An elitist snob?" asked Emony.

"Yes, that. And the next, he was a lovesick fool. We certainly welcomed the change, though."

"For as long as it lasted," the old woman sighed.

Emony glanced over at them and added more silver to the pile. He spied Aylard looking at it with envy. He finished his drink, grimacing, as he could only use one hand for everything, given that his other was broken.

"He'd stayed here for quite a while, even though he was supposed to have left to tour the rest of the kingdom. The lords accompanying him kept urging him to leave, to do his duty. He refused. And then someone spied him standing in the shallows of the lake one day, with Imarah. They said they saw him give her a ring."

"They married."

"Yes," the man grunted. "Just like that. And that must have been the last straw. She was a commoner! He hadn't even introduced her to any of the lords he called fools and churls. I heard they were enraged by his insolence. He'd already been betrothed to a princess of a neighboring country."

"Anyway, I remember the one time I met him in person. It was later on that I brought him water as he trained with his sword. That thing, it was as long as he was, and he was clearly ghastly good at using it. He told me they were trying to part him from his love, make him marry a cur. That he wasn't going to let that happen. To me, he seemed insane."

"I see. Then this story doesn't have a happy ending," said Emony.

"No, it doesn't. The lords started conspiring amongst themselves. The king was often nowhere to be seen, who knows where he went off to for whole days at a time. They planned to put his bastard half-brother – Raynardt – on the throne instead of him, saying Aulduyen was too much trouble. They said the kingdom needed stability. And, well, they succeeded. I heard the king was coming out of the lake one day after a swim with his new wife when they captured them both – forced them onto a boat and went out to the middle of the lake. And I suppose they killed them there. They killed all of his personal guards, too."

"It was strange, actually – the man that told me, he said they needed a fishing net to catch the girl, Imarah. I can't imagine why."

"I heard she had a tail," murmured the woman. "That she was a monster."

"I think I heard that too, though I think it was just that they wanted another excuse to kill them both. They later said that she had bewitched the king, rid him of his senses. I don't know."

"Do you think she might have been a mermaid?" Aylard asked.

"Well... she certainly knew how to sing a tune. But no, of course not! There was nothing all that special about her. She seemed like a good person."

Emony suddenly noticed the man scratch his head, uncertain of something. That same motion continued among many of the patrons of the tavern.

"Yes, she was normal enough."

"She was our friend."

"Normal enough."

"Agreed. Even if she was a little weird, she was kind. And one time, she brought me the biggest fish I'd ever seen."

Emony leaned over to Tiphaine. "You see it too, right?"

"Well, she was a siren," she whispered back, nodding. "She obviously used that."

"Maybe she was as bad as the king," he murmured. "We'll have to ask Verena about it. Why must you make friends with the worst of people, Tiphaine?"

"*You're* lucky I do."

"Mhm," Emony said, "and don't I know it."

"So, this completely normal girl that never left the lake and seduced a horrible king in no more than a minute... What do you really think happened to her? I don't think she died that day."

The old man closest to them scratched his chin again, lost in memories. "I don't know. I never saw her again after she had been taken onto the boat. Her sister Verena must still be here somewhere, though. I saw her swimming a few months ago. The usurpers were looking for her all over, back then, but they couldn't find her. You should ask her. Oh, well, actually, I suppose she might be gone now. The men of the lake…"

Emony put a few more pieces of silver onto the table and lifted his pouch, shaking it so the remaining coins could be heard, before putting it back down and discreetly slipping most of them into his pocket.

"The rest goes to whoever tells me what really happened to Imarah."

All around the tavern, the humans' eyes lit up in surprise, then dulled as they raced madly through their thoughts.

"They killed her!" exclaimed one man quickly. "I saw them take both her and the king onto the boat! She was tied to the mast!"

"No, she was trapped in a net!"

"Where is her body?" he asked.

"At the bottom of the lake, must be," the same man said. "His, too!"

Emony shook his head, tapping Tiphaine's shoulder. "My friend here assures me that's not true. She's a seer, I tell you, and she says the woman managed to get off that boat."

"That can't be!" the man protested, angry, staring at the pouch of silver.

"The traitor knights took a good deal of our fishing boats, but the bodies of the king's personal guards were piled up on the deck of the largest boat," said an old man smelling of fish that hadn't spoken before.

The men murmured in consensus.

"Many of us worked on the boat they killed the old king on. It was full of supplies – they stole them afterward, the bastards."

"I remember that, too! They took my sail!"

"Where did they go?" Emony asked. "Back to Terrena? South?"

The men looked amongst themselves nervously. They would probably only be guessing at this point. After some talking in hushed tones, the oldest of them spoke up.

"Maybe... We don't know for sure where they went, or if they took her alive, but we might know someone who does. If we tell you of them—"

Emony threw him the mostly empty pouch of silver.

"Tell me."

"Garrick," the man said hoarsely, looking astonished after catching it. "Garrick, the merchant. He would know. They took the bodies of the king's personal guards off the boat, to cart them around the kingdom and send a message. They used him and his carriage, and had him drive it after them on their way. He returned to us a while later but without it. The thieves must have kept it, though he refused to say. Still, he might know where they went."

"I want to talk to – huh? What the—"

2

Emony felt a cold liquid trickle down his back. He whirled around in an instant, ready to attack – but he saw it was just Aylard behind him, stepping back in shock at seeing his reaction and spilling more of the ale he was holding.

"Sorry," he remarked upon seeing Emony's murderous expression. "I was just... getting us a refill."

More of the liquid fell on Emony's tunic. Panic rising, he quickly turned to Tiphaine. She shook her head. Turning everyone in the tavern into stone… bad idea. But his skin was already vibrating where the ale had made contact with it. He had to get away.

As fast as his legs could carry them, he sprinted out of the tavern.

The sun blinded him momentarily upon reaching the outside, but he ignored that and ran in the direction of the lake. A few humans walking along the road stared at him, confused, and quickly stepped out of his way.

"Stay here!" he heard Tiphaine shout, probably at Aylard and the rest. He was already far away. The wind was whipping his face as he ran.

He got lucky. Just as he leaped toward the water, while he was soaring through the air, his legs combined into that long, golden tail, ripping apart his newest pair of pants, and the top half of his body contorted into a smaller, feminine frame.

At the same moment, magic wrapped itself tightly around Emony's mind, poisoning *her* thoughts again. The top part of her tunic was quickly stretched by her expanding chest, but by a rare stroke of good fortune, it held. Maybe, just maybe, the king wouldn't kill her for making him lust after her.

And she had nearly resorted to violence earlier when she'd caught Tiphaine trying to sneak Verena's bra into her/*his* pockets.

Emony's unfamiliar new face was the first thing to touch the water, and the clear, cold liquid flooded straight into her smaller-than-normal mouth and nose. This time, she didn't resist it, instead letting it fill her lungs, as panic-inducing as that was.

She slipped underwater and lithely turned herself around, so she was not upside-down but opted to stay under the surface. After a couple of seconds, her madly beating heart calmed down and her breathing slowed. She grew accustomed to the water in her throat and lungs. Her broken arm suddenly registered pain, as it had fallen out of its sling.

Breathing out the agony, she secured it against her chest again, grabbed her slowly sinking ripped pants and fished the bra out of them before swimming further away from the shore, trying to spy anything that might be happening there through the light bent by the water's surface while she put it on.

"So, what now?" she sighed finally, not being able to make out anything outside and instead looking around the water.

The lake was a beautifully vivid blue, teeming with fish and rocky grounds that steadily grew deeper as the shore grew further away. It was beautiful. If only she hadn't just been turned into a female fish, she would have definitely wanted to stay there for a while.

In the distance, she spotted something large floating in the water.

As she got closer, she first thought it was a human, and her instinct was to back away, but then she realized that one of those could not survive, unmoving under the water as it was. She thought it must have been a corpse, then, and she was sort of right – but the cadaver turned its head to look at her.

It was a man of the lake.

Gulping fresh water along with her spit, she swam over to it, assuring herself that it was her friend.

She stopped a respectful distance away, hoping she'd put the bra on right. By the divines, if she'd have to ask Tiphaine to teach her…

Actually, she smiled thinking on it further, *maybe if I pretend to be thoroughly incompetent, I could get a demonstration…*

She pulled herself away from such thoughts.

"Um… My king, can you hear me through this man?" she asked the man of the lake. Seeing the flesh rotting off his face, she noticed the slight tremble in her unfamiliarly cute voice.

The corpse remained quiet but nodded its head in response. Perhaps it no longer had vocal cords. Strange that its ears and eyes still seemed to work, then, even after they had all rotten away.

"My king, I've come to report back to you – I was forced into the water by some humans that I need to remain ignorant of my nature. I will go back soon – but first, I thought I would relay to you some information – we have discovered that your queen really may have been taken somewhere from here, after you died on that boat ten years ago."

The man of the lake stood completely still, unmoved by the waves that rhythmically swayed her.

"The men that may have taken her had a local named Derreck – no, Garrick, that was the name – cart around the corpses of your personal guards for them when they left the village after the coup was done. We hope to find this man soon, to ask him if your queen was among them – though she would have been alive, of course."

Upon hearing the last of her words, the floating cadaver slowly moved an arm towards its front and abruptly punched itself in the face. Suddenly, it started pounding its head forward into its knees, shattering its own bones, before continuing to punch itself again. Its head was fracturing with every impact it laid on itself. Emony could only look on with her mouth open, thoroughly unnerved.

The tantrum lasted for minutes.

Then, when it finally calmed down, it stood unmoving in the water again, as if nothing had happened. Emony couldn't tell what to do or say next.

She heard a woman's voice pierce the wall of bubbles behind her.

"Garrick can't help us," said Verena, who appeared a moment later.

"Verena – my lady. It's good to see you. That's… a shame. We were hoping to spend the day interrogating him. May I ask why we can't?"

The mermaid swam over closer to her and sadly gazed at the man of the lake. "The dead cannot remember. Their minds are gone. That's Garrick, right in front of you."

Emony turned to look at the corpse. He did look a little… fresh?

"He joined the ranks only a week ago. It was an accident," Verena said.

"I suppose the villagers don't know yet, since they say he was a merchant…" she responded, nodding. "They must think he's gone to sell something in another village or town."

Verena swam even closer to her, stopping near her face as she floated awkwardly in the light current, trying to balance herself with her one good arm. *Garrick the merchant* followed.

"I hope that wasn't your only lead?" Verena asked hopefully.

"Merely the first," she responded quickly, eyeing the pair of grimy eye sockets watching her. "I'm sure we will have another soon. On that note, I should probably get back to land to go and find it."

"Yes, that would be great. Come back when you find something new, or if you need any sort of help. We'll be glad to provide it. Hey, Emony, Garrick's house was that way. It's on a little hill. I know, because he would often… we used to be friends, of a sort."

"I see. I'm… sorry, then. I'll be back soon."

Verena shifted around the water nervously. "One more thing. Since you've already talked to the villagers – did any of them mention a settlement called Palehome? It's north of here, the opposite direction from Terrena. A few days march, according to Aulduyen."

"No, none of them mentioned it."

"Make certain it's not important, that we don't need any information anyone there might have. And tell us soon if there might be. We can give you…. I'm sorry, perhaps three days, at the most."

"Three days. Okay. I'll ask around again, and if anyone mentions it's connected at all to the rebellion, I'll let you know."

"Or anything else that might be related," added Verena. "Anything at all."

"Of course. I'll be back soon with my next report."

The dead form of Garrick nodded and swam back to where it had floated from before she arrived. Before Emony could turn to leave as well, Verena spoke to her again.

"Just one more thing, Emony. You understand why I'm asking… right?"

"Yes," she nodded, for a moment looking past Verena towards the man of the lake, who was shifting away. "Yes, I think I do."

3

Tiphaine

"He doesn't like being wet," she was explaining to their assistant, Aylard, at around the same time. "It's because when he was young, only a toddler, his mom dropped him into a puddle and left him there… That's how he became an orphan, you know."

"What kind of a stupid story is that? Try harder, lady Tiphaine, by the divines."

"That's what he told me, though. I'm serious. About how he ended up alone."

"Is he going to tell you that ale is poisonous to him, too? Don't believe him. I saw him drinking it when we accosted you in the tavern when you arrived."

They were on their way to find Garrick's house on the far end of the village.

"Oh, were you one of the soldiers? I don't remember seeing you there."

"I was. I was behind Sir Meheyn, I was wearing a helmet. But really, he runs fast with a broken arm… Well, I suppose it's not his leg. Anyway, have you known each other very long? Perhaps since right after you… hatched?"

"I'm part viper, so I didn't come out of an egg, and no, not that long," she waved him off. "I think I'd been through… I don't know, ten winters before I first met him? So… it was about nine cycles ago. He's three cycles older, so he must have been thirteen. Haha, his chin was completely hairless back then."

She noticed a human about that same age hiding in the bushes along her path, trying to sneak a peek at her without being noticed. The people were so afraid of lamias here. It was completely different from Aeliah. But then, she'd played a large part in making it so, so she couldn't complain.

"How old are you?" she asked Aylard, changing the subject.

"Twenty-three years," he replied. "That's what we call "cycles" here."

"Oh. Okay."

"I'm surprised you've managed to stay friends for nearly a decade. He seems like a loner."

Tiphaine smiled. "He is. Most of Aeliah is afraid of him when he's not with me. He's really paranoid and reclusive, especially around the humans. My friend Lenah and I are probably the only ones he talks to on a regular basis. Whenever we leave him alone, he just goes hunting in the woods."

"He likes killing things, then."

"Yeah... It's his nature. But he's a softy, trust me. I asked him to stop hunting rabbits one time, I said they were too cute, and he really did for a couple of weeks. And he's changed my bandages three times today, and that's hard to do with one hand."

The human snorted. "I wouldn't have thought it. I hope you're not in pain, by the way, those seem pretty tight. I'm curious, has he ever seen your face? Since, you know, he can't do so without turning to stone, being a human and all, like he said."

"Of course he has. He can see me any time he wants so long as my eyes are closed. Oh, but every now and then, when we find... the stuff, the cure for petrification, he'll get curious, and I'll show him my eyes, too. He turns to stone, of course, but he can still see, so I twirl around for him a bit and revive him again. Apparently, I'm really pretty – a real heartstopper. You want to see?"

"I think I'll pass, if you don't mind. He trusts you to bring him back though? You know – I recall the villagers saying something about you putting something in their mouths to bring them – oh – divines! Sorry, I'll pretend I didn't hear that!"

Tiphaine glanced over at Aylard, confused by his sudden reaction. "Hm? Oh, don't mind them.

They have minds of their own, but they're not actually dangerous, the hair-vipers."

"You just said they were vipers," he said, anxiously eyeing the top of her head. The snakes were hissing at him, ready to strike. "Vipers are venomous."

"But only a little bit," she cringed, turning to him, lifting her veil a bit to show him her mouth and extending her fangs. "I am much, much more."

"I'll keep that in mind," he replied, with a hint of fear in his voice that hadn't been there before.

She set down the veil again and continued slithering down the road. She wondered when Emony would join them again. He was probably down in the lake somewhere, cursing his cute face. Or staring at him… herself?

Hopefully just staring. No matter what Lenah says, I'm sure he's still a man in there, she thought.

Then she began wondering which of the two of them might be prettier. It was hard to tell.

"But you're right, you know," she spoke aloud to distract herself. "We did put something in their mouths to unpetrify them. It's pretty easy to free people if they haven't been statues for long. It just becomes harder or impossible if they remain that way for more than a week or so."

"Pretty easy, like how your vipers are a liiittle poisonous, I'm sure."

"Haha. Maybe. Actually, I can't say, Emony would get angry with me. Oh, right, we didn't talk about this, okay? If he finds out we did, he'll… Well, he won't kill you, probably, but you won't have a good time. And he'll call me stupid again."

Aylard, whilst nodding in her direction, waved at and made some strange gestures to some passerby who were keeping their distance from them.

"I'll keep that in mind," he said. "We're almost there. Sorry, do you mind waiting here for a moment? I'd like to go ask those people there about Garrick, but they might not talk if you're with me. I think they might be his neighbors."

"Awww, I want to go too. But fine. Go."

With a nod, the human ran off towards the others, who were still casting nervous glances her way. She slithered a little distance in the opposite direction towards a spot the sunlight managed to touch next to the lake. Her hair-vipers appreciated it, hissing contentedly above her forehead. Stroking a few of them gently, she closed her eyes and stretched out over the grass, taking in the meagre warmth. She wouldn't mind if Aylard took a while…

"Tiphaine!"

The sun really felt so good… She wished she could stay there forever. Maybe with a fire close by, too?

"Tiphaine!" That voice again…

"What do you want?" she yawned, too tired to open her eyes. It was time to sleep. "Are you already back, Aylard? Is it time to go? Let's wait for another minute or two…"

Hm? That's not Aylard's voice…

She struggled for a moment to open her sleepy eyes. Once she did, what she saw in the blurry light was the strangest thing.

A breathtakingly cute girl with a scaly tail and fin the color of the sun was struggling to pull herself out of the water with a single delicate arm.

"Who are you?" she gasped, stupefied.

The small features on the girl's face contorted into the most endearing sort of angry expression Tiphaine had ever seen.

"Are you still asleep?! Help me!" the little mermaid hissed.

She couldn't possibly refuse, she thought, shaking her head and quickly getting up.

Actually, she could have, she realized a moment later, when she came back to her senses. Emony hadn't forced his… her…? *Yeah, her* definitely fit better right now. *Her* will upon Tiphaine with magic this time. Nevertheless, she decided to help pull her out of the water.

"You're back," she whispered, at the same time trying to calm her hair-vipers, which were angry that they'd been woken up.

"I'm back," Emony repeated back to her with a ridiculously girly voice. She really couldn't picture the werewolf she knew was in there.

"And I've spoken to the king," Emony continued. "Sort of. Are you alone?"

Tiphaine shook her head to clear her thoughts again and looked up over the slight incline that hid the pebble shore from the road. Aylard was still talking to the humans a little ways away.

"No," she said, "but I think we have a minute or two."

"Good. I don't suppose you have a towel?"

"Actually, I do. Here – Aylard bought it for me ten minutes ago. I thought you might need it."

"Good thinking. Help dry me off, would you – ouch! Not so rough with the end of the tail!"

"Divines, you're cute. Nice bra," Tiphaine said.

Delightedly watching Emony blush, she let her make her empty threats while she helped her out. It took a couple of minutes, but she managed to get her quite dry. The hair took the most work, since it was the human kind. Then Emony closed her eyes and made an expression of extreme concentration. Soon after, her face and body changed, and her golden tail lost its color as it slowly separated into two human legs.

It seemed *he* had gotten better at controlling his form, she noted, looking away. He wasn't completely dry yet, but he'd already managed to change back. And earlier, back at the tavern, he'd managed to resist the transformation for about half a minute, even though it had taken him by surprise.

"Thank you, Tiphaine," he said. "You've no idea the relief I feel every time I manage to turn back."

"But it's really a shame, Emony, you were so much cuter a few seconds ago," she murmured in reply.

"Do you want to die?"

"Haha. Hey, here are those clothes I brought along in case you wet yourself. Those are the last pants, so be careful – and give me your wet tunic, I'll put it in my bag. Oh, no, you can keep the bra."

"Tiphaine…"

"What? You might need it again! What if the king starts lusting after you? Haha, fine… Anyway, um, you're not going to make me look up forever, are you?"

"Give me a second, it's hard to do this with one hand. Do you have another sling, too?"

"Yeah, I'll get it ready for you. Right. Well, um, we are on our way to Garrick's house. The people at the tavern told us where it is and we're almost there. With a little luck, we'll find him and the queen shacked up in it."

"It'd take a lot of luck. I just saw Garrick. He's dead. He's become a man of the lake. Okay, I'm done, you can look."

"Are you sure it's him that you saw?" she asked, lowering her gaze from the cloudy horizon above him.

Emony nodded, mirroring the uneasy expression she hid underneath her veil. "Verena told me. Anyway, it might still be a good idea to go there. We might find some clues, even if the human is gone. Also, have you heard any mention of a town called Palehome while I was down in the lake? Anything at all?"

She shook her head. "No... I don't think so."

"Absolutely nothing?"

"No, why? What is that place?" she asked, slithering over to him and gently placing his broken arm into a dry piece of cloth.

"Not important, apparently," he shrugged, looking up at her whilst pulling on his new pair of boots. "I'll tell you later. But come to me right away if you do hear something about it."

She agreed, noting that he was trying to hide something from her again, and turned to look back at the road. Aylard was returning, looking around to try to find her.

"It's time to go," she said.

4

Emony

He saw the first sign of the killing before he entered the house. The crimson red of the blood stood out against the white flowers it was staining in the garden. The second sign was the trail of dried droplets that led to the little wooden house, and the third, past the open front door, was the splintered wall lying on the floor beside the back door, which was ripped open and hanging on a single hinge.

The human, Aylard, who had been talking to him leisurely until then, apologizing for spilling his drink, abruptly shut up and unsheathed his sword, carefully stalking forward in front of them. *What a hero,* Emony thought. Unimpressed, he strode past him into the house and peered into the bedroom. The bed was unmade, with blankets lying all around, betraying that someone had jumped out of it in a hurry. Emony tasted the air out of instinct before remembering he was no longer a werewolf – but he didn't really need to be one to smell that something had died there. The dried pool of blood next to the bed was starting to turn. Tiphaine was still slithering before the front door, pinching her nose under her mask, obviously uncomfortable. Shooting her a smile, Emony stepped fully into the small room and closed the door behind him.

Stepping gingerly past the pool of blood, he opened up the small nightstand that lay collapsed on the wooden floor next to the bed. How he missed having two functioning arms.

There was a small leather purse in the nightstand, which he grabbed and pocketed without hesitation. He looked over the other contents as well before tossing them onto the bed one by one: a bowl, a shaving knife, a key, a quill and even two letters written on parchment.

He turned them over and read, holding them still with his good hand. They were old and damp, but still legible. One was a note from the "Bank of Trouwts", informing Garrick the merchant that he owed them a sum of twenty-seven silver pieces, to be paid back by spring of next year. He shook the pocket he'd put the man's purse in. He didn't have enough. The other was a letter to "Lenah of Gulls Landing." It was a love letter he hadn't sent. There was a silver ring tied to it with a string.

Lenah of Gull's Landing. If it was the same Lenah Emony knew… No, actually it wouldn't be that surprising. She lived all over the place. Maybe it was her.

Poor guy.

He lifted the letter to the light of the window to get a better look at the ring. It was real silver, he saw. As a werewolf, he'd never been able to touch it, but he certainly knew how to make it out. Lenah would have hated the thing if she received it. Any witch would have.

After a moment of thought, he rejoined his companions in the main room, keeping both the ring and the two letters.

"Find anything?" he asked Aylard.

"By the look of things, he was attacked," Aylard muttered, glancing in Emony's direction for a moment.

"Obviously. He's also dead. I meant, did you find anything that could help us find out how he was involved in moving the former queen."

The human winced and went back to looking around, shaking his head.

"Tiphaine?" he inquired next.

"No, I didn't find anything either," she said, her hand over her mouth.

"Are you okay?"

She nodded quickly. She was obviously lying.

He resolved to find that new lead quickly. "Aylard, the man didn't die in here. He was asleep when his attacker came in. He woke up as it entered the bedroom – got slashed across the chest and stomach, staggered away, made it outside, and died there. Don't bother with that, help me find out who the man was."

Aylard looked over at him in shock. He returned the gaze – he'd expected the human to be more familiar with death.

"I know, because I'm the one that did it," he joked. It didn't seem that it was appreciated.

Unfortunately, over the next twenty minutes, they found nothing. Emony had Tiphaine leave the house, convincing her, despite her protests, that there could be clues outside, before ransacking the place and finding nothing but more wooden bowls, mugs, some silverware and a small barrel of cider that smelled like it had turned.

Once again, he looked over the pieces of parchment he'd taken.

"What do you care about what happened to that girl, anyway?" asked Aylard. "The rebellion was ten years ago. It has nothing to do with the men of the lake."

"So says the expert," he murmured, trying to read. It was harder when someone was trying to talk to him.

"Look – I haven't seen a woman trying to murder us any of the times we've been attacked. So please explain it to me. Why is finding this girl, Imarah, important? ... Shouldn't we be researching ways to break curses? How to destroy the undead? Well?"

After a few wasted moments, Emony looked up from the letters, smiling maliciously. He hadn't managed to read a thing.

"I'd rather not say. Just trust that it's important and stop asking questions about why. Or, I might just *trip,* and *accidentally* slit your throat.

Tiphaine might be cross with me, but you'll be with the men of the lake. You'll understand everything."

Aylard stared at him in disbelief for a few seconds, then looked away, apparently unsure which expression he should wear on his face.

Suddenly, while he was staring at him, Emony was struck by a thought: That every word the human had spoken might have been consciously schemed. It seemed, somehow, like there was a methodical order to every question…

No, no, he was just being paranoid again. As Tiphaine said, humans always brought out the worst in him. It wasn't his fault, after what they'd done to his parents, but…

"I don't think we are going to find anything here," Aylard said as he was thinking, not meeting his eyes. "We've looked through the whole place. Unless you found something in the bedroom?"

"Maybe I did," he said, narrowing his eyes. That feeling was back. For a moment, he wondered if he should turn into a mermaid and ask him a few questions. Were he still a werewolf, he would have pulled the truth out of his throat… but becoming a mermaid was too unnerving. He decided against it.

"Come then. Let's go."

"Yeah."

"Find anything, Tiphaine?" he asked, stepping out into the garden. His preferred companion was slithering around the grass in the garden, careful not to disturb the bloody scene of the murder.

She pointed over to the patch of flowers stained by blood. "I think he died here," she said. "But it's not where the trail ends. The smell is faint, but it goes that way."

"To the lake," Emony said. "Where he is now."

For a moment, he wondered if she had accepted that Verena was likely complicit in the murder. Knowing her, she was probably trying to avoid thinking about it. There was no point in forcing it on her.

"Aylard, I trust you will report this to the knight commander? Judging by the color and the smell of the blood, I'd say the man died a week ago. Let's get back to camp."

Of course, he couldn't really smell anything. But what was the harm? It's not paranoia if you're right.

Chapter 6

1

Yperian

"I heard your expedition yesterday bore fruit," Yperian said, pouring the mythics some drinks, as had seemed to become custom during their many meetings.

He noticed, once again, that Emony was being very careful with his chalice – unusually so. He hated spilling good wine as much as the next man, but it still struck him as odd. Aylard had reported to him earlier that the man was ghastly afraid of being wet, too. It was strange – and likely due to his true nature. Seeing him handle the silver without care made him suspect he was not a werewolf or sorcerer, as he'd initially suspected. He was likely something else... Of course, he wouldn't reveal anything related to the matter to anyone. For some reason, it struck him that no good would come from doing so.

"The merchant is dead," Emony said. "He was killed and taken by the men of the lake. He's one of them now. Unless, for whatever reason, he decided to fake his own death and run."

The lamia turned to look at him through her jeweled mask, the vipers on her head hissing quietly, while Emony busied himself with tying a new bandage around her stomach. Yperian saw that her wound had already mostly healed – startlingly quickly. The man's broken arm, unfortunately, had not.

Perhaps he really is human, Yperian thought. But he doubted it.

"That's not it. It was human blood, I could tell from the smell," said Tiphaine, raising her arms to make things easier on her companion.

Yperian leaned back into his chair. "I assumed that's what happened, anyway. A shame. Anyway, my man Aylard tells me you're searching for a girl, one that likely died in the rebellion ten years ago. May I ask why?"

"She's involved," said Emony, tying a knot.

"How?"

The snake looked down towards her friend. "Should we tell him?"

He shrugged. "Maybe not everything, but... why not?"

"So, um... This girl, Imarah, she's connected to the men of the lake. If we find her, and we bring her to them, we might be able to end all the bloodshed."

"Provided she's alive?"

"I... don't know. But even if she's not, we still need to find her and bring her here. Yes, even if she's dead. It's the only thing that matters – if we do that, the men of the lake might stop attacking."

Yperian leaned forward and laid his chin on his hands, thinking.

"I cannot possibly see why. But I suppose the reason is simple: magic. A set of forces and rules I couldn't possibly understand. I will not ask you to explain. So, this merchant of yours, the one that died, he was the lead that might have led you to the girl? Aylard said it was his carriage that the knights used to cart around the dead ten years ago, and that she may have ended up on it. I happen to know that quite a few of the knights involved in the coup were from Terrena. I'm even acquainted with some of them. I'll send a few men to ask them about the matter, but it would perhaps be easier if I knew more about the merchant than just his name. It has been ten years."

"I doubt it, but maybe these will help," said Emony, taking some pieces of parchment from a pocket in his jacket. Come to think of it, Yperian couldn't imagine where the man could have gotten yet another set of clothing. At this point, he looked downright regal. But… that wasn't important. *Was it?*

"They're letters, one of which Garrick wrote himself. It seems the man was literate."

"Not terribly unusual, for a merchant."

Tiphaine leaned in close to Emony. "Do you really think it's for Lenah? The one we know?"

"You know what she's like. It may well be. Maybe not, though, there was a silver ring tied to the letter."

"A silver one? Lenah would've hated that. Let me see it. Oh, but it's so pretty!"

"Then keep it."

"Seriously? Thanks! I'll treasure it forever."

"You better, or Garrick's ghost will come after you."

"The Bank of Trouwts... I believe that business is in Levara. Oh, right, you're foreigners. It's a small town southwest of here. About as far away as Terrena, though in a different direction. Not many go there, there are lots of swamps in that corner of the kingdom. It's plagued by diseases, more so than by bandits. The perfect place for a brave merchant, though, come to think of it. And this... a love letter? For the lady...? The king's royal advisor? No, never mind, it can't be. Hm, it's not half bad. I like the double meaning here. But Gull's Landing... that is somewhat closer to here than Levara. More of a village, similar to Coldbarrow. It's to the northeast – by the frozen sea. That's the ocean, you know. Only that, that far north the ice never truly melts. It's too risky for a ship to go there."

"Not further north..." grumbled the cold-blooded Tiphaine.

"Northeast – is it close to Palehome?" asked Emony.

He needed a map, Yperian realized. He was relying far too much on his shabby memory. Still... "I don't think so, not really. I suppose you could go to Palehome on your way to Gull's Landing if you wanted to, but you would have to take a detour. A rather pointless one, even for a merchant – the savages of Palehome don't speak our language or use our currency. Speaking plainly, that's the rear end of Evaria."

Emony seemed to gaze at him uneasily. "Is there already snow up there?" he asked.

"I would imagine so. Palehome is up on a mountain, so they must have snow all year round."

The man and the lamia shared a look. Yperian wished he knew the context behind it.

"Bummer. Well, what about Gull's Landing?"

"No snow there yet. There will be soon, mind you – but not yet. An envoy coming from there passed through Coldbarrow on his way to Terrena, only two weeks ago. He said that the climate was refreshing, whatever that means. It's a much more commonly travelled path than that to Palehome, if you're looking to visit."

"I think we're going to have to," said Emony. It seemed he wasn't going to spare his cold-blooded friend any suffering. "On the off-chance that's the Lenah we know, we could use her help, and if it's not, perhaps it was someone who was close to the dead guy. Sorry, Tiphaine. After that, if we don't find anything, we can go to Levara."

"As if it's not cold enough here," the lamia grumbled.

"We'll need some more warm clothing," Emony told Yperian.

"Understood," he nodded, not dissatisfied in the least. Their leaving would be a welcome respite for the villagers, if nothing else. "We'll pack you some provisions, then. In the meantime, I'll send a few of my men to Terrena, and have them ask those knights about the merchant. Perhaps I could have them ask King Raynardt, too. He's quite intent on having this situation resolved quickly, and my reports up until now have brought nothing but bad news. If this would help end the threat of the undead, he would be glad to help. And even if he knows nothing, we could at least petition him to send us more men."

"Thank you. That sounds good. Well then, please point us in the direction of Gull's Landing tomorrow. We'll leave at dawn."

2

Emony

By the sides of the dirt road that was their path, three days' walk from Coldbarrow, two beanpoles were driven into the ground. Each held a sign pointing in a separate direction – one, depicting a crudely drawn picture of a bird, pointed directly along the road they were already following, apparently to Gull's Landing. The other pointed towards a path that wasn't there, in a direction where no carriage had left its mark on the frosty dirt. A snowflake drawn in red was on that sign.

They chose to follow the road.

"So that's the way out of Evaria," said Aylard, leaning out of his saddle and glancing in the direction of the mountain range. "Doesn't seem like there's much of a world out there. The commander told me about a settlement out in those hills, but I forget the name."

Emony shrugged his shoulders and kept walking. "I'm sure they're civilized folk."

"Ha! Far from it! I used to hear stories as a child, actually, of barbarians raiding in the night, burning down villages for the fun of it. Not that I take them at face value now, but no food can grow out of the permafrost, so I suppose stealing must be the only viable way of life up there."

"Or hunting," said Tiphaine, slithering a little too close to the horse and madly scaring it with her hair. Immediately, the beast tried to throw Aylard off of itself.

"Divines! Calm down, Starling!" the human shouted at the animal carrying both him and all their supplies, holding the reigns with all his might. Tiphaine winced and moved further away from them.

Emony, looking over her for a moment, tossed her his coat. She was cold-blooded, after all. Startled, she didn't manage to catch it, but she did put it on after lifting her mask over her lips and mouthing a silent "thank you" with a smile. Emony noticed she was still wearing that dead man's silver ring.

Sentimental idiot, he thought, returning the smile.

"So, what are we looking for in Gull's Landing? Cod?" asked Aylard.

"A woman named Lenah. If we're unlucky, she might just be an insufferable, immortal old witch with hair Tiphaine is jealous of. We need her alive."

"Hey! That's not true! I love my hair-vipers."

She really did. She'd once told him they reminded her of home. Of her mom.

Her mom, huh... Emony looked ahead uneasily.

The human next to him, Aylard, expressed confusion. "Well, I don't see why we would go all this way to kill her. What do you mean, "immortal"? In any case, she's not the girl from the rebellion?"

"No."

"You're not going to tell me anything? I only mean to help," he said.

"You're being very helpful," Tiphaine called, keeping her distance from him and the horse.

Emony, wondering again if he was being too paranoid before making a decision, made a mental note to really become a mermaid once during the trip so he could ask Aylard if he was a duplicitous fraud. Better to do it sooner rather than later. And he'd been so happy to keep his legs and sane mind for a whole day.

"Perhaps we could ask those people if they know her? They seem to be coming from Gull's Landing," Aylard asked, pointing at a group of travelers moving along the road in their direction.

Emony stopped for a moment, considering it. What if they were his friends and coconspirators? No, that was ridiculous, he was just being paranoid. Aylard had done them no harm.

Yet, he thought, remembering the source of his paranoia.

"Go, then," he said, though distrust was still filling his mind. "Remember, Lenah of Gull's Landing. And if they ask, it's Garrick, a merchant from Coldbarrow, that's asking."

"Right." Aylard pressed his heels against the horse's chest and galloped ahead of them. Emony, an uneasy expression on his face, went and joined Tiphaine.

"It must be annoying, trying to ask the locals for anything with me around," she said. "I wonder if that is the appropriate reaction to my kind – to keep your distance, and cower in fear."

He shrugged, eyeing the hissing snakes on her head. He had long ago stopped fearing them in the slightest. Currently, they had gotten all tangled up and were fighting each other to find out who could stand tallest above her. He wondered if they could recognize him after seeing him so many times.

"Sure, it is," he replied. "For years, I've been soiling myself every time I look at you, Tiphaine, if I'm going to be honest. It's been terribly difficult trying to hide it."

She chuckled. He looked back towards the humans ahead of them.

"But if you'd like, I'll slaughter every one of those cowards over there for making you feel this way. My broken arm is no obstacle at all."

"Emony…"

"Don't worry, I'm just joking. Actually, I'm not. Just say the word. Hm? What is that idiot doing? … Ah. I thought knights were supposed to know how to ride horses."

"Aylard's not a knight, he's a commoner."

"Whatever you say. I can't be bothered to learn the difference. You've been talking to him a lot these past few days."

"Shouldn't I have? Are you getting jealous?"

"I wonder… Maybe I am. Do you have a problem with that?"

"Nope. Not at all – but I can tell that's not what's really troubling you. Emony, I know something's up, what is it?"

"My paranoia is acting up again," he lied, skillfully, by revealing a lesser truth.

"I noticed," Tiphaine sighed. "But it wasn't Aylard back then, all those years ago. You know that, don't you? It wasn't any of the humans we've met here."

"That's the thing – I don't know that. Not for sure. I can't remember the faces from back then. I don't even know how many humans there were. It would have had to have been a lot, to best two purebred werewolves…"

He glanced over in the direction of where Palehome must have been for a few moments before returning his gaze to her.

"But I trust you. If you say it wasn't this *one specific commoner*, I'll believe you."

"It wasn't. I promise he had nothing to do with it."

"You have no way at all of knowing that, but okay. Fine, I'll try to play nice."

"Great. Now, then, if you wouldn't mind, I'm freezing. Furs and coats can only help the cold-blooded so much. Give me a hug, doggy?"

Emony smiled and gently pulled off her cold metal mask, before reaching under her furs and coats and wrapping both arms, broken and not, around her.

"Don't think I don't know you're playing me," he said. "You can't win – you know how much I hate the sound of your laugh. It's always accompanied by misfortune for me."

"Not every time," Tiphaine murmured into his ear, leaning her head on his shoulder. She really was cold.

"Really? Do you remember that time – urgh, never mind. He's coming back. Close your eyes."

Far too soon for Emony's liking, Aylard came riding back towards them. As he came close, Emony noticed the discomfort on his face.

"What is it?" he asked, not letting go of Tiphaine. "Is she dead?"

The human shook his head. "No, but she really is a witch. A sorceress."

"Damn. What a pain, it really is her. Poor Garrick – horrible taste in women."

"She's your friend, Emony," Tiphaine said.

"Absolutely. My best friend – and matchmaker."

Tiphaine giggled by the side of his head.

"Actually, speaking of matchmaking," Aylard continued, "these merchants I just talked to said the witch has a great deal of suiters. The men seem to love her. This despite her being – entirely in the open – as a witch.”

“She must be giving them that love potion,” Tiphaine laughed.

Terrible memories surfaced in Emony’s mind.

Aylard continued: “They say she’s staying with an envoy from Terrena, the very man sent from the capital to deal with her. They have a cottage on the outskirts of town.”

“Surely, she couldn’t have poisoned the whole town? Tiphaine would kill her out of jealousy if she were that popular.”

At that, a mass of hair-vipers began coiling in front of his face, angrily hissing at him. He couldn’t even swat them away; he was too busy sharing his body heat.

“Well, now that you mention it, they only mentioned the men liking her. And I know from experience that the women of Gull’s Landing are the jealous type. Perhaps we should hurry, before they kill her.”

Emony smiled. “Don’t you try to help them, Tiphaine. You said it yourself; she is our friend.”

In response to his taunt, her vipers messed up his hair as she threateningly ran the edge of a poisonous fang along his shoulder. But there was still a day’s worth of walking ahead, and she needed warmth. He won.

3

“That snake-thing stays away,” repeated the town guard, staring at the three of them with his spear pointed in their direction. “Are you deaf? Monsters are not allowed here. How many times must I repeat myself?”

"A few more times, apparently," stated Emony, annoyed. "But it won't make a difference – she's coming with us. It's cold out here even for me, and I have warm blood in my veins."

"You say that like it's a bad thing – but a dead monster can only ever be the opposite."

Emony glanced over at Tiphaine for a moment and shrugged before taking a step closer to the human. "I'm done playing nice. Are you feeling witty?"

Tiphaine quickly grabbed him again and held him back. The town guard stared at them in disgust.

"We have a letter of intent and pass from the knight commander of the Coldbarrow field legion!" shouted Aylard. "You must let us into the village, to not do so would be to break the law!"

"Law, you say," the man huffed. "That applies to humans. And I'll be daft if I ever call that thing one of us! It stays outside – lucky I don't kill it, as the laws I know demand! It can slither over to Palehome if it wants, those fiends can take it in. We've got enough problems already with the king's damned witch! Now go on, monster! Scram!"

They had wasted too much time already. Aylard was reaching for his coin pouch, preparing option number two. Emony had rapidly become disgusted by option number two. He jumped straight to number three instead, opting for the most personally satisfying solution.

Quickly retrieving his unbroken hand from Tiphaine's, he grabbed Aylard's sword from its scabbard and leaped forward, reaching with it for the guard's neck before the fool could react. But as soon as it collided, instead of slicing through, the blade stopped and crashed off the human, ringing Emony's arm like a bell.

"Argh!" he shouted in pain, the vibrations reverberating through his arm. "What the—"

He glared at the human. He was suddenly grayer than the dull clouds in the sky. Only a small piece had been chipped out of his stone neck.

"Tiphaine!" he hissed, whirling around.

"Don't look! Nor you, Aylard! I didn't want him dead, okay? Be angry if you want, Emony, but I didn't! Okay, now you can look."

"You would have killed him," gasped Aylard, staring at Emony, patting his waist, unable to locate his weapon. "We could have worked something out, or gone around him… But you would have killed him! He's a human being!"

"And I'm not! So I don't care!" he shouted, shoving the sword back towards him.

He stalked over to Tiphaine, staring angrily at her golden mask for a few moments before redirecting his anger towards the stone man again.

He leaned in close so his two companions wouldn't hear his words. "That snake you just called a monster gave you another chance at life right now, fool. But don't worry. There is no need to feel grateful. As soon as she tries to sneak away from me to free you, I will be there again to end you."

He toppled over the statue into the dirt and glared back at his two companions. "Come on. Let's get moving."

Lenah's house in Gull's Landing was a large one, easily twice the size of the one she had in Aeliah. He could see smoke rising from the stone chimney, and colored glass windows allowing light inside. A metal door stood, baring their way, closed and locked. They had been knocking on it for ten minutes, standing around in the cold, before the footsteps Emony heard inside finally deigned to come open it. Typical.

"What do' y wan?" asked the man who opened the door, however, a tall, somewhat fat human with crumbs on his face and messy hands, with no shirt shielding him from the cold. The smell of some sort of smoke was strong on his breath – and that was gray, as if it were coming out of a chimney. Emony suddenly found his foul mood abating, turning to pity.

What has she done to him?

"Good tidings to you, sir," said Aylard politely, taking the lead, while he opted to stand behind him and hide Tiphaine from the man's line of sight. "We beg your pardon, we've come to speak to the lady Lenah."

"Lady? That's rich," Emony snorted.

"Not herrrre," the man said, swaying and leaning onto the door to close it. Aylard stepped forward and prevented him from doing so.

"May we ask where she is? We've been assured that she lived in a cottage on the outskirts of town. Have we come to the wrong place?"

"No, this is definitely the right place," said Tiphaine, eyeing the troubled human.

The man raised his head toward the sky, seemingly confused. He squinted with his bloodshot eyes. His pupils covered nearly the entirety of his eyes.

"I don't think it's that love potion of hers, Tiphaine. It looks worse. Divines, she managed to make something worse."

"No. It can't be worse than the love potion. No way."

"Not here. There's…. nobody here. Nobody real. Listennn… Come back in the… in the morning, okay? Come in the morning. You're not here, either, anyway."

"It's… already noon," Emony replied.

"Oh?" The man suddenly looked like he was going to hurl. "Oh… Oh, then come back… back in the evening."

"Urgh, damned witch." Rolling his eyes, Emony stepped past Tiphaine and Aylard and brushed past the man, entering the house. While the poor sod weakly protested, struggling to speak coherently, he took in the scene – and the heavy smell of smoke clinging to the dim, thick air. A table in the middle of the large room was covered with washcloths soaked in wine, tipped-over jugs and goblets, messy plates, fancy cutlery and wax candles dripping onto the floor, where shattered pieces of glass were littered around, all over the room. Smoke was rising in many small quantities from rolled-up leaves lying around on toppled chairs.

It was definitely the Lenah he knew that lived there. He grimaced. After turning him into a fish, she'd gone and had a party.

Emony looked back towards the human at the door, who was nearly tripping over himself trying to stand straight. Tiphaine, of all people, was helping keep him steady, he couldn't even see clearly enough to panic at the sight of her.

He shrugged, a small hint of sympathy touching his heart. His experience had been very different, but the man's plight was not entirely unknown to him. Lenah's potions were always something else.

He strode over to the table, took a goblet and poured a drink. The wine smelled good, but he knew better than to ingest it.

With Aylard behind him, Emony strode further into the house. Beside countless wooden chalices lying on the floor and more of those rolled-up, smoking leaves was a small, expensive-looking woman's shoe – but only one.

For a moment, he wasn't sure if he should keep going, but he could still see Tiphaine patting the human on the back, watching him puke in front of her, and Aylard gazing uncomfortably at him, silently pleading with him to get further away from the two of them. He didn't want vomit on his clothes, either, so, shrugging, he continued forward.

The room split into two halls, one going left, the other right. Behind the corner on the left, he saw the second shoe, draped on a coat hanger next to a door, along with a long, ornate black gown.

Emony, glancing over at Aylard for a moment to let him know he was to be quiet, silently opened the door and peered inside before shutting it just as stealthily. She was in there.

He knocked on the door gently. "Lenah? It's me. Are you decent?"

"Yes, come in, Pauron," answered her sleepy voice.

He opened the door and stepped into the bedroom, walking over broken glass and littered clothes. "I'm not Pauron. The human is vomiting outside with Tiphaine. And you said you were decent."

A young, pale and freckled face, with ocean-blue eyes and lips, rose from the bedcovers, a stream of hair of the same hue following behind it.

"Oh, hi, Emony! I lied. Is that drink for me?"

Emony sighed and brought it over to her. He'd have thought she'd had too much already, but given she could talk, she was sober enough, unlike her newest lover.

"My lover?" she spat suddenly, looking at him in disgust, throwing off her blanket and revealing more of her nudity. She looked pretty stunning. "Absolutely not. Not that one. Pauron's just a court advisor. And a prude. Please, just hand over the wine. Thank you. Now clean up your thoughts, Emony, you've already got Tiphaine. And you too, man-hiding-behind-the-doorway."

He lifted an eyebrow. "You're not exactly making it easy for us. Aylard, just remember she's a good century older than she looks."

"Rude," Lenah growled.

"You can—"

"Read your thoughts? Yes, yes. But I can see you've already heard that I'm a witch, so why are you surprised? What are you guys doing here, anyway? Oh, Emony, you haven't managed to fix that yet? Was Verena not able to… Oh. Oh. Oh, my bad. So that's where all the black magic is coming from? Looks like I dropped you in the middle of something. That must be the first time you've ever had your arm broken, right? Let me play with it later. Hey, what's your name, in the doorway?"

"Ay—"

"Right. Aylard. So, Aylard stays in the dark, is that right, Emony? But you know I love gossiping. My silence has a price and I will collect. And I want to see Tiphaine."

The annoying witch scrambled out of the bed, long silk robes materializing out of nothing around her body as she stood up straight. While he watched, her blue hair brushed itself around her neck and jewels appeared out of nowhere over her new plunging neckline.

She drank deep from the goblet he'd brought her before abruptly throwing it away, walking over to him and invading his personal space with a hint of amusement in her eyes.

"Haha, it's not working, is it, Emony? Go on, try remembering how old I am. You know, Tiphaine would be devastated if she could hear you right now."

He shrugged. Tiphaine couldn't blame him for his thoughts, he couldn't control them. And Lenah was clearly being provocative.

"But will she see it that way? Why don't we find out? Tiphaine, come here! You have no idea what Emony is thinking about right now!"

Emony slammed his unbroken hand into the wall a few inches in front of her, blocking her from leaving before she could skip past him. Lenah only started giggling as she turned to face him again.

"Well, in that case, we'll have to find another way to have fun."

4

Though he'd seen it many times before, it was still unnerving, watching the room clean itself up, after the mess that it was in merely minutes earlier. The wooden chalices flew across the air of their own volition, landing on a table that cleaned itself up, the spilled wine lifting itself off the latter and floating out the window. Wax unstuck itself from the wooden floor and rejoined candles that lit themselves while the ashes in the fireplace regained the color and shape of logs and burst into a raging hot flame.

Two chairs materialized behind Emony and Aylard. Tiphaine, obviously, did not need one, as she was already warming herself on the floor by the fire.

While he and the human sat down, Lenah sat down on the edge of the table in front of them, rolling up a leaf and setting a drop of black liquid on it lightly aflame.

"Where did the guy from before go?" Emony asked Tiphaine.

"Look up," answered the witch, watching the smoke waft from the leaf she was holding.

Emony did as she said – and there, on the ceiling, was the human, sleeping soundly on a straw bed for which gravity had reversed.

"That's new," he said.

"We need the space. Here," Lenah said, offering him the leaf she was holding. "This is new, too. Breathe in the smoke."

Obviously, he didn't take it.

"Oh, come on, don't trust me? This is nothing like the love potion, I promise. It'll be fun. In fact, it will be really fun. And if you don't do it, I won't tell you about Garrick."

Emony squinted at his shameless blackmailer before glancing over at his companions for a moment. "Fine, but just me. You leave them out of this."

"Hahaha! No, that's not how this works, doggy. We're all going to do it. Here, if it will soothe your fears, I'll be the first. Look, this is how you do it. Just breathe in, breathe out."

She exhaled smoke from between her blue lips and offered him the leaf again. Sighing, Emony hesitantly took it, knowing full well something unbelievably stupid and unpleasant would happen.

He breathed in the horribly smelling air.

Instantly, a wire of magic slipped past his mental barriers and forced him to close his eyes. A strange feeling of wooziness fell over him.

Upon opening his eyes again, which he could only do with difficulty, he saw that the world had changed.

The colors were… accentuated. More vibrant than he had ever seen, even far more than when he'd been a wolf. And his hand, the one he was holding up in front of himself, holding the leaf… it was a liquid. No, he was wrong, actually, everything was a liquid. Everything in the world. His fingers melted away from his palm without pain. Seeing that, he wondered, curiously, if he was about to die. It felt like there was water in his head.

Am I drowning? This is so weird!

From seemingly far away, he heard the sound of laughter. He looked around the unfamiliar room, which had somehow expanded. Tiphaine, beside him, was staring at him, a mixture of worry and curiosity on her face. And Aylard was refusing something from Lenah – actually, her hair was even more blue than he'd thought. But he was still there, in the weird liquid room. His body was, at any rate. His mind, on the other hand, felt so far away…

He heard that laughter again. He was starting to feel giddy himself, though he couldn't tell why. Suddenly, he felt tingling all over his hands, neck, and the back of his head.

"Strange," he tried to say, but realized he couldn't. His mouth was already speaking something without his knowledge, and now he'd ruined it. He'd…

Then he figured it out. That laughter. It wasn't Tiphaine, Aylard or Lenah. It was him.

"What's so funny?" Tiphaine asked him as he snapped back to reality for a brief moment.

You wouldn't get it, he realized as he drifted off again. It'd be pointless to try to explain with words. But Lenah was smiling at him knowingly with those blue lips.

Do you feel the same thing? he mused, daring her to answer his unvoiced thoughts.

She gave him a small nod without a word and turned back to his companions. She could keep her composure, feeling this way? He really couldn't understand how.

"It will be okay, I'll give you a little less than I did him," the witch told Tiphaine, her voice just as much a liquid as the flames of the candles. He could *see* her voice. Reality was so distorted. He closed his eyes, trying to center himself – and that was a mistake. All around him was darkness, endless expanses of space…

He opened his eyes again. The whole world around him was breathing. He felt numb, but his hands were tingling like they were hot and cold at the same time. The subtle colors shifting through the air… were beautiful.

Looking around, he saw Aylard and Tiphaine share a leaf by the fireplace. He hoped to the divines that she would be okay.

Lenah got up from the table. The world seemed to stretch behind her as she walked over. Then she laid down on the ground in front of him, a pile of cushions appearing under her. Suddenly, Emony's chair disappeared out from under him and he was falling, falling, falling, until finally he too landed on a mass of cushions. Curious, he looked over at Lenah, who just smiled, then at the snakes atop Tiphaine's head. They were as calm as… Strange. Those things never stopped hissing. But it seemed like they did.

"Hey," Lenah said, lying in front of him, thoroughly careless about her revealing neckline. "Do you trust me yet?"

I've never trusted you for a day in my life, he thought happily before watching the thought fly away into the fireplace.

The witch's blue lips curved into that smile again. "Ha, that's probably wise. But give me your hand anyway. No, not that one. The broken one."

After a couple of moments, he decided to do so, for the sake of the mission, whatever that was, and began struggling with his sling. Eventually, he finally managed to stretch his arm out towards her. It seemed he was immune to pain in that moment. The next, he could feel the witch's light touch on his skin. Blue sparks sizzled out of her fingertips onto his arm. She caressed it gently before letting it go.

"There," she said. "You know how bad I am at healing magic, but I think I've done it right this time. You know, I think I'm actually somewhat better when I'm using this stuff."

He lifted his hand, curious, and made a fist a couple of times before turning his wrist and cracking his fingers a bit. It seemed like the arm really wasn't broken anymore. Then he felt something else. A liquid, sitting right in the middle of the palm of his other hand. He glanced over at it for a moment, stupidly curious, before looking up and seeing Lenah spill a chalice of water onto it. His skin started to tingle far more intensely than it did before. Rapidly panicking, he jumped up to his feet in an instant, nearly losing balance while doing so. He was about to transform.

He heard a squeak of laughter – Lenah's. He really did hate her. She glanced over at him and pointed in the direction of the bedroom. He ran towards it, falling over himself in the process and getting up again so he could trip his way through the door that opened itself for him. As soon as Emony made it into the room, he collapsed onto the floor in front of the bed, his boots and pants ripped apart and his legs combined into a scaly golden tail. At least *her* tunic held, so her tits weren't out.

The witch followed, closing the door after herself with a wave of her hand and smiling at her.

"That's what I wanted to see. My handiwork... I designed that new face of yours, you know. And all the rest. And I really did do well – you're so cute! Are you sure you want to turn back? I made you the first male, surface-walking mermaid in existence. That's pretty cool, isn't it, Emony? Oh, but you're not using my enchanted clothing. That didn't hold up? Don't worry, I'll make more."

"Lenah... Stop it. I'll admit it, this smoke thing you made is pretty cool, but please make it stop and help me get dry," Emony said, lacing magic into her voice. She was incredibly surprised that she had managed to string the words together into a sentence. "We've got a job to do."

Blue sparks flew off the witch in all directions, catching the magic.

"Nah!" she laughed. "Don't worry, Aylard won't see anything, he's pretty far gone himself... By the way, how do you like this new shield of mine? You can't sing me into obeying you, Emony. As much as you might want to, what with such things crossing your vulgar mind..."

Emony gulped, trying to think about anything else, but *she* quickly found herself unable to think clearly enough to remember even what she was trying not to think about. Her mouth was dry and the world was spinning. That was as far as she got.

"Damned hedonistic witch. Stop smiling like that, it's not attractive on a woman your age."

"Evidently, it is," Lenah shrugged, crouching in front of her and floating a chalice full of water right beside her head. Emony took it, gratefully, and drank from it.

Lenah twirled her fingers and a wind picked up, suddenly lifting her off the wooden floor, moving her backwards and dropping her on the bed. The witch walked over and sat down next to her.

"So, what do you want me to tell you about first? About Garrick? About how he adores me? Or about how Tiphaine, and how she feels about you? It's the same story, really."

She heard Tiphaine laughing hysterically in the other room. That was a nice sound.

"Garrick is dead," Emony replied to Lenah, wondering why her face looked like a gently breathing… she lost the thought.

"Oh. That's too bad. Hey, you're pretty far gone, Emony. You can't even string two thoughts together. Normally, I'd let the party continue, but I suppose we do have a few errands to run, don't we? The king of the lake wants to destroy Palehome, hm? And you were counting on me... I'm sorry, Emony. I've been sensing the black magic all the way from here, it's stronger than anything I've ever seen. This is going to be bigger than a few little villages. Those people are goners. Oh, and I'm sorry I dropped you and Tiphaine right in the middle of it all. The ley lines only showed me Verena. I'm glad you're still alive. I was just about to go over and rescue you two."

"It's fine. As it turns out, Verena introduced us to someone that can help me with my little mermaid problem. Maybe even with Tiphaine's Eyes – apparently, he's just that powerful. It's a shame he's a mass murderer, but nobody's perfect."

Lenah took a deep breath and sighed, flicking her wrist. The water that kept Emony a fish flew away from her, and she regained her/his human form. A nearby closet burst open and a pair of pants launched themselves at him.

"Yes, I can see what you've been up to. Look, I'm going to help you, Emony, it's time I started doing my job. But I have to try to minimize the human death toll. If you really mean to take the side of the king... I hope we don't end up on opposite sides of this. Anyway, we haven't yet, so let's play nice and rejoin those two. I'll help you get sober. By the way, it's been four hours. Your sense of time is way off. Don't try running anywhere, okay? It won't end well."

5

Tiphaine

She spotted Emony and Lenah coming back as she was lying on the floor beside Aylard, gazing at the man sleeping on the ceiling and laughing.

To her, it looked like the man's liquid and breathing face was dripping onto the floor, but at the same time somehow coming back so that it never ran out. For a while, she was scared that it was really happening – they were at Lenah's house, after all, but it turned out it probably wasn't, as Aylard was seeing something completely different.

She heard a crash.

"Oh, divines. Sorry," said Emony, who'd tripped over her tail. Slowly, he managed to get up and sit down at the table next to their witchy friend. She noticed he wasn't wearing his sling anymore, and he had a new set of clothes on. It looked like Lenah had been busy with him.

"Now, what was the spell..." the witch murmured, looking for something on the table. Tiphaine could barely hear her, but she could tell they were going to talk about something important. Eventually, she got sick of being left out and joined them, even leaving the fireplace to do so.

"…Oh, right, that was it. Now, Emony… Be cured! Did it work? No? How about now? Be… cured! Now? Urgh. Please be cured? Now? Oh, thank the divines, finally," Lenah grumbled as she materialized a chair for Tiphaine.

"Now, what were we going to talk about? Oh, right, Garrick. Garrick wasn't the smartest of merchants, but he was pretty opportunistic. He often traveled to Levara. Oh, you already know that? Okay, well, he'd always come back here whenever he made enough money to spend a day or two with me – he was a pretty lonely human. No, don't bother trying to talk out loud. I hear you. To answer your question, no. He never told me, and I never thought to look. But one time, I did notice something that might be of help to us. I thought nothing of it back then, but… He was having trouble – ah, you already know about the bank, too. Why are you even here, then? So, anyway, he's been dealing with the Bank of Trouwts for years. He always paid off his debts, but not always on time. The bank made good money off him, but they wanted assurances before they lent him any. They wanted to know what he was doing, how he was making his returns. They had a ledger; they'd constantly write things down in it. There's a chance there might be something useful in there."

"Do you think the bank still has it? The information we're looking for is ten years old."

"They might."

"Lenah?" Tiphaine asked, suddenly curious about something entirely different. "Right now, is it hot or cold? I can't tell."

"It's pleasantly warm," she said. "Don't worry about it. You'll be back with us soon,

Tiphaine. Oh, don't you be so worried. You survived, didn't you, Emony? It looks like the effects are nearly gone from your mind, and with them, your openness and good humor. Don't worry. I'll be sure to tell her nothing of what we spoke about... Or what we did."

Emony gave Lenah his murder-stare again. The witch ignored him, pointing her own gaze at Tiphaine.

"But really, Tiphaine, what we did... What Emony wanted to do..."

Tiphaine turned and stared at Emony, briefly considering taking off her veil.

"She's lying," he mouthed, irritated.

"Oh, but not entirely. Don't worry about it though, Tiphaine. You were right when you were talking to Aylard that time. He really is a softy! After waiting so long, you two finally had your first kiss next to that undead king, and he messed it up! So sweet!"

"I will kill you in your sleep," Emony hissed, murderously staring at Lenah with that wide, fake smile that creeped Tiphaine out. Still, she couldn't help blushing, remembering that particular memory.

"So, anyway," the witch smiled, changing the subject, "I vote that we go to the Bank of Trouwts, ask them to give us the man's ledger. They won't want to, obviously, but I'm sure we can persuade them. If necessary, we can bark up the wrong tree... Put them in a new and unusual situation – like fish on dry land."

"Urgh."

"By the way, no, I'm afraid you can't spend the night here. You are friends, and you are right, it is late, and I would actually be glad to have you, but the thing is, I can't stay here either. I hear a mob of angry humans coming here with pitchforks – quite a lot of women among them, come to think of it, and I don't think I want to be here when they arrive. The king's seal will only get me so far."

Tiphaine looked around and listened closely. Her eyes widened. Lenah was right. A lot of people were coming.

"You really have a way with human women," Emony grumbled. "How, by the divines, can the king's seal not be enough to keep them from trying to kill you? Whatever, just cure Tiphaine."

"One more healing spell, coming right up," Lenah said, pretty blue sparks suddenly flying off her hands and sizzling through the air. They danced all over Tiphaine's skin for a moment while the world blurred. Then, a few moments later, a sense of dull normalcy overcame her.

"Welcome back to reality," Emony said. "Feels weird, doesn't it?"

"Mhm. Super weird. How do I know I'm really here?"

"I couldn't tell you. But we have to move. Get up slowly. I'll help you."

Lenah interrupted: "Emony, I approve of what you're doing, but there are hundreds of angry women coming. Grab the wine and the leaves, as many as possible. Oh, and that love potion over there, in the little flask, for old time's sake. Tiphaine, pick up your human friend. We're leaving through the backdoor."

Tiphaine nodded and quickly slithered over to Aylard, grabbing his waist with the end of her tail, as she once had Emony's.

"You got him? Good. Lenah, we're ready to go," Emony said, his arms already full of various nefarious things.

"Good. Now, where was that...? Oh, right. There it is. Hey, before we leave, Emony, I must warn you – right now, you're being paranoid for no reason. Aylard's trustworthy – but that may change if he learns about Palehome. Are you sure you want to take him with us?"

Tiphaine looked at the two, not understanding. "Hm? What are you talking about? Emony, you mentioned Palehome a couple of times before... Urgh, fine, don't tell me anything! Just come on, let's go! They're getting closer! Yes, we're taking him!"

"Agreed. I trust Tiphaine. Let's go," Emony muttered.

"Okay. Oh, but first, put the love potion in his pocket, Emony. It'll be really funny if he mistakes it for alcohol," Lenah said, still not feeling rushed in the least.

"You're a hideously evil little creature, you know that?" Emony gasped, shaking his head, though he sauntered over behind Tiphaine and did it anyway with a wide smile.

As he did so, Lenah snapped her fingers and all the furniture around them rushed to push itself against the front door. "Come on, this way," she said.

She led them to a door on the opposite side of the hallway, beside the bedroom. Hearing the thudding of countless footsteps on the stone path outside, Tiphaine was already growing increasingly nervous – but just before she went through the door Lenah had opened for them, she remembered something: "Wait, Lenah, that guy, your friend! He's still on the ceiling!"

"Don't worry, they'll find a way to get him down eventually. Come on," Lenah said, putting her hands on Tiphaine's back and pushing her forward.

Suddenly there was a great pounding on the door.

"To the dirt with you, witch! That love potion doesn't... Just open the door!" a female human voice shouted outside.

"I'd really rather not," Lenah said and ushered them all through the door.

Chapter 7

1

Emony

"Where… where are we?" Emony asked, shocked, as his eyes adapted to the suddenly weaker light and he saw the pale moon rising above the endless fields of wheat spreading before him. "This isn't… There were no fields… Are we still in the north?"

His thoughts were suddenly interrupted by the sound of Aylard vomiting behind him, and Tiphaine, still wrapped up in her tail. For a moment, he thought he also saw a shiny door there next to them, but it was gone as soon as the thought crossed his mind.

"Gross," irked Lenah, running over and hiding behind Emony, watching the man puke. "But normal. Don't worry, Tiphaine. Humans have a weaker constitution than we do, it always happens."

She was eyeing Emony as she said that last bit. He almost took offense.

Luckily, though, he felt fine. He nodded. "So, where are we?"

"Just west of Terrena, in Hewlet's range. It's the closest spot I've got to Levara."

"Where is my horse?" grumbled Aylard hoarsely, struggling to free himself from Tiphaine's tail, standing up and abruptly tripping over nothing and falling again.

"You're screwed, Aylard. Just let Tiphaine carry you. The horse is a couple hundred miles away."

"Oh, no. Please, no."

"So, this is teleportation. I wasn't ready for it the first time, and it's no different the second," exclaimed Tiphaine, gingerly wrapping herself around the human again.

"Well, get used to it. I feel like hanging around you guys for a bit, but I have no intention of walking unnecessarily. And I hate hiking in heels," Lenah said.

"So, conjure up something else. You obviously can."

Lenah's face contorted as if Emony had just said something obscenely foolish. He decided to shrug it off and stay quiet – she knew what he thought, anyway.

"Yes, I do," she said. "Now carry me. I've brought us three quarters of the way there, the least you could do is cover the rest."

"You're kidding, right? What are you, a hundred and *twelve*?"

The witch grimaced and beckoned to him with her finger. In an instant, gravity began pulling in a different direction, and he was shooting toward her in freefall. Then he stopped, barely catching himself in front of her, crouching on the ground. She climbed onto his shoulders like she had planned it.

At least she wasn't heavy, Emony thought. She was certainly lighter than Tiphaine, what with her massive, long tail.

Lenah lightly punched the top of his head, apparently having heard the thought. He'd have to be careful, lest she tattle on him. She'd done so many times in the past.

"Fine, then. Let's go. Which way? Of course, you're going to squirm around. Come on, this is serious, Lenah. Lives depend on it.

You already said we can't save those people in Palehome – let's not add to the pile."

Hearing that thought, at least, she stopped messing around for a bit.

2

Aulduyen

He had waited long enough.

Three days were given to Verena's pets to report back any sign of the importance of the village of barbarians up on the mountain, and the man-siren had then said the only place of interest was Gull's Landing, five leagues away, by the frozen sea.

So why wait another day? His queen was waiting for him somewhere out there, and he knew what he had to do to get closer to retrieving her.

Verena had asked him to be patient, to wait for the pets to return from their trip, but that would be pointless. Who knew if they would return in the first place, fearful as they were of his power? Their voices had trembled when they spoke to him, as if he was some dreadful monster. He was not, of course. He had been forced into all of this. All he wanted was his queen.

But now was not the time for mercy. It was time to act. He'd gathered enough strength to bring forth rain again – and with it, the army could make their way to the snows of the mountain, where the solid water could likely sustain them just as the lake did.

Three days of a human march separated him from the nearest source of thralls – he and the puppets he already had could make it there in two. And it was time to do just that. It was bad enough that he couldn't start with Coldbarrow, but his queen would without a doubt be mournful if he did, caring as she was. She would pity even the cowards that had turned their backs on her as she was captured to be executed. No doubt she would pity those barbarians, too, but he still had to move forward.

After she'd return to him, he would right a hundred wrongs for every one that he committed. No, better a thousand. Perhaps that would appease her, if only a little – but thinking of such things now was pointless. Now he had to be cruel, he had to commit those wrongs.

Aulduyen clutched the pearl-laced locket that Imarah had worn on their wedding day. A vision appeared before him – her face, breaking the clear water's surface in that beautiful moment when she said "I do". It was distorted only by the minute flaws of his memory. She was perfect, he knew. She was gazing into his eyes with such happiness she could fill the world with it.

If only time had stopped in that moment.

"I do this for you!" he shouted, staring at her empty spot on the sandy bed they used to share. "Oh, I know… You were afraid of this part of me, I know it! That's why you sang to me so beautifully, to shine a light upon my blackened soul! But without you, my queen… I'm sorry. Black is the only color I know."

He carefully put down the locket upon the spot where she'd laid her head, filling his own with songs of love, the songs he'd been so desperate to hear.

Black tears streaming out of his eyes and tainting the water, he kneeled before the bed one last time before he went to war. "But the black, too, must serve its purpose. You understand, don't you? Love must prevail, my queen. I must have you back."

Two sunsets later, it was the children playing with their dogs outside the wooden village palisade that were the first to spot them. They were dressed in thick furs to keep the cold at bay, happily running around with their pets to keep warm.

Aulduyen imagined they must have been a truly horrific sight, a thousand skeletons and rotting corpses barreling up the snowy mountain towards them with swords in their hands.

The kids began running, their short legs barely taller than the snow, their dogs barking wildly in fear ahead of them, trying to drag them away. Only two out of the fourteen made it behind the frozen walls. The brave men at the gate, fearfully shouting as they were, had waited for them, at least, before closing it.

But it brought no safety.

Aulduyen called forth his power, and from the churning, dark sky above the mountain, a burst of lightning descended to the ground, smashing through the frosted wood and throwing the men who guarded it to the ground, clutching their burned limbs and howling in the pain.

But such pain is nothing, compared to what I endure, he thought. Still, pain was pain, and his queen would not want him to inflict it without purpose. With a swing of his great sword, he struck the ground and launched himself into the air, soaring towards them like a comet. He sliced apart the men and the huts behind them as he landed, and then, only moments later, the puppets were all around them.

Streaming over the collapsed gate, the corpses surged in all directions, as per his orders, attacking every living thing in sight, overpowering them with the strength that was brought to them by strings of magic and water.

Walls, houses and barricades were being shattered everywhere he looked, the shields of warriors falling as the men died, blood staining the snow. Panicked screaming of every variety sounded over the thralls' rampage, overpowered only by the rolling of the thunder overhead.

Chaos quickly consumed the battlefield. After surveying the carnage for a few minutes, Aulduyen noticed the living held strong in a single spot, destroying his thralls with battleaxes and hammers when they came close. Aulduyen had them stay away and finish off the other survivors instead. He'd not lose his queen's soldiers for nothing.

Seeing the dead stop charging towards them for a moment, the three men, protecting a woman and child, ran towards a small building by the palisade. A stable, by the look of it. They trembled in fear as they noticed him approach. One of them grabbed a bow from the ground and loosed arrow after arrow in his direction. Four, he avoided, as it was no trouble to do so, another two he swatted away with his hand, the last, he let pierce his heart.

The men continued gazing upon him in terror as he approached them.

"Dad!" the child screamed, already up on the horse with the woman. That one word, he understood. One of the men was shouting something back in that foreign language of theirs. Aulduyen stopped and stood patiently before them in the snow, grasping his sword and planting it in the ground before taking the arrow out of his heart, letting them have their precious moment.

The apparent father, seeing him, turned to face him suddenly after shouting something to the woman and child. "Please," he begged in Aulduyen's tongue, in a harsh accent his mind found distasteful. "Please. Them… Free."

Then, as the two other men joined the first with hammers and axes in hand, the woman and child attempted to gallop away. Aulduyen took up his sword again.

The village had been completely consumed by his puppets within a half-hour. A fire had started, spilling forth from the fallen torches and cooking pots strewn about the settlement before reaching the huts. The frosted wood was crackling and hissing, blackening with every passing second. The thatch roofs and tents threw flames high in the air, warming the cold mountain. The screaming had stopped. He had the thralls bring the dead to him, laying them to rest on the snow for a few moments before their bodies could be used.

Looking over the corpses, he saw that one – the woman, the one that had tried to escape with her child, had not yet been taken by oblivion. She was gurgling blood, her stomach split open where his sword had slashed through her. She was in pain – but it would only be seconds now.

He knelt beside her and gently brushed away her hair from her eyes, attempting to comfort her in her last moments.

"Imarah?! Is that you?!" he suddenly shouted, seeing her eyes.

Her eyes – they had that color. But no… No. The shape was wrong, and everything else was too. She was not his queen. Still – she had her eyes.

"Rest, woman," he said softly, calming himself. "Worry not, death comes for you all. With your sacrifice, a queen without compare shall be freed from her gilded cage. Now go. Go and join your son."

Her eyes were starting to flitter shut. He did not know if she had understood him. Probably not –

but in any case, she was gone. Aulduyen stood up and walked away, towards the center of the pile of corpses. He lifted his hands towards the stormy sky.

"Arise!"

3

Tiphaine

The world had become a pale shade of white. It was an empty void as far as Tiphaine's mind could see. There was nothing there, no smells, no wind, nor any sort of presence at all, except her and the vipers on her head.

A pool of black slowly appeared before her, though, staining the white ground.

Strange tendrils of magic corrupted the white nothingness she stood on, and began to spread, gain shape, and become three-dimensional.

They rose from the ground, shaping themselves into a human form. The black made way to blue, and after a minute, it was Lenah she saw standing before her.

While she was frozen, not knowing how to move through the nothingness, the witch finished gaining her pretty form, and her blue lips stretched into a smile as she walked closer.

"Beautiful mind you've got here," she said. "It's just how I remember it. I hope you don't mind, I thought we might spend some time together while we sleep."

"We're… in my mind?" she asked, forming the words. She couldn't feel her mouth move at all.

"Yes. We've been here quite a few times before, don't you remember?"

"No."

Lenah shrugged. "Well, I can't blame you. For you, dreams fade quickly after they are dreamt. It's quite tragic, really. We can do so many things in here, but soon after you wake up, you'll forget all about them. Or even if you remember, you'll think – it was just a dream…"

"I do forget dreams pretty quickly. Unless I hold on to them deliberately, or write them down…"

"That's good! But you know, it may be best if you don't hold on to this one. I thought we might take another look through your memories. I remembered something from the last time we did this, and I need to have another look. You might not like it."

"Have we really done this before?"

"Yes. Many times, over the years. And I've done it with Emony, too, but you don't want to know what we were doing in *his* mind…"

"Hey."

The next moment, she felt something distinctly *wrong*. Like something really, really… bad… was clawing through the inside of her head, pulling something out. A second later, however, the feeling was gone, and a giant bookcase stood in front of her, reaching for the sky, thousands of tomes littering it and filling in the white expanses of the emptiness.

"Hm… where to start…"

As Lenah took one of the books off a shelf and looked through it, the whiteness of the world flashed in its entirety to life, revealing a scene Tiphaine had witnessed many cycles ago. It was flickering, fading out for moments at a time before coming back and flickering again. She recognized it. She saw her mother's face smiling down at her as she wrapped herself around her arm. She was so small, she barely made it from her hand to her elbow. Her vision was blurry. There were tears in her eyes – the sound of crying filled her mind, and then a male voice – her dad, comforting her.

"I've seen this one before. It was a few years before you inherited the Eyes," Lenah said. "You were so cute. You still are, of course, but back then..."

"You don't know what I look like now," Tiphaine murmured. She'd heard it before, that she was beautiful, from many nervous humans trying to curry favor with her so she wouldn't "eat" them. "You haven't seen my face in months, Lenah."

"Do you think your veil followed you here? I can see your face right now, dummy.

Tiphaine's hand shot up to her head, making sure it wasn't true. She had no ravenwood on her. If her face really was exposed, her friend, looking at her, would be stuck petrified, but...but that wasn't happening. The witch wasn't turning to stone. She stared over at her, confused.

"Like I said, this is just a dream. They're not your real eyes."

"Can I... can I see my face, then? I haven't seen it in a while, either."

The feeling of undivided wrongness overcame her again. The next moment, a mirror stood before her, and she was gazing, still afraid that she might turn to stone, into her own green eyes. It was the first time in about a decade since she'd seen their color, since she'd only been able to see them when they were stone. Emony had told her about them, but... they really were the same shade of green as her tail and hair-vipers.

"I'll leave you to it," Lenah laughed. "Unfortunately, there's no use using makeup here, it won't follow you to the real world. But that really is what you look like, Tiphaine, minus any dirt and foreign elements."

She eyed the eyebrows and nose she'd always been afraid to look at and made a few different facial expressions. She felt that maybe, just maybe, she might really have been able to compare to mermaid Emony, though that was a weird comparison to make.

The whiteness of the world flittered to life again. Lenah was watching another scene from her childhood. It was far clearer and in more detail, with much less flickering. She recognized it instantly, though she wished she hadn't. If only the memory had been less familiar. But it was one she remembered every day.

She was slithering across tall stones with her human father, still just a little girl of nine cycles. Her tiny fangs were freely poking out of her mouth, her hair-vipers biting the air in excitement. Her dad was unwrapping a large piece of cloth onto a warm boulder and letting her sun herself on it as he unpacked their lunch.

And then… the vision violently flickered. A single flash of lightning covered the sky.

"The Eyes," said Lenah, looking at young Tiphaine with pity.

She was reaching for that piece of bread her dad was holding out to her, laughing, when his hands turned gray. Slowly, her happiness turned to confusion and fear as she began crying in front of her suddenly deathly still dad, hugging him desperately, pleading with him to move. But he couldn't.

And she couldn't move him. She was far too small, so, still crying, she sobbed to him that she'd get help, before scampering through the forest as quickly as she could to find her mom. All around her, wherever she looked, birds were falling out of the sky, turned to stone.

And when she finally reached her mother, who was hanging up a sheepskin onto a string beside their little house, unaware of what was happening… it happened to her, too.

The older Tiphaine, watching the scene unfold in front of her, got goosebumps all over her cold skin and looked away. She couldn't watch any more. The scene stopped moving forward.

"I'm sorry," said Lenah, hurrying towards her and pulling her into an embrace. "I don't want to make you relive this. It's just… What comes next, it may be important."

"You mean Westmire?" Tiphaine asked. "You know what I did there. Just the name says it all, it's the city of statues!"

"I know even more than you do about what happened in Westmire, Tiphaine, but no, not that. I meant right after this. I'm so sorry."

"Then... then go on. Memory, go on," Tiphaine sobbed, her voice shaking. The scene began to move forward again.

She was still wailing on her mother's tail, hours later, when a group of soldiers came marching along the road with a carriage rolling behind them.

One of them ran forward towards her, asking her what was wrong. She recognized the voice – it was a friend of her father's.

He was the first of them to turn to stone. She still didn't understand what was happening, but then, as the tears started streaming out of her eyes again, the carriage abruptly stopped moving and the soldiers' talking ended in sudden silence. A single terrified man that had been in the carriage managed not to look into her eyes before he ran, screaming, into the woods.

And then the young her cried –

Standing beside the current Tiphaine, Lenah swung her hand, and the vision broke, shattering all around the two of them and revealing white nothingness in its stead. She tightened her embrace. Tiphaine just sobbed on her shoulder.

"You know what the funny bit is, about it all?" Tiphaine asked a few minutes later, still horrified. "Every one of those trees was a ravenwood oak. Every single one. If I had tried even for a moment to help them, I could have brought them back. I could have saved them all."

"You couldn't have known. Nobody told you. It's not your fault."

"If it wasn't for me, it wouldn't have happened. It *is* my fault."

Quietly, she turned away from Lenah, looking towards the empty ground, the giant bookcase stretching towards the nothingness in front of her.

"Though someone did tell me something similar, once," Tiphaine said.

The nothingness gained color again, revealing a memory from another time. It was a little less than a year later, in a different place, on the edge of a tall cliff above a frozen forest. A full moon hung in the dark sky. She was standing at the edge, still surrounded by living beings she had petrified. She had already decided, they would be the last.

She was gathering her courage.

That was when she heard something snarling behind her, and there, in the clearing, prowled a giant black wolf.

She had turned to it without covering her face, a mistake she had made a million times by then, but it didn't turn to stone. It avoided looking at her eyes. Then, noticing where she stood and the tears dripping down her cheeks, its vicious, murderous growl suddenly died in its throat.

The scene changed.

"This kind of wood drinks up dark magic," a young Emony said the next morning, in his human form. "It concentrates it, and it turns it into life for the tree."

Tiphaine hadn't believed him for a moment, though she'd desperately wanted to. But Emony kept stuffing the tree bark into the little rabbit's mouth, and then suddenly, the little thing began struggling in his grip.

It was alive again. She'd never seen a thing as beautiful.

"A witch told me about it. It can help if you haven't been petrified for too long. A month is too much, but…"

It worked on him, too, the day after. He couldn't remain on guard all the time. Careless as she was, she had petrified him over a hundred times before they arrived at their destination much, much later. It was back at her home; outside that little house she grew up in. The seasons had changed by then, the leaves had fallen onto her mom and dad's statues. The soldiers and the old carriage they had been in were gone. Someone must have moved them, maybe buried them. They hadn't honored her mother or her father, a little further away, with the same. She'd been relieved, really – she and Emony were carrying large sacks on their backs. But no matter how much they tried to give her parents, just as Emony had told her it wouldn't, the ravenwood did not work.

Lenah glanced over at the real her, worriedly. "You don't need to see this, I'm sure you have happier memories. But you're forcing the scene, I can't change it."

She ignored her. The next memory was inescapable.

"I'm so sorry, Tiphaine. I tried to tell you…" Emony was saying.

Young Tiphaine began crying again, wrapping herself around her stone parents.

A few hours later, the sun was starting to go down, and Emony started a fire for her right there beside them.

"Whenever you've done it to me, I've been conscious in the stone," he said quietly, his hand laid gently over her shoulder. "I couldn't move, but I was still there. I don't know if it's still like that after all this time, but… they might hear you. And if ravenwood doesn't work, and nothing else would either, apart from… from… And if nothing else does either, then maybe you should say goodbye."

And so, there she sat, wrapped around her mom and dad, her eyes tightly closed as the tears flooded down her face. Emony had positioned the two to look into each other's eyes. She kissed them both, one last time, as he changed his form and became a wolf.

The scene faded away. The void that it had filled was not white anymore. It was darker than any night she'd ever awoken in.

All she could see were Lenah's blue eyes, glowing in front of her.

"I'm sorry," she said quietly. "Even if I needed to do it, I'm so sorry for making you go through that again, I can see the pain drowning you. I'm sorry, Tiphaine. But here. Here, look at me. Let me at least give you this one thing."

She awoke to a dull yellow sunrise shining through the window into the small wooden shack they had stayed the night in. The place was warm. Aylard and Emony were already awake, and they had started a fire right in the middle of the wooden floor. Her tail had instinctively wrapped itself around Emony again.

"Good morning," he whispered, glancing in her direction with a little smile. "You're leaving me breathless again, with how tight you're holding me."

"But you're so warm," she yawned, easing up her tail's grip around his chest.

Lenah was also just slowly waking up beside her. "Morning," she said, leaning back away from her groggy hair-vipers, which were trying to bite her. "You sleep well?"

Tiphaine numbly shook her head and readjusted her veil so she could see better through the crystals. For some reason, everything was blurry. "I don't know. I guess."

Emony was still staring at her, a curiously gentle expression on his face.

"Hey, Tiphaine? You're crying."

4

Yperian

"So, the scouts were not mistaken? They really left? The men of the lake – they left?"

"It would seem so, knight commander. Nobody has reported any sign of them in the past three days. The last word we got were those of the forward observers, saying they were on the move, headed north."

Yperian laid his head in his hands. "Argh, and I didn't believe them! What are they doing?! What goes on in the minds of those corpses?!"

"I don't know, sir. But the observers said they marched in formation."

Shaking his head, he dismissed the captain. He was so confused. He'd been assured that the men of the lake were tied to it, unable to move far from it. That they couldn't live on dry land.

It was true that it was raining the day that they got the report of them leaving, but surely the rain could not last forever. There were no lakes north of Coldbarrow – where could those monsters go?!

Slamming his desk in frustration, he got up from his chair, taking his sword, and made his way out of the tent. The guard on duty got up from the stump he'd been sitting on just outside, sharpening his blade.

"Leynor, follow me. We're going to talk to the forward observers."

"Huh? Those madmen?"

"Yes, those madmen. But we'll call them brave to their faces."

They strolled through the camp, observing the salutes of soldiers running past them on errands. They were having trouble rebuilding the barricades around their camp, almost as much trouble as they had convincing the villagers to run for the hills when it looked like it was about to rain.

The locals seemed to lack a healthy fear for their lives. Still, if they did die, they would become soldiers in the army of the dead. He couldn't afford to be too kind to them. He'd had to fight one of the retired fishermen already, a corpse that had been missing half its head. He did not want to relive that.

"We need to end this war, somehow, before winter," he said, half to himself, half to Leynor. "If the men of the lake come back. Right now, it's fine, while the people have crops to eat, but once those are gone, they'll want to start fishing again."

"The lake will freeze over," said his adjutant.

"That won't stop them. The northerners have their ways. They have to survive in this frigid back end of Evaria somehow, and they aren't sent provisions from Terrena as we are. No… Once there is hunger, the men will set out and start fishing again – the danger be damned. Hunger always overcomes fear. They will walk over that frozen lake. And then they will die and become our enemies."

"Perhaps we'd be wise to enforce a curfew, then, to keep people in their homes when rain is on the horizon, and only let them close to the lake when surrounded by soldiers."

Yperian snorted. "And become known as tyrants? That will only embolden the youths. A better choice might be to evacuate the village altogether… If the men of the lake come back, that is."

"I'm afraid King Raynardt might have your head if you propose that."

"Yes, well, the king, his lords, and the idiots on the council don't know what we're really facing here, do they? I send them reports of dead people attacking us and they think I've found religion!"

"Ha. Well, bringing people back from the dead is something normally reserved for the divines. Perhaps it's one of them we're fighting."

"An ugly divine, if so. No, those corpses aren't alive. They're just fodder, controlled by someone else. The seers did say the lake was a hotspot of dark magic. They mentioned something might be under it, according to the old fishwives' tales. Yeah, I know. I felt the same way. But you know what? I am starting to believe it.”

“Knight commander! Knight commander!” shouted a young man, darting into the encampment with his sword at his belt and his armor only half-on. A watchman.

“You’re in a hurry, young man. You’ve left half your armor behind you – I’d reprimand you if you didn’t save us a trip. We were just heading over to talk to you.”

“Knight commander, I’d like to report the latest status from the forward line on the lake!”

The boy looked terrified as he saluted. That was a bad sign.

“What is it?”

The boy gulped down spit and straightened his shoulders, speaking loud and clear: “The men of the lake have returned! And there’s more than twice as many as there were before!”

Emony

"I'd help you if I could! But I can't, so stop complaining and pull! Put your backs into it!"

The trout's ugly head was being pulled onto the surface, and dragged forward towards the air while it splashed around and furiously swam circles in the water.

"You still haven't said why you can't help us!" growled Aylard, tugging on the rope beside Tiphaine with all his might. "Are you actually afraid of water?!"

"Yes! I am! Now you tell me, why are you so weak?!" he retorted, "I thought you lived in a fishing village! You're ten times its size, now get it out of the water!"

Lenah chuckled, sitting on the rock beside him. *She* could have helped if she wanted to. Getting wet wouldn't turn her into a fish.

"Careful," she warned, a smile on her face. "Loosen the line now, or it might break!"

"This fish is a monster!" shouted Aylard, obviously not listening. Luckily, Tiphaine was. The line held.

The trout dived back into the water, jerking them forward towards the riverbank.

"Pull!" shouted Aylard.

"No, don't pull now! You'll lose it!"

Emony was truly disgusted, watching the pathetic display. He'd always done his and Tiphaine's fishing, he'd have had the thing out of the water twenty minutes ago. Being a mermaid was the worst.

Aylard dug his heels into the pebbles and pulled again. The line jerked around in the water, scattering droplets of water into the air. Emony took a quick step back.

"Careful… now pull!" shouted Lenah, still far too happy.

Aylard and Tiphaine hunched up and heaved with all their might. They quickly started to get closer to the end of the line.

"Pull!" struggled Aylard. "Let's reel it in!"

And then the line snapped. The human and the lamia fell with their backs right onto the ground. Emony shook his head, disappointed.

Then Lenah chuckled and raised a hand, and while they could only watch, half of the water in the stream flung itself into the air and floated above them.

"By the divines," gasped Aylard. The trout, confused, swam right out of the mass of water and fell at their feet, flopping around on the pebbles.

"Couldn't you have done that sooner?" he asked.

Lenah spared Emony a glance, giving him a moment to move away, then dropped the water back into the stream with a flick of her wrist.

"You all make terrible fishermen," she said. "You could all stand to learn something from me."

"As if that would help…" he muttered.

"More black magic," gasped Aylard. "The number of crimes sanctionable by death I've seen in the past few days…"

"Haha. I've got the king's seal. I've got permission to do this. By the way, you call *this* black magic? You really know nothing, Aylard. Let's just cook the fish and go."

Levara was just as the knight commander had said. The clear stream they had followed for the past three leagues soon adapted to the flatlands, slowing down and growing wider, before splitting up into many smaller streams, which, in turn, ended in huge puddles that were covered with tall grass.

Soon enough, the dirt on either side of the path, laid with rotting wood, became soft, wet, and full of life.

The croaking of frogs was the only thing that overpowered the endless buzz of mosquitos and dragonflies. The pools of messy water were the ideal habitat for their kind.

A town stood in the middle of that marsh, standing on a bed of wooden poles that held it aloft. Steps led down to the path from the houses, welcoming them, away from the stench below, onto the raised platform that was only slowly sinking into the mud.

"I can't imagine why people don't like coming here," said Lenah, pinching her nose. "I can't even think of all the diseases I would find if I dissected one of these frogs."

A small, dark shape flew over them silently, swiftly dodging the men and women walking by but being suddenly struck out of the air and caught by one of the vipers on Tiphaine's head.

"A bat!" Lenah shrieked. "Tiphaine, your hair is eating a bat!"

As the witch was screaming, an amused Emony watched Tiphaine race through her mind to find out which emotional reaction would be most appropriate before cycling through all of them one after the other.

Funnily enough, she ended up not being able to snatch the bat away from the vipers, and they ended up fighting over it atop her head while she could only rub her arms together where they had bit her for trying to steal it from them.

"This is a seriously rotten day," she mumbled as they made their way towards the bank.

Emony smiled. That was ironic, considering the stench all around them.

Guards shouted at them and threatened them with death after the townspeople had complained that a giant snake was roaming the streets, but this time, the knight commander's note was enough to quell any bigoted complaints they might have had. The men, their hands never leaving the hilts of their swords, led them to the Bank of Trouwts with an escort, to show the people that the situation was under control.

Of course, inside the bank, the whole process started again.

"We only want the ledger with the information about Garrick's dealings. Garrick of Coldbarrow, the merchant. He used to come here often. Give it to us, and we will be on our way," Emony repeated for the third time, rolling his eyes. He'd thought bankers were supposed to be smart.

"Yes, we know you're not supposed to give out your client's information," added Lenah, reading the man's mind. "But look, Garrick is dead. He was my lover, and he – Aylard, here, is his brother. We want to take over the business."

"What?"

The banker looked thoughtful for a moment. "Well, if that is true, we might be able to make an exception... but how do we know you are who you say? This is highly unusual."

"Do you know what Garrick looked like? He and Aylard are practically identical. They're twins. Come on, I'm sure you've got the man's description written down somewhere, how else could you deal with these sorts of situations?"

"Actually, no. Parchment is far too valuable to be wasted on every single serf that wants to take on a meager debt."

"Ah, speaking of parchment. Here, I've got some. This was his."

"A letter of notice. Twenty-seven pieces. I'll have to take a look at the books to confirm this. So — would you like to pay off the debt, young man?"

"Not me. Him," Emony said, pointing at Aylard.

Aylard, dropped into the central role of the act, stared at the banker, rattled. "Yes… Sure. I'll pay off my brother's debt. That's why we came."

"Ah. Well, I don't see why anyone would come to give money back for someone else… Excellent, early returns are always very welcome. Of course, it doesn't mean we can reduce the rate."

"Of course not."

The banker turned and got up from his chair, walking away, looking for something. As soon as his back was turned, Aylard whirled around to the three of them standing behind him.

"I don't have that kind of money!" he hissed. "I don't make that much in a year!"

Emony shrugged. He still had some that was given to him by the knight commander, but he didn't want to part with it. He'd treated Tiphaine to some exotic meat earlier since she'd been traumatized by the bat, and he wanted to do something similar again later.

"He was your brother," he shrugged simply.

"No, he wasn't!"

Tiphaine couldn't help the human, either.

"Hide me," whispered Lenah, once all eyes were on her. "I don't want to become known as a criminal." Glancing around, they all huddled around her. After a few moments of muttering some hushed words and drawing circles in the air, a fist full of gold appeared in her hand.

"I can't do silver. Even the disappearing kind is bad for us witches. Here, take it, Aylard. Oh? Yes, you can keep the ring, Tiphaine. I don't care if it was meant for me. It's hideous."

She handed the conjured gold to Aylard.

"Wait, are you saying this is going to disappear?!" the human gasped.

"Yes, but not today, so go on and use it! No complaints! Quiet! He's coming!"

The banker walked back over to his chair, not noticing their chatter. He was holding three roles of parchment tightly bound by strings of tied grass.

"These are the ledgers written for a… Garrick of Coldbarrow. A merchant, by trade – and a frequent client. The last amount written… is indeed twenty-seven silvers."

"I'm afraid I only have gold," Aylard said. "I'm sorry, I can't demand of my clients that they pay in a currency of my choosing."

A well-placed lie, and perfectly delivered, Emony thought, a hint of paranoia creeping in. Lenah smiled at his side and glanced his way, obviously hearing it.

"No matter. We offer exchange services as well, as it is a frequent problem."

The banker took the gold from Aylard's hands and tested every coin separately against his teeth. None of them bent in the slightest. Apparently satisfied, he put them on a scale, and then finally began writing something down in the ledger.

"Thank you, I'll go get your change. With this, your debt is settled. Thank you for doing business with us – Aylard, is it? Also of Coldbarrow?"

"Yes. But before you go – I'd still like that look at my brother's book. There are a few things I need to check up on."

"Certainly. The ledger cannot leave the premises of the bank, unfortunately, but while you are here, feel free to browse it. Now, about that change."

Aylard took the parchment from the desk and stared at it.

"Soon, I'm going to become known as a criminal. Anyway, I can't read," he said. "What am I looking at?"

Again, Emony got the feeling he was lying. His eyes were gazing at the parchment far too knowingly, though he seemed to be trying to hide it.

"Give it to me," he said, taking it from him and looking it over.

"You know how to read?" Aylard asked.

"Despite appearances, I'm a noble," he answered.

But there was nothing in the ledger that would be useful to them. The accounts were far too new. The banker was slowly making his way back towards them, silver coins in his hands. Lenah cringed at the sight of them.

"Sorry, could you get us any of the older records?" Aylard asked the banker. "What we are interested in, specifically, are those from the time of the rebellion in Coldbarrow. Ten years ago."

"Ten years ago? Oh, my, that will be some trouble. I'm afraid we will have to charge you for a service of that nature. Archiving is difficult—"

"Keep the change, then," Aylard said.

The man bowed again and left.

Chapter 8

1

"So, King Raynardt paid him to keep quiet? About what? What could the merchant have known?" asked Aylard.

"Oh, any number of things," Lenah said. "Lots of games were being played back then, what with the rebellion and the succession of power in question. I remember, it was the spring of that year when the humans really began becoming intolerant of witches and mythics. I had to go to ask that brat and ask for his seal. It was embarrassing. Urgh, I hope I don't catch anything. These mosquitos are a menace."

"It was because of Westmire," Tiphaine murmured.

"Yes, come to think of it, that did happen around the same time, didn't it? The city of statues. Right, I remember the fishermen complaining back then. First, they complained because our idiot king married a commoner and got killed by his brother, and then Westmire happened, like divine punishment. They say everyone in the city was turned to stone. A troupe of angry… well, you know," said Aylard.

Tiphaine slithered around uncomfortably as they walked through the mud along rotting wooden beams. "Don't be nice about it for my sake. It wasn't a troupe of lamias, it was all—"

"Very unfortunate," Lenah interrupted. "But what they don't tell you is that soon after, people from all over began to flock to Westmire to gawk at it. First came the curious, then came the thieves. Of course, if an entire city's worth of people is suddenly turned to stone, naturally, people will come to steal their things, but you know something interesting? None of the jewelry the people there owned was as valuable as they were. The poor petrified sods were sold all over Evaria for truly exorbitant sums of gold and silver."

"Yeah," Emony murmured to himself. "That's why… never mind."

He couldn't do a thing to stop what had happened, young and ignorant as he had been back then. He hadn't met Lenah and learned about ravenwood yet. By the time he did, it was far too late…

Too late for what?

He shook his head.

What was I just thinking about?

"We went there together, to Westmire, remember, Emony?" Tiphaine asked. "After we buried my parents."

That's right, we did. I wanted to see my home one more time, and my parents—

Suddenly, the thought escaped Emony, leaving him staring at Tiphaine in utter confusion. Why had they gone there? She certainly wouldn't have wanted to go. Why would he have?

"What's going on?" he asked, suddenly shuddering. Why was he suddenly feeling so cold?

"Is something wrong?" Tiphaine asked.

"I don't know," he said. His mind was racing and he had no idea why. He'd forgotten something, he knew, but he had no idea what it was. He turned towards Lenah. Perhaps she could help.

The witch was staring at him in horror.

"What's going on, Lenah? Are you in my head?" he asked. "Fix me, if you are."

Slowly, with an expression of deep unhappiness, she shook her head. "I can't. I made you a promise, Emony."

Suddenly, Emony's head began to explode with pain. Lenah's eyes began to glow, and blue sparks began sizzling off her in every direction.

"Lenah, what's going on?!" Tiphaine cried.

"I'm sorry! All of you, forget—"

"—Yeah, that's why… Do you remember, Tiphaine? For a time, we roamed the countryside, sticking ravenwood in every statue we could find. I don't think we ever managed to get to anyone in time, though," Emony said.

"Ravenwood?" asked Aylard.

"It's wood from a special tree, full of dark magic," Lenah explained.

Why did I mention it in front of him? Emony thought. But it was too late to take it back now.

In any case, they had wasted their time back then. After about a week of something being petrified, ravenwood stopped working. He'd had Tiphaine help him experiment to figure that out later on in Aeliah, using rabbits. Although, Lenah did say that, true to the ignorant human guideline of "Kill the caster, break the curse", when Tiphaine died, everything she petrified would be freed. So one day, a lot of humans would end up finding their expensive statues running away from them.

"Anyway, if King Raynardt is involved, he may know something," Lenah continued, a look of unhappiness on her face. "We should go and ask him before many more people die by the hand of that other crazy king. For now, it seems like all roads lead to…"

"Just as that crazy king said. Terrena."

They made it out of the marshes by nightfall, deciding to make camp before continuing to the shack the next day, which they would use to teleport to Terrena with Lenah's absolutely incredible, magnificent power, which she would graciously use, showing off her glorious—

"Thank you, Emony," Lenah said. "That's quite enough – you don't have to insert sarcasm into everything you say. I can feel that you're grateful."

"I don't know what you're talking about, I didn't even say anything. Perhaps it's your own thoughts that you're hearing right now?"

"Be quiet, I'm trying to sleep," mumbled Tiphaine. "It's hard enough doing it with my veil on."

"Fair enough, then I'll watch over you guys for a while. I can't sleep with all these mosquitos. Tiphaine, get your tail off of me, you can wrap yourself around Lenah tonight."

"Aylard's already on watch…"

"Even better. I won't be bored."

He couldn't trust him anyway. For some reason, his paranoia was back and stronger than ever. He gently unwrapped Lenah's tail from his legs, waist and chest and left the tent, walking over to the human that was sitting on a rock, watching the nearby river quickly flow past them in the bright moonlight. The man's ears, at least, were pointed in the right direction for a watchman – he noticed him approach.

"Not tired?" Aylard asked, yawning.

"Not at all. How are you passing the time?"

"I'm just wondering what might be going on back in Coldbarrow. It's a full moon tonight."

Emony glanced up at the moon. He hadn't even noticed it until then – something he wasn't used to. As a werewolf, he was always acutely aware of the lunar cycles. He felt no urge at all to transform and howl at it. That was a shame.

"Ah, well… so, what do you think is going on?"

"Death, unfortunately. The men of the lake never left us alone for more than a day or two between their attacks."

Emony stretched his tired legs. "You know, I think they might have, this time."

"You think they stopped killing people?"

"Oh, no, no. I just think they might have stopped killing *your* people."

"Ha… And would you tell me if I asked why? I didn't think so. You know, I found it strange – that the men of the lake mostly refrained from killing the villagers. We'd heard that they were terrorizing them when we arrived, but they never outright killed almost any of them, though they obviously could have wiped them out. Us, on the other hand… They lifted their rusted swords against us the first day we arrived. So, they must see something different in us. They possess an intelligence of some sort. I imagine they might just be a bit like me in one aspect. They're serving their king."

Emony flashed a smile at the human's pointed look. "Did you deduce that all on your own, or was it a result of your eavesdropping?"

He shrugged. "Everyone listens in occasionally when their friends are talking right in front of them and they're left out of the conversation. Can you really blame me? You do keep an annoyingly large number of secrets."

"For good reason, human. Hey, do you remember that time in Garrick's house, when I told you to stop asking questions?"

"When you said you'd slit my throat if I didn't? I remember. Is it time for that?"

"Maybe it is," Emony said, discreetly tensing his hand, daring the human to make the first move. Aylard didn't move a muscle.

A minute later, he found himself slightly disappointed. He could have used a little bout of violence. It'd been too long since the last one.

"You know, I've seen you kidding around with Tiphaine all those times, manipulating her into telling you things. You control yourself well, but your eyes, they speak the truth. You're afraid of her. And of Lenah, and of me."

He shrugged, not denying it. "You of all people would recognize fear, wouldn't you? I heard you've inspired quite a bit of it in your life."

Emony smiled and opened his waterskin, taking a drink before offering it to the human.

"What, did Tiphaine tell you?"

"Not outright," Aylard laughed, a little too loudly, as Emony's not-yet-sleeping, favorite companion complained about it.

"Sorry! So, anyway, you're not howling at the moon right now?" Aylard asked.

"Nope."

"How come? Is the witch keeping the wolf at bay?"

He rolled his eyes. "With all of her black magic. Idiot, not all magic is black."

The human glanced at him again, wiping his mouth and handing the waterskin back to him.

"It is, as far as I'm concerned. I've never seen a single good thing come of any of it. What do you say is the difference?"

"Black magic is bad. Dark magic is less so. Regular magic is neutral."

"The witch mentioned earlier that ravenwood harbors dark magic. And though you and Tiphaine covered the villagers' eyes while you were bringing them back to life, quite a few later reported that you stuck something like tree bark into their mouths. So that would have been dark magic, reviving them?"

"You really should stop asking questions."

"Well, allow me a few more, and I'll answer one of yours. One you haven't even thought of asking."

"As if I could trust a word you say," Emony said, shaking his head, "or you knew anything I didn't. But go ahead, ask away."

"Does ravenwood revive people that have been petrified?" Aylard asked.

"Sometimes."

"Did Tiphaine cause the tragedy at Westmire?"

"Obviously. At any given time, there is only one lamia in the world cursed with the Eyes, and that's been her for the past nine cycles."

"Are you originally from Westmire?"

Emony blinked, disconcerted for a moment, and gazed at the moon's reflection in the river.

"Why would you think to ask that?" he inquired.

"I'll take that as a yes. I've recently found out that a large enough quantity of silver can protect a human from a witch's curses."

"Interesting. Well, the answer is no," Emony said, narrowing his eyes. "I've never been to Westmire. But you really do know too much."

"You might not want to trust your blue-haired friend quite so fully. Do you know what she's capable of?" Aylard said.

"Just about anything. Mass destruction, ritual sacrifice, suspending a soul between life and death…"

"Messing with your mind," Aylard added.

Obviously, Emony thought, remembering how being turned into a fish had changed him.

"I wonder what I should reveal…" the human continued. "But you know, in case you're only still listening to me because you plan to silence me forever, I should tell you that if you do so, the king of Evaria will be told a truly awful story about a monstrous snake that turns people to stone. Also, that killing her would bring thousands of petrified citizens back to life."

"I did notice you talking to all those strangers. You didn't really use the word "monstrous", did you? Tiphaine would be so upset," he replied.

"No, I didn't. I said her human-looking bit was the prettiest in the world."

Emony laughed. Well, that was probably true.

"So? What if I don't take your sword and scramble your innards? What happens then?"

"I don't really know. I suppose I'll keep following you around, so long as we're on the same side."

Emony burst out laughing. "Ha! All this eavesdropping and scheming, and you think we're on your side?! I have thoroughly overestimated you, human!"

"Emony!" shouted a sleepy Tiphaine from the tent. He glanced back over at her. Her tail was already wrapped a couple times around Lenah, the nearest source of warmth. He could see the quietly snoring witch had deployed a protection spell to avoid suffocating.

"Sorry!" he called back before lowering his tone again and speaking to the human.

"Okay, but seriously – yes, we share a common goal right now, but we are far from being allies. Your thoughts regarding magic, though ignorant, have merit. The differences between us are quite unreconcilable."

"Why is that?" Aylard asked quietly.

"Because I know what you humans are truly like," Emony growled, a vivid memory of his slaughtered parents entering his mind. Angrily, he stood up and walked a few feet away from the human before he took his rage out on him. "You're vicious, bigoted killers, the whole lot of you, and I have no trouble watching the king of the lake slaughter you all."

"Then why are you working against him?" Aylard asked.

"I don't recall ever saying I was doing that. You know something, Aylard? You're not very useful to me here. I'd feel a lot better if you were gone, so I'm going to tell you something to make you leave. Recently, Palehome has been wiped off the map."

"What?"

That finally got a reaction.

Emony tensed his hands again. "As I said. Palehome is gone. Everyone there is dead. The king of the lake wanted more soldiers."

The human glared towards the ground, unease and anger clear on his face. "Palehome... You knew it was going to happen, didn't you? The knight commander said you mentioned it before you left, but you didn't say why. You let those people die."

"That's right."

The disgust became ever clearer on Aylard's face. Suddenly, he unsheathed his blade, swinging it through the air and pointing it at him.

"Quietly! Remember, they're trying to sleep!" Emony laughed, hopping away.

"Why didn't you say anything?!" Aylard snarled. "They could have been evacuated!"

"Lenah, if you can hear me, put Tiphaine to sleep," he said, ignoring him. "She doesn't need to see or hear this."

"More black magic? What are you after?!"

"There it is, the "black" magic again. All I want is to break a couple of curses."

"What curses? The king's?! The one in the lake?!"

Emony shook his head, watching Lenah run out of the tent towards them. So much for all that snoring. "Stop this, you two! Aylard, you don't understand!" she shouted.

The human pointed his sword towards her. "You knew too, didn't you? You can read our minds, you had to have!"

"She did," Emony admitted. "Though, if anyone is, it's her that's on your side."

"Am I supposed to believe that?"

He shrugged. "Or we could try to kill each other."

Emony studied the human's face. The muscles in his cheeks were tensing. He was definitely going to attack, furious as he was. He smiled.

And he was right.

Emony jumped to the side, avoiding the sword that came slicing through the air towards him, and spun swiftly in a pirouette. The human followed him with his blade, slashing the air, trying to reach his chest. Really, it was more difficult than he'd thought it'd be to dodge the blows, a consequence of him no longer being a werewolf.

The clean steel reached within a hair's length of him as he jumped away again, laughing all the while as the wind ruffled his hair. He liked a challenge. The Steel flashed in the moonlight at least twenty times while Lenah kept shouting at them to stop. She wasn't using her magic to force them to do so though, so he took that to mean she actually approved.

"Haha, feel like you can hit me, human?"

Aylard was already panting, tired by the movement and weight of his sword. "You're slower than I thought you'd be," he growled, before striking again.

Emony took a quick step back, avoiding the blade, then suddenly surged forward, crashing into the human's chest with his shoulder, knocking him to the ground and gracefully taking the weapon for himself. Then it was he who stopped it before the other's chest. Aylard, looking impossibly shocked, surrendered.

With a smile, Emony planted the sword into the ground between the man's legs.

"That was fun. Not bad for such a fragile little form of life. How would you like to be a hero?"

"I'm done listening to you monsters."

"Oh, come on, don't you want to save human lives? I'm giving you the opportunity to do so."

"To do what?" he asked.

"Palehome was only the first. If we fail our mission in Terrena, if we don't find Imarah there, the king will want to search for her himself. He'll want more soldiers to help him do so. My guess is he'll attack every settlement north of Coldbarrow except Gull's Landing."

Aylard got up from the ground, retrieving his sword, and after a moment of staring at him in suspicion, he laid it to rest in his scabbard. "How do you know any of this?"

"It's true, Aylard," Lenah said, coming over to them and looking them over for injuries. "Trust me, it's true."

"Trust a witch? You've got to be joking. Only an hour ago, I saw you get burned by the touch of Tiphaine's silver ring. Then you did something to their minds, making them forget something! It's clear you possess dark magic."

Emony raised an eyebrow at Lenah.

She ignored him. "You know?! Were you faking… Well… Yeah, I do have dark magic, and lots of it! I've got the black kind, too, but that doesn't mean I'm evil! Life is worth protecting."

"Tell that to the people of Palehome."

"They were already lost. The king is too strong, Aylard. I don't think any of us can beat him right now. Until we build up our strength, we have to give him what he wants."

"You want me to serve the undead?! I'd sooner die!"

"A poor choice of words," Emony snorted. "I can help you with that as soon as you like. Look, for Tiphaine's sake, forget the big picture. Lenah can send you back to Coldbarrow tomorrow. Try to get the northerners to run for their lives. Or, if you want, save yourself. Go south. It's your choice. Just… leave."

2

Aylard

He was doing just that, angrily walking through the dim light along the river, away from the three monsters, when they came. The full moon was lighting his way, but his eyes were not as sensitive as theirs likely were – he had trouble seeing far into the distance. The best he could do was avoid trees and fences that appeared in his way.

For that reason, he heard the horsemen before he saw them. There were two of them, he could just barely make out their shapes in the darkness. He couldn't hear any sort of armor clanking around as they moved, but he saw the glint of spear points in the moonlight just in front of the black poles they held.

"Well, well, a lone merchant," the first of the two said, the larger of the two shapes. As he approached. Aylard let his horse blindly trot closer to him. He got the rotten feeling that his fear was about to be confirmed – that they were bandits. It was thoroughly ironic, being in more danger now that he had left the witch, the werewolf and the lamia cursed with the Eyes.

"Good evening," he said loudly, giving up on hiding and instead pretending that he could be trying to alert others of their presence.

Could I be, though? Would any of them come for me? he foolishly thought.

"Peasant," continued the larger silhouette, "I'll have you pay me for the protection I offer. Without me, there's no way you'll reach Terrena safely."

The smaller of the two horsemen sniggered.

"I'm very grateful for your protection!" he declared. "I was afraid I might have lost my way! Are you a knight? I'm afraid I don't have much on me at this very moment, but—"

"Shut it. Everyone knows people only travel by night when they've got something to hide. Whatever it is, it's mine now. Give it to me."

"I honestly don't have anything on me. Here, I'm emptying my pockets. My companions are further down the river, I left my silver with them."

The smaller brigand spat at his feet contemptuously. He could hear it.

"Buying yourself a few minutes to run, little man? I see your sword. I'll be taking it now, unless you want to try using it."

The larger man's spear poked his chest.

Given how easily Emony had beaten him earlier, he realized he obviously wasn't the warrior he'd thought he was. Still, the brigands would likely kill him anyway, right after he handed them the sword, and then dump his body into the river.

On the other hand, maybe he could reach the water alive.

"As you wish, good sir!" he exclaimed, slowly unsheathing his blade and gingerly dropping it to the ground, displaying no hostility at all while slightly distancing himself from the spear tip, before suddenly dashing madly away from them towards the river glinting in the moonlight.

"After him!" one of them bellowed after a moment.

Do they not care about the sword?!

"Get him! Go, faster!"

The galloping of the two horses was right on his heels. They were getting closer, fast. Grimacing, he pounded the ground as fast as his human legs could manage, throwing himself forward and forward. Within seconds he reached the bank, and he jumped.

He was just feeling the cold rush of the wind on his face, wondering if he'd really made it, when the metal pierced his shoulder. Blood poured out of him for just a moment before he hit the cold water.

And then he was taken by the current. His shoulder hurt far too much and he was gasping for air. He couldn't move his arm. He was struggling to reach for the surface, the water slipping through his fingers and his blood pouring into the cold water.

The air was quickly escaping his lungs, his heart was beating much too fast for his breath to keep up. And then he swallowed water.

The brigands were laughing on the shore, he heard them for a moment when he reached the air to take a breath, but then he was underwater again. He saw rocks in the river, and the powerful tide was bringing him straight towards them.

He tried desperately to swim, to move out of the way, but he could only move one of his arms and legs, and that wasn't enough.

He hit the jagged rocks in force. They cut through the skin on his side. He could feel his ribs breaking.

The men were still laughing, following him along the riverbank.

Trying desperately to breathe, he only swallowed water again. The tide was getting even stronger. His strength was waning.

His head slipped under the surface.

The water was moving him quickly, his mind screamed, but it didn't really feel like that then. Things were getting fuzzy. Everything was slower underwater – except for the blood and life rapidly spilling out of him. All the noise dulled, the light got weaker and muddled. He desperately held what little breath he had, though his lungs shouted at him to let it go.

It was peaceful, somehow. The world was growing quieter. The water was carrying him...

somewhere. He hit more rocks. There was a terrible pain coming from his shoulder, his side, and… and his lungs.

He couldn't hold that breath any longer, yet he knew it would be over if he stopped. He closed his eyes tightly shut, struggling for one last second.

He heard a splash as something hit the water somewhere nearby. Were the brigands throwing things at him?

Humans could really be cruel, he thought. He didn't want it to be over. He really didn't want it to. But it would be, all the same.

As those thoughts faded from his mind, something more solid than the water, yet still gracefully soft, suddenly embraced him. It would probably be his final comfort, he knew. The water was starting to creep in through his lips.

How could it end up being humans that killed him, and not the three monsters he'd kept for company? His head was exploding with the pain of keeping his mouth shut. That soft thing was at his back, pushing him upwards. He really wanted to open his mouth. He had to; it was far too painful not to. But that would mean death—

His head suddenly burst through the water's surface.

He gasped for air instinctively, filling up his lungs more than they had ever been before. The water was leaving his ears, streaming down his face, the muddled peace of the river was gone in an instant. He was breathing hoarsely, flailing his arms, trying to do… anything. Anything he could do with his few more moments. He didn't go back under. He was being held up somehow by small hands that were not his own. Those hands must have belonged to the soft thing behind him.

"You bottom-feeding, night-raiding scum! I hope you choke on your own muck! Come closer, I'll kill you!"

It was the voice of a girl. It was coming from right behind Aylard's head. He hoped he hadn't gotten someone else killed by dying too slowly himself.

"Escape..." he tried to say.

He heard the pounding of hooves. The bandits were coming.

"Hey, we've got a girl over here!" one shouted. The smaller one, if he remembered the voice correctly. "Come here, little lady, get out of the water! The current only gets stronger, you know! But we'll save you!"

"Don't... don't listen..." He couldn't move his throat into the right shapes to make words with it. The blood loss was starting to take him. There was another fog setting in.

"Quiet," the girl said to him, a mesmerizing tune escaping her lips right beside his ear. "Just focus on your breathing. You're going to be okay."

He had to obey. He had no choice. She was still holding him above the water, though with her small frame, she couldn't possibly... He realized something strange. No legs were kicking against the water behind his own. His heels were grazing against something else. Something with scales. A tail? It wasn't Tiphaine's voice, though, it couldn't be her. His head rolled back, and he saw a young human face. He didn't recognize it, but the girl looked so beautiful... and so very, very angry. And then she was smiling. She must have been a hallucination. Was he already dead?

"Well, come closer, then," she suddenly shouted, looking past him, towards the shore. "Come closer, save me!"

A second dark silhouette arrived in Aylard's foggy field of vision, announced by the muddled pounding of hooves.

"What have you found here, brother? Another prize?" the horseman laughed.

"Come closer, you two," the girl's beautiful voice sang. "Come drown yourselves in this river."

Right before he lost consciousness, Aylard heard two splashes hit the water.

3

Verena

"Are those all men from Palehome?" she asked her brother-in-law as he arrived home, sauntering through the gates of Acu'enah with his sword over his shoulder and an army of corpses behind him.

A mad smile appeared on his lips.

"Wait outside, curs!" he boomed through the water, sending ripples throughout the lake, before he turned back towards her, planted his sword into the sand and walked over to her, gently grasping and kissing her hand.

Then he showed her another smile as he pointed towards the right side of the horde.

"Those there were the people of the mountain. Those, there, we found on the way, and those at the far end, on the way back. They were carrying gold, to Terrena, of all places! I had them bring it here instead, I know my queen loves her trinkets. With that, we will be able to make many of them! This is a great day, Verena. We have come one step closer to bringing back our queen!"

"How?" she gasped, swimming to the gates so she could see the entirety of the horde. "All this death… What did it accomplish?"

At that, Aulduyen quickly ran back towards her, planting himself in front of her eyes and laying a hand on her shoulder. She shuddered at his touch.

"I'm sorry. I… I know it pains you to see this. I should have known better than to show it to you. Please, come, let's talk in the palace. Clearly, I am a fiend, suited for the evil I must inflict, but be assured – you will never be the same."

Aulduyen swiftly led her into the throne room, shutting the ornate doors behind them. The dead horde slipped out of sight – but not out of mind. Aulduyen sighed, unhappiness suddenly clear on his face as he leaned his back against the door.

"Perhaps it would be best if I explained. I cannot bear to see you fearful of me. Verena… As the villages and towns fall prey to our army, even the bastard king will be forced to react, and as he sends man after man to defeat us, our army will only grow larger. I do not wish to harm the innocent, Verena. But once the world sees that our victory and conquest are assured, they will come to see that the only way to stop us is to give us what we want. They will search for my queen. They will do everything they can. All men, living and dead, will serve our ends. Our queen will be found."

Verena stared at Aulduyen, watching the glimmer in his eyes.

"But how many will die, before that happens?" she asked quietly.

Aulduyen slowly walked over to her and gently grasped her hands with his own.

"This will be over soon, Verena. I swear it. Soon, very soon, this butchery will end. But not yet."

She looked into his dark eyes and nodded. They stayed there, close together, for a long time. Then she unlinked her hands from his own.

"I… I want to go to the surface today. I want to go meet the human commander, the one that Emony sang to," she said.

Aulduyen tilted his head. "To what end? A show of force? I have gotten stronger since I left. It seems that with every death I cause, my power increases."

"I don't want a slaughter. Before they left for Gull's Landing, Tiphaine told me Emony had the human commander ask his friends in Terrena to try to find Imarah. They haven't come back yet, so I'll go ask him myself if the men found anything."

"Go, if you believe it wise. But wait, I beg you, a couple moments. I will bring forth rain to protect you. You are far too precious to be lost because of your grace. Humans can be vicious to those with the best of intentions."

She wanted to protest, to say that she didn't need the protection of corpses, but she nodded anyway. She knew he wouldn't relent. He would never give an inch when it came to her safety. Because she was Imarah's sister. His queen's.

"Imarah," she whispered to herself. "Is this anything at all like what you intended? Those songs you sang for him – they took him so far…"

Only an hour later, she was outside the human's camp, waiting to be let in through the wooden gates. It was her first time on the surface in years.

The clouds in the dark sky above were swirling angrily above the lake, the powerful surging of the wind conjuring a deep, gigantic maelstrom over the entirety of its surface. A tremendous downpour was soaking the mud all around the surrounding land. The sound of it was overpowered only by thunder. These were all Aulduyen's methods of warding off any attempt at harming her.

Earlier, right after she'd pulled herself out of the water, a legion of corpses had picked her up, as gently as a feather, and carried her on their broken shoulder bones directly over the soaking wet land towards the human's camp.

The storm only picked up as they came closer, the ghastly gusts of wind threatening to unearth trees they passed on the way up the hill.

She'd looked with a mixture of embarrassment and horror over at the human soldiers staring at her, terrified, from behind their wooden walls and palisade.

They had clearly expected a vicious assault, seeing the weather as a harbinger of their deaths. Now they were watching the horde of rotting corpses carry a mermaid, like some sort of evil royalty, to their gate.

Her convoy stopped there. Ten puppets had arrived there before the rest, waving dirty cloths before the panic-stricken humans. They kept their bows drawn, but they didn't shoot.

It seemed as though ages had passed while she lay there on the men's shoulders, before the gate. The humans kept staring at her in fear, when suddenly, a bolt of lightning punched through the sky and destroyed the barrier before her, splinters flying in all directions and smoldering logs being thrown into the air around the encampment. Men had been standing behind the gate. Those men were now lying on the ground, groaning in pain. Nobody dared move to help them.

"I've come to talk!" she shouted before Aulduyen could bring forth any more destruction. "Only to talk! Where is your leader, the knight commander?!"

The rain continued to soak the ground.

Finally, a human, identical in equipment and armor to the rest of them, stepped forward. He stared at her, appraising her coldly, as an enemy. She resisted the urge to look in any other direction.

"I am the knight commander of this field legion," he said curtly. "Have you come to negotiate?"

The corpses standing to her sides began growling, an ugly gurgling sound leaving their rotting throats.

"Yes. There is no need for violence," she hastily replied. She could barely hear the words she said over the rain and the shaking of her voice.

The man nodded with hesitation and glanced over at his men around the palisade. "Stand down, then, men. Remain vigilant. Honored emissary, the command tent is this way."

The human led her to a large pavilion of red cloth at the far end of the encampment. There was so much rain caught atop it that it barely stood straight.

"We can't enter," she said before he could invite her onto the dry ground inside. "Can we talk here? I'm sure the rain will calm down."

The roaring of the thunder and wind slightly weakened at her behest. Aulduyen must have been watching her closely through the eyes of the things that carried her.

"Of course. I hope you don't mind if only I remain under the cloth, though? I hate it when water gets in my eyes, you see."

"It's fine," she nervously smiled. She remembered Aulduyen himself had a similar problem ten years ago, when she and Imarah were just introducing him to the lake.

"Thank you. Well then, I'm sorry we don't have any chairs suited for your kind here. Wine?"

"Please. It's been years since I've had any."

While the man slipped inside the tent, the corpses in front of her began to kneel on the ground while others behind her stood hunchbacked or straight, creating a throne for her atop their horrific shoulders and backs. She looked around. The soldiers all around the encampment were trying to keep their gazes fixed on the outside of their walls, but were sneaking frightened glances at her constantly.

"I'm sorry, we've only got the Terrenan stuff left," the knight commander said, coming back out of the tent. "I doubt it's of the quality you must be used to."

He walked over to the side of her throne and offered her a chalice. *Silver*, Verena could see from first glance. She couldn't let it touch Aulduyen's puppets.

She took it from the human's hand gratefully and chugged down the wine in a heartbeat, the liquid slightly burning her throat. She coughed. The man, though clearly surprised, kept his face completely still.

"More?" he asked.

She nodded, licking her lips. He took the chalice from her hand and disappeared back into the tent again.

"It's good," she said after sipping from the next chalice in moderation. "It's hard to drink anything but water, down in the lake."

"I see. That must be unpleasant. If you wish, we could arrange a supply line for you. A lady of your stature surely deserves nothing but the finest things in life."

She shook her head. "I'm a commoner. Acu'enah has been drowned for centuries, you can't really call it a kingdom anymore if only two or three people are living in it."

"Centuries? You certainly don't look it."

"No! No, I only meant… Never mind. I'm your age. Listen, um… I don't remember your name, but… Tiphaine is an annoying, wretched little beast."

The man made an expression of utter confusion for a moment.

"That's what I'm supposed to say, isn't it? I hope I didn't misremember. Emony told me that was it, I hope he wasn't joking…"

Understanding colored the human's face upon hearing her explanation. "Ah… No, you're right. Emony did tell me, before he left, to be courteous and to obey whoever told me those specific words, in that specific order. I suppose I ought to. What can I help you with, my lady?"

She nodded, sipping more of the wine, hoping it would soon start to calm her down.

"Have you heard any news from Terrena? The people you sent to ask about Imarah – the girl that was kidnapped ten years ago? Have you learned anything yet?"

"I'm afraid not," he replied, shaking his head. "Messengers need time to get to Terrena, and time to get back, even leaving out the time spent there gathering information. I'm afraid I've nothing to share with you yet – but I sent five of my best men. They should send at least one back soon."

"How soon?" she asked. The rain was picking up again, lightning flashing above the clouds. Waiting was never something Aulduyen was good at.

"A fortnight, perhaps. Or, if you prefer, I could send some more men after them on our fastest horses, have them return sooner. They could be back in a few days, if by chance they've managed to find something."

Verena glanced over at one of the corpses carrying her, one that was little more than a skeleton, with clams growing on its ribs. It turned towards her, strings of invisible magic running through its empty eye sockets. It stared for a long time, then nodded at her before looking straight ahead again.

She looked over to the knight commander.

"Three… days. Sooner, if possible. We want to know about the queen. Please – just give us what we want. You might live."

4

Aylard

The pre-dawn light did little to warm the cold air. A breeze was slipping through his clothes, freezing his nerves as he cringed at the sight right in front of him.

"Are you in pain?" Tiphaine asked, her rusty golden mask inches from his face. His vision was still blurry from the blood loss, but he could recognize the vipers coiling around her and hissing at him.

His shoulder stung, as though a part of it were missing.

"Yyy…. I caaant…."

"Talk? Then stop, you're too much of a nuisance as is." A male voice.

"Emony! He's a friend!"

He wanted to shake his head. That wasn't true.

He grimaced and turned onto his side. He could feel something coming up. Curling into his stomach, vomit began to pour out of his mouth. No. No, it wasn't vomit. That was the wrong color. It was blood.

"Lenah, can't you do something? You helped Emony with his hand!"

"That was one cleanly broken bone. This… is bad."

The blue-haired witch laid a warm hand on his chest. He shivered at the touch.

The werewolf, somewhere behind them, cursed.

"We have to make it to Terrena," Lenah said. "There are healers there who will be better equipped to help him – mortal ones, at that. We need to take him to one of them. But for him to survive till we get there… I'm going to chain his life to yours, Emony."

"What? No! Keep your black magic off of me!"

Tiphaine's voice: "Emony, please! Lenah, you could use mine, too, if you need it!"

"Urgh. No way, not that. It'll be mine," the werewolf growled. "At least we're going in that direction already."

"Why are you complaining, anyway, Emony? If you really didn't care at all, why did you sic your pet mermaid on him?" Lenah asked.

"Because I do stupid things sometimes, Lenah! Don't think I don't regret them!"

Mermaid? Was that...?

The witch patted him on the chest. It hurt.

"That's right, Aylard. You remember it quite clearly."

"That's impossible," he croaked.

"After everything you've seen, this is where you draw the line? Look, the next few days are going to be unpleasant. I'm going to link you to Emony, you're going to be leeching off his black little soul for a while. You already owe him your life, so play nice and don't start dying too quickly, he won't appreciate that. Okay. Let's get going. First things first, though. Tiphaine. You... won't be welcome in the city."

"What?" the lamia and the werewolf said simultaneously.

"Yes... Unfortunately, Terrena is still quite the hotspot for mythic haters. I know the king, and while Emony and I can pass for human, you, well... not for a second. You would be too much."

"Can't you—"

"No. There's no way."

"... Damn it all. Tiphaine—"

"It's fine. Then... I'll... I'll go back to Coldbarrow. I'll go and talk to Verena, I'm sure she'll want to know how we're doing. We've been gone for a while."

"While you're there, please try to tame the king. Tell him we're close to finding Imarah," Lenah begged, embracing the lamia.

"I'll tell him. I hope it's true, though."

"But who's going to be our pack mule after you're gone? I don't want to carry the human."

"You're going to, Emony! I'll make you a statue for a whole day if he dies!"

"By the divines, Tiphaine... Fine, then. Don't squirm, Aylard. I hope all that blood you lost in the river made you lighter. Lose some weight, do you know how… never mind.”

Rough hands slipped under Aylard’s back and knees, lifting him into the air. Surprisingly gently, he was slung over the werewolf’s shoulder.

“Emony,” said Lenah. “We have to make haste. There’s something else that I absolutely need to see there as soon as possible.”

“Then let’s get to that shack before the human bleeds out. I can smell the death on you already, Aylard. Don’t you dare abuse my soul for your gain. Do it, Lenah.”

The witch did something to Emony before walking over behind him, in front of Aylard’s head. She gave him a small nod before brushing his forehead with her thumb. After stepping back, she knelt on the ground and laid her hands on the grass. Her blue eyes instantly turned black. Every vein on her body darkened. Sparks sizzled out of her hands, crackling through the air and ground before reaching him.

Aylard screamed.

When he woke up, he could tell that hours had passed. They were moving. The werewolf’s legs were thumping on the ground, making him bump rhythmically and painfully onto his shoulder. Everything was blurry.

“By the divines!” someone shouted. He heard steps running towards them. “What happened to him?”

“Brigands in the night,” said Emony with a tired voice. “We need to get him to a healer, quickly. Can you let us through the gate? We’ve been travelling all day. I fear for his – and my – life.”

Another set of footsteps could be heard walking over to them. A dismissing tone was clear in the voice of the new man. "Not until you've been checked. Nobody passes the gate before being searched and passing the mythic test, that's the king's order. The next one is in a couple of hours."

"We don't know if he has that long," the Emony growled.

Aylard croaked for added effect.

"Perhaps an exception could be made?" asked the first guard.

"No. There's no way through, not unless they've got a letter of safe conduct."

"What if we threaten—"

"Emony. Shut up. Friends, it seems we are in luck, then. We have a letter of safe conduct. Aylard, which pocket do you have it in? In your coat? One moment, Aylard, try to lean on your side. Ah, here it is. There. Will that suffice?"

He could hear the men untying and unrolling the parchment Lenah had taken from his coat pocket.

"Damn it, what is this? There's no seal."

"It's a letter of intent from our knight commander," the wolf said. "Says we are on official business."

"So you say, but I can't read, and I don't see a seal. It could be a love letter, for all I know."

"I promise you the parchment says what he said it does," Lenah said. "Let us through. You can see the poor state our man is in. We have to find someone to make him better—"

Emony interrupted her: "Look at it this way – either we'll be out of your hair, or we'll be telling King Raynardt all about why we failed our mission. We were coming this way to speak to him, in the first place. Lenah, show him your seal too, why don't you?"

"Right, I completely forgot!"

Seeing the witch holding up that thing for him, the human guard rolled up the piece of parchment.

"I can't tell if that's real or not, either, it's got to be at least ten years old! Fine. Go, and don't cause any trouble. If I find you making a ruckus in the city, I will personally tell the city watch to have you all executed – and keep that parchment safe, if it really says what you say it does."

"Thank you…"

Aylard lost consciousness again.

It was warm and stuffy in the healer's room. The air was stale, and the bedrolls smelled of sickness and medicine. A fire crackled in a small hearth positioned before the line of bedrolls laying on a big pile of hay. Sick men and women were coughing, laying atop them while the healers worked.

"I'm honestly surprised you're alive," the man said, pricking a needle through Aylard's skin, sewing the spear wound shut with the skin on his shoulder. "You're deathly pale, there must be very little blood left in you. And your wound is deep. I've seen corpses in better condition. But you said you fell into the river? The current has been awfully strong these past few weeks, with the constant rain we've been getting. You're lucky you managed to get out, though clearly, you've had a brush with the rapids, too. I don't understand any of this… but in any case, I strongly advise you to spend the next few days here. I'm sorry – sir? Could you lay your friend onto the bedroll over there? By the fire."

Emony, apparently standing close by, snorted at the word "friend", but picked him up and did as the healer said. He was looking pale, too.

"Thank you," the healer said. "I'm afraid that nowadays, I myself lack the strength of youth. Now, as I've mentioned, the treatment and lodgings will be paid for by the king's grace – but I'm afraid the same cannot be said for anything more than a daily meal. Any amount you could spare would go a long way towards his recovery."

"Here. And there's plenty more if you come to need it, just keep him alive."

"Thank… Thank you. That will be more than enough. I'll do my best – though as I said, I really don't understand how he is still alive at this very moment. Now, then, I must leave you with him. I have to go get some things."

As the healer hurried away, Aylard's "friend" stepped closer and threw a blanket over him.

"Going to smother me?" Aylard asked, uncovering his head. His voice was very hoarse.

"Don't flatter yourself. You're not worth the effort," Emony said.

He sat down on the floor in front of him, leaning his back on Aylard's legs, making them ache. He seemed to be in pain, too.

"You just had to go and meet some bandits, didn't you? Is this part of one of your schemes?"

"Ha! Oh, damn. I hurt too much to laugh right now."

"Then don't."

"Then stop speaking nonsense. Why would I plan to have myself killed…? All I want is to save human lives. And keep my own. Urgh. Talking hurts, too. Anyway, the witch said you and a mermaid saved me?"

The werewolf grimaced. "Don't bother being grateful. You'll never see her again. But to think, the one time you were about to make yourself useful, you almost died... And then got my life chained to yours. I thought you were against the use of black magic. Filthy sympathizer."

"I'd like to thank her. The mermaid. And you, I guess."

"I'll pass on the message," Emony said as the healer's assistant approached. "Hm? Oh, okay. Fine. Hey, you, drink this."

He tossed him a vial full of some dark brown liquid.

"What is it?"

"Poison, straight out of Tiphaine's hair. Relax, idiot, it's a painkilling elixir. According to Lenah, in any case. She's already got herself another minion. For all I know, this'll make you run around flapping your arms like a bird, like you did that time in Gull's Landing."

"Please never mention that again. Can you help me? I'm having trouble lifting my head."

"You're a serious pain in my behind, you know that?"

The werewolf stood up, taking the vial and, after he smelled it, placed it to his lips.

"It smells like a strong drink," he told Aylard.

Which was exactly what it was. The alcohol burned his throat as it went down. It was painfully intense. Likely expensive, too.

"Thank you," Aylard said, after choking on the last sip the werewolf poured down his mouth.

"By the way, there's a small flask in your pocket. It might smell like alcohol, too, but for your own good, never drink what's in it," Emony said, getting up.

"I noticed it yesterday... Or was it the day before? What's in it?"

"A highly defective love potion."

"Huh. Am I going to fall in love soon, then? Did the witch give it to me? Where is she, anyway?"

"She's gone to ask around about something. We're to have dinner with the king one of these days, we're moving up in the world. But don't you worry about that or the potion. Just keep the thing around and don't drink it."

"Why not?" Aylard asked.

"Like I said, it's highly defective. About this, I wouldn't lie to my worst enemy."

"Right… Then I guess I should give you a piece of advice, too… Since you saved my life… Chained it to yours, whatever that means… Divines, my throat hurts. What did the witch do, anyway? I feel terrible. She said it was black magic. According to your definition."

"It is, but it's one of the lighter shades of black. So long as the magic holds and I live, you can't die," Emony explained. "Now, what were you going to say? You know how much I love listening to human advice."

"Ha… It's about the witch, Lenah. I already tried to tell you once, but I have a feeling you don't remember. Back when we were leaving Levara, she messed with your head. Tiphaine's too, but more so yours."

The werewolf shook his head, his lips creeping into a smile. "No, she didn't."

"She did. I only remember, myself, because I was holding onto all that silver the bankers gave me."

"Ha… Well, what did she do? More witchy party smoke?" he asked.

Aylard shook his head. "I think she made you forget something. Something – I think it has to do with Westmire."

"Westmire's great, I hear. Lovely scenery."

"No, Emony. She said she'd made you a promise, that you'd never find out."

The smug smile suddenly disappeared from Emony's lips.

"And though you told me you're not… This is just a guess, so I might be wrong, but I really think… that you're not originally from Aeliah. I think you used to live in Westmire."

The werewolf's hand suddenly shot up to his head. Goosebumps appeared on his arms, and his face contorted into a fiercely agonized expression as he held it.

"You're wrong," he gasped. Blue sparks suddenly shot out of his head towards the ground, sizzling in all directions. "She wouldn't."

Aylard stared at the werewolf, disconcerted, unable to avoid the sparks of magic, which were hurtling off him.

"Emony, look at what's happening!"

He fell to the floor, the blue sparks burning the wood beneath him. He groaned in pain.

"No, no! That didn't happen! We never went there! We never went to Westmire together. Even if we did, they were gone by the time she arrived the first time, anyway! That's a stupid story, made up by an idiot!"

"I didn't say anything," Aylard whispered.

Emony turned to him with crazed eyes. "Why would I…?! Are you stupid?!"

The werewolf blinked, and the pain and rage suddenly left his face. "Was it for her? It was, wasn't it?"

"Emony?"

He didn't notice him.

"No… no, it wasn't. I had to. I did, I'd already made my choice when I killed hers. But it wasn't for her, it was for me! It was all for me!"

"What are you talking about, Emony?!" Aylard rasped. Emony was staring vacantly into space.

"I didn't want to want to kill her. So… so I made it so it wouldn't do me any good. It wasn't humans… It was me."

Emony stared at him quietly, his mouth agape. The seconds turned into minutes, but he moved nothing but his eyes.

Finally, after wildly shaking his head for a moment, he looked lucidly at Aylard again.

"Did I make the wrong choice?" he asked, tears suddenly welling in his eyes. He quickly turned away from him, hurrying towards the window and staring at the sky. "I didn't, did I? Her life… I couldn't kill her – and a hundred years is a long time! Should I have left them like that? No. I'd do the same thing again if I had to. But it… hurts…"

"Emony." Aylard said, struggling to put his weight on his elbows so he could look at him.

The werewolf suddenly saw him. Slowly, the horror disappeared from his face.

He walked over, back towards Aylard, and pushed him back down onto the bedroll.

"Don't strain yourself, human. Everything is fine. You made a mistake, that's all. You should never have told me that," he said quietly.

"What did I tell you? You haven't made anything clear at all," he replied.

"Nor will I. I'm a horrible monster, remember? I killed some people, that's all you need to know."

"You know, for some reason, right now I'm getting the feeling you haven't killed half the people you pretend to have. Quit the murderer act."

"Ha... I don't remember telling you any numbers – but hey, just between us guys – it is pretty high. And those two people were special to me. Just as those two were special to her…"

"Sure... whatever you say."

A pained expression settled on him again. Then, the werewolf smiled at him maliciously, trying unsuccessfully to hide it, and patted him roughly on the chest, provoking a painful groan from Aylard.

"Anyway – get better soon. Lenah wants you with us when we meet the king. Apparently, I was wrong, and even after everything, you can be trusted. We don't even have to threaten you. But for old time's sake – you try to expose me, and I'll kill the king, all of his guards, and then I'll go after everyone you've ever cared for. Sleep on it."

"Urgh. Fine. No problem. Wait – Emony."

"What is it? Want to be buddies? I've just had some mind-shattering realizations, I could be convinced."

"I want to speak to the mermaid."

He grimaced again. "Never mind. I don't need another friend of that sort. Look, the mermaid is long gone. If you ever do see her, she'll probably kill you. Just recover. We have a job to do. Palehome is gone, but there is still the rest of the world to consider. I really don't know if Tiphaine will be able to convince the king not to destroy it."

Chapter 9

1

Yperian

"We need to evacuate the village. Today, before the monsters get a chance to stop us. Leynor, give the order. Take the men, go to every house and tavern, and scour the fields. Nobody stays behind."

Yperian stared over at the lake from the hilltop, the lake he had seen swirling like a colossal whirlpool the very day before. It was becoming increasingly clear that the enemy was unbeatable. That undead horde couldn't be stopped, not even delayed. It was by their undead… grace… that the humans had survived even this long.

But they had to leave.

"Sir, if we do that… Those things will notice. They control the weather, by the look of it, they'll definitely attack us. They don't wait for the rain, like we thought – they bring it."

"I know. Our chances are slim. We may all die the very moment we try to leave. But I still think it's our best chance."

"Sir knight commander! Knight commander, I bring a report—"

"Speak. Do not delay with formalities."

"Sir… Roughly a third of our forward observers have abandoned their posts. We can't find them anywhere. They've deserted."

Bad news. But not unexpected.

"Very well. Thank you, squire. Carry a message back to those that remain – tell them to start packing. They'll know what that means."

"Yes, sir!" with a quick salute, the squire ran off.

"I'd rather not see that boy become a walking corpse," Yperian said to his adjutant. "I knew his father, in a previous war. But that was one in which we had a chance at victory. In this one, we don't. Give the order. Tell the people to ready as much food and water as they can carry on foot all the way to Terrena. We leave tonight. We take no breaks. If we make it there and King Raynardt takes my head for my cowardice, so be it."

"Understood, commander," Leynor said. "Let's hope it doesn't come to that."

"It's one of the better outcomes, really," he murmured.

"Hold your fire, archers! That's an ally!" called one of the watchmen on top of their guard tower.

Yperian turned towards the entrance to the encampment, where the wooden gate had been blasted off its hinges the night before. The cursed lamia, Tiphaine, slithered into the camp, looking around at all the destruction. Though apparently unharmed, she was alone.

He made his way over to her, noticing her snakes coiling above her head. He wondered which one of her emotional states they could be betraying. Could he dare to expect any good news?

Almost certainly not.

"Knight commander," she said as she saw him approach. "I've returned a little sooner than my friends. What happened here? Were you attacked?"

"The situation has progressed unfavorably. The enemy has been in contact. You might care to hear about this – their ranks do indeed include a mermaid."

"Is that so… Well, what did she say?"

"That we have three days to tell them of that girl from the rebellion, Imarah. Of course, we've already sent riders in the night, to Terrena. Hopefully, those sent there before them will have something to say. Still, since we must expect to receive bad news, we are planning an evacuation."

"I see… I didn't think this would happen, I thought we had more time… But the villagers are unharmed?"

"Yes. For now, the monsters have not come for them. They haven't brought their real strength to bear against us yet, either – but it's become certain that we fight them. They could wipe us out at any moment."

"Are there more of them now than there were before? I thought you were evenly matched… Listen, Emony and Aylard have also gone to Terrena, following the leads we've found. There's a chance they might find something there even if your soldiers don't. They're going to meet with the king. Maybe we can negotiate with the… um… the mermaid."

"The mermaid is not the one in charge. She was an enemy, to be sure, but definitely not the one truly leading the undead army. She was afraid of her own men. There must be another. The "king" that everyone whispers about. Perhaps it really is the late Aulduyen."

The snake nervously glanced at him for a moment before shaking her head. "Whoever he is, I'll talk to him. I'll buy you more time – but please, don't do anything rash. Trying to run might antagonize him."

"You're right, of course, but we must do what we can to keep the people safe. We cannot live at the mercy of the undead!"

"I know… What should I do… Please, just give me today. You said they gave you three days, right? If the riders come back with nothing… I'll go and talk to the king. I'll convince him it's not worth hurting you or the villagers. Just… wait for me."

There were no good options, but he still thought that trying to escape was the better choice. So why did his mind force him to obey the snake? Couldn't he refuse?

2

Tiphaine

She'd been worried she might have forgotten where they were, but she found the steps carved into the lake easily, by following the path of destruction. Rows and rows of trees were collapsed in a straight line from the encampment to the water. The soldiers were running around all over, shouting, grabbing various kinds of equipment and taking it all with them to the encampment.

She quickly slithered over to the lake, hoping that what she was doing was a good idea. The steps cut into the stone on the lakebed lay before her, sinking into the depths. Nervously, she dipped her head into the water to see if she could still breathe in it. Fighting all of her instincts, she opened her mouth and let it in.

It was terrifying. The feeling of water slipping down between her vocal cords made her feel like she was about to drown. But she breathed out, and breathed in again. She wasn't drowning. Not really. Gathering her courage, she slithered forward into the lake, and opened her eyes in it.

The bright water was full of life, just as it had been the last time she'd entered it, but there were more than just fish and crabs there now. She spotted the bodies of soldiers strewn all over the lake, floating in the water at various levels. They were watching her. Swallowing her spit along with plenty of water, she nodded towards them and moved forward along the path, towards the sunken palace.

A while later, the algae-covered walls of Acu'enah stood before her, an army of corpses standing in the water just in front of them. She could hardly breathe, though that had nothing to do with her being underwater. The abyss she had just crossed over was spewing black magic into the water like a million evil sorcerers.

Trying to catch her breath, she saw Verena swim gracefully over the walls of the palace to greet her.

"You're back," Verena said, coming back down to her level at the seabed. "It's so good to see you, Tiphaine! I wish it were under better circumstances. Do you bring any news? Please tell me you have something good."

She shook her head nervously. "Nothing definitive. We've been to Gull's Landing and Levara, and the path led us to Terrena. I can't get in, so I came back – but it's okay – we've met up with Lenah. I'm sure they'll be able to find something soon."

"The humans said they sent some men to Terrena, too. Divines, I hope they come up with something. Tiphaine, I'm afraid that, as time passes, our methods may become increasingly brutal. I didn't think our quest to bring back Imarah would look like this. I'm so sorry I got you involved."

"It's okay. But, Verena, I have to talk with the king."

"Aulduyen? Why? I'm... I'm not so sure that you should."

"I really need to. It's the humans. The soldiers on the hill. They want to evacuate the villagers tonight – they're all terrified, I could see it on their faces."

The mermaid nodded. "They have every right to be. My expedition... I'm not sure it helped. But if they leave, I fear Aulduyen might... He'd consider them all traitors. Wherever he looks, he sees only Imarah. Only his queen. Anything or anyone that might not want to help him get her back..."

"It's gotten worse, since we left? He stayed his hand, then. He promised he'd give us time."

"I recall – but you've seen how much bigger the army has gotten. The towns and villages to the north – they are all gone. Except for Gull's Landing, as you said you would be going there, everything has been laid to waste."

Tiphaine looked at her with horror. "Surely not! How?!"

"The compulsion has taken root in his heart, Tiphaine, I know it. It's as I said, the only thing that matters to him is his queen. She sang him a song ten years ago, I don't know how it's still affecting him after all this time, but that has to be it. It has to be, but I don't know how we can get rid of it! If we don't find Imarah quickly... I truly don't know what he might do."

Verena shook her head before worryingly staring at her again.

"Coldbarrow might be lost if the people decide to run," she continued. "If you think you can stop that, then go. Talk to Aulduyen. But please, do nothing to offend him – say nothing about Imarah. He's in their tower, the tallest one in the palace.

Wait for him at its base. He will come to you, don't enter without permission."

Tiphaine slowly nodded before slithering past the statues of mermaids, into the palace.

What could she possibly say to the man responsible for so much death?

"So, the humans of Terrena barred your entry," murmured the king, sitting derisively on a chair on the opposite side of the marble table. He'd led her into the "war room", a smaller chamber within the palace, in which a stone table stood, a map of the world outside the lake carved in it, with pieces of rusty metal floating with the tide on the markings of cities. "They've made their choice, to stand in opposition to my love. A grave mistake."

"My king… I'd like to ask you not to go to war with them. I don't mean not ever, just… not yet. Emony, Lenah and Aylard are all there, and they're doing their best to find your queen. It will be harder to do so if the people get ready for war."

"Lies. You attempt to deceive me, snake," the king retorted. "In an attempt to protect your friends, no doubt. If an army lays claim to the fields around a city, demanding nothing but a girl, there is no doubt she will be given to them in exchange for the people's lives. Imarah would be returned to me with honors, if she were there. It makes things more difficult for your friends to find her. It would be easier, and I have nearly accumulated enough strength to go through with this. The only danger is that typical of war – death. Death and destruction. Which might fall upon those friends of yours in the chaos."

"It may be that way," she stammered, bowing her head. "But… I beg you all the same. Please give them more time."

He got up from his tall chair, walking through the water around the table towards her. He gazed into her eyes, a thin, pitying smile on his face. "It is such a fragile thing, isn't it? Life? It is truly the height of foolishness that love should be so strong in demanding it remain whole."

Tiphaine looked away from his dark eyes, towards the stone floor.

"You understand me, I can see it, as can your companion. However, there is something you do not recognize. You are not the heroes of this love story. You are side characters. You are on the right side, but still, your desires matter ever so little when unaligned with the return of my queen."

He slowly stepped away, walking back towards his chair.

"Do I really understand you, though?" she asked quietly.

"Hm? What do you mean? Speak your mind."

"I'm not sure I understand you," she said, a slither of courage – or madness, probably – entering her mind. "I don't know if I would slaughter thousands of innocents for a chance at finding Emony. I know he'd never want me to, in the first place. Would your queen really want it of you?"

"No, of course not – but she will not bear witness to any of it. These sins are mine, and mine alone."

"Are they?" she asked. "Are you sure she will see it that way? When it was she, a siren, that sang to you, to make you fall in love?"

The king sprang out of his chair in an instant, the impenetrable stone table thrown against the wall like it was nothing, destroying half of the entire room with a resounding blast, and surging forward through the water.

"You dare make such accusations of my queen?! You dare believe, in my presence, that she would wound me so?!"

Even the snakes on top of Tiphaine's head stood as still as statues, dead quiet, while she watched, paralyzed in fear herself. The king's rage boiled over, the water around him darkening to a pitch black. The dark magic emanating all around made her feel sick to her stomach, and it hadn't even touched her yet. Only a little more and she would vomit out even the blood in her veins. That would be the death of her, she knew. But ever so slowly, the nausea faded. The king suddenly calmed down and looked towards the destruction. He scratched his chin, thinking about something.

"Ah, no, I see, that wasn't an accusation. My apologies. I lost my composure for a moment. You have a point. Her blaming herself for the evils I commit is something that must absolutely be avoided. Your argument may have merit. So, what do you propose?"

His strange, erratic manners somehow made Tiphaine even more fearful. There was no telling when he would next explode. The king sat down gracefully on the stone floor where his chair had stood before it had shattered.

"I'm sorry, I don't know. But perhaps until we figure something out, we should refrain from doing anything too cruel?"

"An obvious approach, but evils must be committed in order to retrieve her. So, should I restrain myself, or should I not? Should I break free from her song, to prove to her that my actions were my own? But that would be... indescribably horrible."

Tiphaine gulped. "Maybe sometimes the hardest decisions are the right ones."

The king sighed, running a hand through the curls of his hair. "You may be telling the truth, snake, but I suspect you only speak the words that would serve you. Without her song in my ears… how would I survive for even a moment? What would I live for, in the first place? This pain I feel… There is no way you could understand. The only thing that matters is her."

Still sitting on the ground, he quietly wrapped his arms around his knees. "I suppose your friend, the siren, has sung to you once or twice since her… his… transformation? By accident, at least?"

She quietly nodded.

"Then you know there can be nothing more beautiful than a siren's song. The way it can fill the world with color, even when everything in it is black… Imarah sang to me on plenty of occasions. I wouldn't be here if she hadn't."

Tiphaine left her seat and made her way a little closer to the king. She curled up her tail and sat down on it across from him, on the floor.

"I haven't heard that much about her. The villagers said she was nice, but they didn't really know her."

"Bah, no, they were never close. She told me she sang a song or two to them when she was young, that they should see her as a human even whilst witnessing her golden tail. She wanted to be their friend. But it didn't work as well as she'd wished it would. She only truly had her sister, Verena, until the two of us met. She was lonely. And me… I had no one at all. But then, we saw each other that day… And this whole, damned world made sense…"

"It must have been true love. You got married pretty quickly," Tiphaine smiled.

"Not quickly enough. Every moment I spent apart from her then was a complete and utter waste."

The king shifted on the stone floor. Suddenly snapping out of his thoughts, his sharp gaze rushed towards the jewels covering Tiphaine's eyes.

"I'm well aware of your suspicions, and that Verena shares them. But you're wrong. Imarah never forced a song on me."

"I'm… I'm sorry?"

"Do you think it wise to look at me as though I am a fool without equal?"

"No! I'm sorry, I never thought—"

"It's quite alright. I am a fool. But not for the reason you think. Embracing my queen that fateful day was the best decision I ever made – even though the path led me here."

Tiphaine shook her head. "I don't understand."

"Of course, you don't. You were born normal, and normal you remain, but I was not. My days were always full of nothing. Before I met her, I was an empty husk of a man, unwanted by everyone and of use to no one, least of all myself. But she… At my request, she simply sang a few words to me, and this whole beautiful world revealed itself to me. It had been gray, only gray, and all of a sudden, I saw it in countless different vibrant hues! There was no way I couldn't fall in love with her after I'd seen her face and she'd done me such a kindness. And far be it for that to be all. In time, the person she revealed herself to be…"

"I… I see…" Tiphaine stammered.

"Oh, you don't need to pretend to understand. Nobody does. Only know this, and tell Verena, should she be interested – normally, yes, a song will fade from your mind after a short time. But

I clung to Imarah's melodies with all my might. I cling to them still, though the abyssal magic I've acquired is trying desperately to strip me of them. I choose to do so. It is my will that keeps her songs in my ears. It is because I can see the truth, that love is the only thing that matters. I'm afraid, snake, that I must deny your request. My love can be cruel, but it will conquer."

3

Emony

Emony was just starting to regain a sense of normalcy – however much he… she could manage, closing her eyes, lying in the bathtub of the private chamber in the form of a mermaid.

She was in the middle of convincing herself that she would not be a pervert if she rubbed soap all over her female chest – she had to do so to attend the king's banquet. She had no choice, and her mind was magically poisoned, anyway.

But then someone annoying came in.

Lenah entered the room just as she reached for the soap.

Emony cleared her throat to let her presence be known.

"Oh, don't mind me," Lenah said, tossing her silk black dress onto a wooden stool. "I'm quite well acquainted with the female form. As, by now, are you."

Emony looked away from her, refusing to be provoked, and reached for the towel she had earlier hung by the tub.

"Leaving so soon? But I think you'll need a while to dry yourself off. Especially with me throwing water at you so you don't manage it."

Emony rolled her eyes and grimaced in her direction. The blue-haired witch was standing completely naked in front of the tub, smiling at her.

"You're going to expose me, now?" Emony asked.

"Ha! You know, if you were to crawl out of the bathhouse, using only your hands and dragging that tail across the floor, that would be an amusing sight! I swear I would ensure there would be no consequences to it."

Emony frowned again. "Unfortunately, these arms are far too slim to manage it." She leaned back into the tub. "I miss my strength."

"Yes, poor you, Emony. Becoming a frail little mermaid, another victim of Lenah, the evil witch... If only there was a single good thing about it..."

Lenah came closer to the tub and dipped her toe into the water.

"There's not enough space for the both of us. Go away."

Those blue sparks crackled around the witch again, catching the magic she had laced into the words. Lenah put her whole foot into the water and eventually sat down on the end of Emony's tail, facing her.

Well with that, she had nowhere else to look.

"Would you pass the soap?" Lenah asked innocently.

Emony did so with closed eyes, to spite her.

"I love seeing that embarrassed expression on your new face. Just the irony behind it is enough for me – the menacing werewolf, the scourge of Aeliah, sulking in the bathtub in the form of a girl, afraid to look at me. Ha! That is why we are friends."

"Are you really that bored?"

"Yes, I am, and I have been for nearly a century now. But you can't be too surprised, you've known other witches."

"Intimately."

Lenah chuckled while smothering the soap onto her arms. "Oh? I hope it wasn't that tramp, Marietta. You could do so much better – oh – I know her. Would you mind if I told Tiphaine about that?"

"Get out of my head."

"Haha, nah. It's an interesting place. While I poke around, would you like me to answer one of those questions swirling around in it? The reason you're having such an easy time looking at my face right now?"

"It's because I remembered your age, you old hag," he said.

"No, that's not it. You certainly didn't have it so easy this morning, and you knew how old I was then, too. I'm sorry, Emony, I'm afraid your suspicions are correct! My mermaid spell affects the mind, too!"

"Please shut up... But you know that I already know that."

"Oh, Tiphaine will be devastated! Ah, no, never mind. I see your feelings for her haven't dimmed a bit. So, it's because Aylard told you."

"He told me," he replied.

"And? Who have you chosen to hate? Tiphaine, for petrifying your parents? Yourself, for killing them? Or me, for making you forget?"

"Nobody. I've actually always wanted to be an orphan, so…"

"Ha…. Then aren't you lucky that she chose to slither through Westmire? Now that you know, are you going to tell her?"

"No, and neither will you. We continue the lie. I'm from Aeliah."

"Whatever you say… Though I wonder how exactly your relationship will work out, built on that lie. Personally, I am most curious about the logistics. Her mother was a lamia while her father was human, so it's clearly possible, but how, precisely, that is the question—"

"I will murder you in your sleep."

"Okay, okay," the witch shrugged, spinning a finger and making the soapy water in the tub swirl around them like a whirlpool. "Just don't come crying to me later asking me how it's done. Actually, please do. I'd be happy to explain, in vivid detail."

With a final smug smile, Lenah got out of the tub, dripping water onto the stone floor for a moment before sending it flying back into the tub with a flick of her wrist. And just like that, she was dry. Emony so wished she could do that.

"I'll be taking my leave first, then. We still have the chamber reserved for another hour or so, so don't worry about any more interruptions."

"Thank you."

Lenah, still smiling for some reason, materialized clothes around her and left.

"You left your other dress here!" she called after her.

She didn't come back. Emony leaned into the tub.

Ignoring that, she finally started to clean herself, wondering if the soap and oils would really stay on after she transformed back into a man. Lenah had assured her they would.

And then the door opened again.

"Ah, Lenah, you forgot—"

It wasn't Lenah.

It was Aylard.

"You—"

The human stared at her, dumbfounded, from the open doorway. He was impossibly shocked, just as she was.

"G-get out!" Emony shrieked, throwing a barrage of magic his way. "Get out of this bathhouse!"

Blue sparks crackled around Aylard, catching the words and protecting him. The human looked nervously around upon seeing them. He didn't seem to know Lenah had put the spell on him. *Damned witch!*

"Get out, now," Emony growled again, suddenly irritated also by the fact that it was impossible for her to sound threatening with her current voice.

Aylard turned around quickly and closed the door in front of himself, leaning his forehead against it. Did he not know how to use a door?!

"I'm sorry," he exclaimed, "I didn't know the room was occupied. I apologize. A… friend… told me it wasn't."

"Well, now you know that it is, so get out."

"I will. I promise. I'm sorry about this. But before I leave… I want to say something to you. For modesty's sake, I promise not to turn around."

Emony laid back further into the soapy water filling the tub, scowling. She couldn't do anything, she was downright teethless, stuck in the bathtub.

"Fine. Say it."

"I… I wanted to thank you. For saving my life in that river. You pulled me out of the water."

"I also killed a few people; would you like me to repeat the words to you?"

Aylard shook his head, forcing his eyes shut while he faced the wooden door. "No. I beg you, do not. I promise not to threaten you in any way. I… I'm sorry – I'm just confused. Why did you save me? I'm human, and you're… not."

"A friend asked me to. That's all there is to it. Now leave."

"Which friend?"

"It doesn't matter."

"Tiphaine would be the most obvious guess, but a witch, Lenah, put her to sleep. And it was clear when I returned to consciousness that she had no idea what had happened. Was it really Emony?"

"Stop thinking about it, it's done. Just leave."

"Please, just tell me why you saved my life! I don't understand what's going on! We're supposed to be enemies! Sirens like you are what…"

The damned human looked desperate. And worse – Lenah was more correct than even she knew. Her damned fishtail was affecting her mind. She cursed the damned thing as she spoke honestly.

"I saved you because I thought it was the right thing to do. Tiphaine wanted to keep you alive, and… Emony asked me to help you… but I would have done it anyway."

A hundred moments passed in silence.

"You thought…" Aylard shook his head slowly against the door. "You thought it was the right thing to do…? I cannot even begin to understand. I'm sorry for disturbing you. I'll go. Just one more thing. If you ever need anything… At the very least, I pay my debts. May I have your name?"

"No. You may not. This is the last you'll ever see of me, anyway."

At that, the door suddenly opened in front of Aylard, hitting him in the face and making him fall to the floor, dumbfounded. Startled, Emony leaned forward to see if Aylard had hurt himself. He was still injured, after all.

Suddenly, he was irked again.

Lenah was standing at the door, beaming a revolting smile.

"Don't be such a sourpuss, friend!" she announced. "Aylard, this here is Emm… Emm… Emma. I think you two will be seeing more of each other soon!"

"Lenah, I really will do it – I swear it, I will murder you in your sleep. Get out!"

Chapter 10

1

"I met Emma," Aylard said, changing the bandage on his shoulder, glancing up at Emony from his straw bed. "My guess is Lenah arranged it, but if you had a hand in it too… thanks."

"I most certainly did not. That damned witch just does whatever she wants. Give me that."

He took the old bandage from the recovering human, smelling it as well as he could with his nearly useless nose. He couldn't smell any rot…

Whatever. He wouldn't really mind if he did die. With a grimace, he threw the messy cloth into the corner of the room, onto some random sick person.

"Can I ask you something?" Aylard inquired.

"Clearly. You just did. But I might not answer next time."

"How would she have gotten into the bathhouse? How and why would she have managed to get into Terrena, in the first place? What would a mermaid be doing on land?"

That was a question he couldn't answer.

"Maybe Lenah teleported her there or something. Anyway, your condition is improving. Painfully slowly, I might add."

"As it turns out, I'm human."

"Sucks to be you. You're lucky to be alive. I had Lenah unlink us, by the way. No more black magic keeping you that way. Where did she go, anyway? Oh, right. I expect they'll be bringing your breakfast soon. Make sure it doesn't taste funny before you eat it all, she might have put something in it like she did in mine yesterday."

The witch in question strolled into the room at that very moment. Aylard was in the middle of checking his pocket to make sure the flask with the defective love potion remained unopened.

"What do you want?" Emony asked, suddenly irritated.

"Just to see you two, grumpy… Oh, no, that's not it. I'm here to bring a few messages. One is for Aylard, from Emma."

He could already feel the day taking a turn for the worse. "Don't be ridiculous. She's got nothing to say to this human."

"Oh, but she does…" Lenah said, walking over and patting Aylard right on his injured shoulder, making him wince in pain. "She wants to wish him a painless recovery. And she says she'll be in touch."

"She will not be in touch," he growled.

"I think she might."

"She will absolutely not. Nothing in the world is more unlikely," he said.

"Emony. I'm not a threat to her."

"What? Well, of course you're not," he cringed. "If you tried anything, she'd make you strangle yourself with your own hair."

"No, I'm serious," Aylard continued. "Whether we meet again or not, I owe her my life. I'd never hurt her. Lenah, could you tell her I'm grateful for her well wishes? And tell her I'm sorry for barging in on her like that yesterday. Tell her… I didn't see anything… What? Why are you looking at me like that? What is wrong with you?! Damn it, shut up! It's not like she's at all similar to you two monsters in the first place! She's… good! Or at least something resembling it!"

Caught off guard, both Lenah and Emony burst into laughter.

"You're a top-notch idiot, Aylard," Lenah chuckled. "But I'll make sure she gets the message. One more thing. I need you two to get ready. We meet the king at sundown. I'll conjure you some better clothes."

The bastard king of Evaria was a fat man. He was around forty years of age, Emony guessed, but his health certainly wasn't holding up. He was sitting on a large, cushioned armchair carved out of ravenwood, his stomach reaching all the way to the oak table in front of him. Next to him stood a slightly younger man, far slimmer and more muscular, with a smaller beard but much more armor and weapons. Emony wondered how good he was with his sword.

"So, you're working with a lamia," King Raynardt said, breaking the long silence that had stayed in the dining room nearly since they had come in.

"Yes," Emony said. He was supposed to pose as a human.

"And why is that? Why do you need to work with one beast to defeat another? It's never been necessary before. Lamias turn people to stone, remember Westmire? The thing should be executed, not collaborated with."

"That's not very accurate, my king," started Lenah, twitching, "But more importantly—"

"The lamia… is a useful asset," interrupted Aylard, sitting at the table across from Emony. "We would not have gotten half as far as we have without her – … it."

"Oh? And where have you gotten? Absolutely nowhere, as far as I've heard. You've sent men back here, begging for our help, and for one of my statues! And I gave it to you, damn it! You should be able to deal with this on your own from now on. What nonsense. "Men of the lake"? What are those? Men that have drowned, you say? So drown them again!"

If he judged the king to be of average human intelligence, Emony would have to act like an idiot, he realized. He looked over to Lenah, searching for advice. She shook her head.

"I'm afraid, my king, that it is not that simple," continued Aylard. "The men of the lake cannot be defeated so easily. Swords do not kill them – not even by beheading. The best we can do is cut off all their limbs, but even after that, the fiends do not really die, and they can put themselves back together in time. I've fought them myself, it's impossible to win. I'm afraid… We must ask you for your help again."

"Before they come here," said Emony. "I've no doubt they will eventually. We sent the lamia to negotiate with them—"

"Negotiate with them? With the undead? Now I know what's happened. You've gone mad! Lady Lenah, what kind of company do you keep? How did you meet these idiots?!"

The witch shifted uncomfortably in her seat.

"My king… you've heard of the "king of the lake" by now. The situation truly is grave. He is someone I fear as well."

"The king… Even you cannot beat him? Some dead pretender?"

She shook her head. "I can feel the effects of his magic even here, halfway across the kingdom. It's the darkest kind there is, and there is a great deal of it. If he marches south, there will be deaths measured in the thousands. And you know him."

The king looked grimly towards the witch. Emony still didn't know what their relationship looked like – it was said that the king hated magic and everything to do with it, yet the two of them knew each other well. Behind his back, Lenah called him a brat. He sat up straight in his chair.

"What do you mean, I know him?" the king asked.

"It's your half-brother, Aulduyen," he said.

"Curses, that arse? And he's leading an army? I thought I'd been done with him ten years ago… Lenah, I've been receiving reports from my emissaries. They've been arriving in villages and towns to remind them to pay their taxes, only to find them empty. Blood everywhere, the places burnt down… but no bodies. You're saying this is the cause? The men that came before you knew nothing of it, only that the corpses attacked the garrison I sent to Coldbarrow and terrorized the villagers. I thought this was a minor issue!"

"The dead become his soldiers," said Emony. "He controls them like puppets with his magic. If he's already started to attack… Palehome has been destroyed, then?"

"Palehome? Huh. So, you've no idea what's been going on, either. And I thought at least you would be well informed. Yes, Palehome is gone, but that's the least of it. If what you say is true, so is just about every other village and town north of Coldbarrow! That unfortunate little village must be nearly the only one left, and even they cannot pay their dues right now! Well then, it's safe to say that old fool has got plenty of soldiers. So, what does he want? What any undead wants, I suppose. Death and destruction? No, but Yperian sent men to my castle asking about some dumb girl… Why?"

"He wants his wife back."

"What, that lowborn strumpet he married in the village before he died? The mermaid? You've got to be joking! Ha! Well, admittedly, he cared far more for her than he did for the throne, the dull fool. Well, he's in for a surprise! The siren is a statue. I was going to have her brought here to be executed ten years ago, but the convoy met a stray lamia on the way. Maybe it was your "asset". In any case, I had the pretty sea monster on display in my garden. Up till three days ago, when Yperian's knights came over, petitioning me for it!"

"A lamia?" Emony gasped. "Are you sure—"

"My king, Raynardt! The king—" Lamiah begun.

"The king, the king! I am the king! Cease giving the title to that fool! He's a pompous, undead vagabond, that's all he is! Even when he was alive, he never cared for anything but a good fight! If he wants one even now, he can have it!"

"This may be unwise—"

"Was it, without a doubt, a lamia?!" Emony demanded.

"Yes! It was a lamia; some merchant survived the encounter and told me about it! Now not another word! I've already called out to the lords and ladies of the kingdom. Their armies will be amassing here soon. He wants his girl back? I already gave her to him! Is he unhappy that she's a rock? Then he can attack, and he can die again! What is he going to do with her, anyway? Take his throne back, put her on it? Can he bring her back to life, too?! Well?! Don't look amongst yourself like you've got some conspiracy going! Can he?!"

"Not with ravenwood," Emony said, trying to shake the sickening feeling he was getting out of his head. "If she's really been petrified, it's been far too long. But Lenah, Tiphaine inherited the Eyes nine cycles ago, in autumn. You say ten years, but how long ago, exactly, did this rebellion happen?”

He saw the witch’s blue eyes begin trembling. “Emony… You don’t want to know…”

“What are you talking about?” demanded the king.

“No… This can’t be happening… But… but Verena said the king might be able to help Tiphaine, to free her from the curse. She said he had enough black magic to do it.”

“The king could help?! Are you friends? What, are you playing both sides?! Lenah, explain yourself!”

“It’s the Eyes,” Lenah said to Emony, shaking her head. “Nothing of this world can break it. It can only move on.”

Emony got up from his chair without a word of warning.

“Lenah, Emony, was it her?” Aylard gasped. “Was it really her?”

“I’m sorry, King Raynardt,” Emony said. “I have to go. It was a mistake, bringing the statue to the king of the lake – it will only serve to enrage him. I will make sure it does not reach him,” he said.

“What is wrong with you, you damned vagabond? Where do you think you’re going? You want to make decisions on your own? I’m in charge here! Your people asked for that damned statue, you got it! Now you think you can leave your king’s table whenever you want? Sit down!”

Emony eyed the weapon on the king’s guard. He did not stay still.

"Emony! Wait up! Wait up, damn you! Do you know what you're doing? Do you know where she is?" Lenah shouted behind him.

"We sent her to Coldbarrow! I'll start there!"

"Wait! Urgh, you idiot, stop moving!"

A bolt of blue lightning suddenly zapped Emony from behind, making him stumble to the ground on the steps out of the castle. His forehead hit the stone floor, hurting him. Footsteps ran over towards him and stopped in front of his face.

"Stop running like a chicken with your head cut off – don't you know I can teleport you there?! Urgh! Look – I'm sorry! But… Tiphaine… It really was her! I saw it in her memories a few nights ago!"

"Damn it, does the king know?"

Aylard ran down the stairs behind them, closing a door behind himself and barring it shut.

"What's going on?!" he demanded. "Was it Tiphaine who petrified that girl?!"

"It doesn't matter! Does the king know?!"

"He... He might! There are other things that can petrify people, but not for decades! What if he starts going down the list?!"

"Dammit, does Tiphaine know that it was her?!" he yelled out from the ground.

"No, but… Emony – it's too late! Those knights left with the girl three days ago!"

"So what are you saying?! That she's already dead?! Urgh, go away, Aylard! You can't hear this!"

"Shut up! I'm on your side right now! Lenah, fill me in! Is Tiphaine in danger?"

Emony felt Lenah's magic fizzle out and he quickly regained control of his limbs again. In an instant, he got back up from the ground.

"No! Lenah, don't you dare tell him, we can't trust him with this! He cares too much about the other humans!"

"So do I! But be quiet!" Lenah shouted. "I'm looking through his mind, give me a moment!"

Aylard suddenly fell onto the ground beside Emony, groaning in pain. A second later, he was foaming at the mouth as black sparks fizzled out of his chest. His eyes rolled to the back of his head.

"Okay! Done! Sorry, Aylard, I was in a rush – but you can trust him for now, Emony! Let's go, before Tiphaine or the king start guessing!"

"What? No! Not with him!"

"Emma can sing to him later if you still don't trust me! Teleportation!"

An instant later, an unnatural, revolting warmth filled his mouth and lungs. They had appeared right in the village square in Coldbarrow, just like he and Tiphaine had weeks ago, but the place was hotter than a desert. The night air was so thick with black magic it was practically visible.

"This means trouble. Lenah, dammit, couldn't you bring us closer? The encampment is on the hill three miles from here! The lake… Lenah? Lenah?! Are you okay?!"

The witch was hunched over beside him, coughing madly into the ground.

"Go! Just hurry, Emony, I'm fine! Divines, there's so much of this darkness! Go and talk to the king! See if Tiphaine is there! We'll go see the humans. We'll have to walk, I can't use that kind of magic in this. And where is everybody?"

"The village is empty," said Aylard, quickly looking around. "They must have been evacuated. The knight commander mentioned that being a last resort, I remember. Didn't you say Coldbarrow was safe, Emony?!"

"I thought it was! I don't know what happened! And I don't care. I'm going. If you find it first, destroy that statue!"

"Emony, if we do that… Who knows what he'll do?!" gasped Lenah.

"Nothing to Tiphaine," he growled. "Now go! If she's in the lake, I'll find her!"

"I thought you were afraid of—"

Without listening to another word, Emony ran off and jumped into the lake, creating a tail from his legs as quickly as he could and swimming madly off into the depths.

The king's puppets were crowding the dark water in far greater numbers than they had when she had been there last. There were corpses floating around everywhere Emony looked. She ignored them all, focusing on her task as she darted as quickly as she could towards the underwater palace.

Soon, the castle walls became visible underneath her. The water was dark, but strange lights glowed from it as they had before, making it easy to navigate. The black magic that had filled the air was even thicker in the water, making her feel like throwing up blood. In order not to come off the wrong way to the king, who was likely watching, she slowed down when she came close and made her way as casually as possible to the rotting wooden gate before the palace. She tried to slow down her breathing. *I have nothing to hide… I'm on his side… I have nothing to hide… Divines! No bra! If he kills me now because of that… But I have to risk it.*

Standing before the gate, a fresh corpse bared her way, but suddenly, it bowed down low towards her and stepped aside, letting her pass. With that, the king surely knew she was there.

She swam into the courtyard with the statues of mermaids on either side of the marble path. It was completely empty, aside from them, not a living soul was there. She went further inside, towards the palace. Then, all of a sudden, the huge, magnificent doors opened in front of her of their own accord, a torrent of water pushing them ajar from the other side.

"Emony!" exclaimed Tiphaine, right across from them.

She was leisurely standing in the ornate hall with Verena at her side. Emony was impossibly happy to see her again. Tiphaine slithered overexcitedly across the marble floor towards her. Emony dashed forward as well, embracing her tightly.

"What's this for, Emony?" she asked. "I'm happy, but... no, it doesn't matter. I've missed you, too! I know it's only been a few days, but... I was worried. But... you've returned so soon? What are you doing here? Are Lenah and Aylard with you?"

"It's all okay," Emony said, relaxing her embrace, nodding hastily before looking around. Verena was swimming over to them.

"We need to leave," she whispered before the mermaid could make it within earshot. Tiphaine tilted her head at Emony in confusion.

"It's nice to see that you're back, Emony," said Verena, reaching them and giving her a friendly greeting. "I hope you are well. Did you retrieve anything of value from Terrena? We weren't expecting you so soon, you really do travel quickly."

"It's Lenah's doing. She teleported us here. Actually, we need to get back to her right now. It's very important. Tiphaine? Come on."

"What's going on?" Tiphaine asked.

The gilded doors that were slowly closing behind them suddenly pushed themselves wide open again, flooding the hall with unnatural light. There, amidst the swirling water, stood the king.

In his arms lay still a beautiful stone statue of a mermaid.

Verena's arms shot up to her mouth, only slightly covering her gasp of surprise.

"Our queen has returned!" the king bellowed. "My love, my guiding star! She has come back to us!"

Tiphaine was speechless, as was Emony. Her mind raced to find out what she should do. She couldn't face the king in battle, she didn't stand a chance. She couldn't escape, either, there were far too many corpses in the water. She had no good options. Starting to tremble slightly, she remained quiet and lowered her head, bowing to the king and queen.

"She has returned to us!" Aulduyen boomed happily, making the world shake. "Imarah, you've made it home!"

Verena swam over towards them quickly to inspect the statue. She and the king were becoming more ecstatic by the second.

"Emony, you found her," said Tiphaine happily, though with a hint of confusion. "But she's... petrified, am I seeing that right? How did that happen?"

"Tiphaine," she said, as quietly as she could without indicating that she was whispering. "She's been petrified for ten years. Listen to me. The first chance I get, I'm going to kidnap you."

"Oh, come, do not speak so shyly before me now, you two!" shouted the king, gazing at them and smiling madly with delight. "Our queen has returned! I have you to thank for this, I know it. I will reward you both exquisitely. Whatever you desire is yours, you need only ask. Oh, but first! First, we must celebrate, together! We must have a feast! A feast, worthy of my love!"

3

Tiphaine

The feast was… unnerving. The king sat beside his throne at the end of the long table with the petrified queen at his side. He was talking to her constantly, as though completely unfazed by the fact that she was a statue. The many fish that lay on their plates were those that Verena had managed to catch at a moment's notice, cooked over a black fire that the king lit with magic in the water.

Verena had asked if her sister could hear her – and she did say "maybe", but, watching her join the king, she felt like she may have given them false hope. No one could be revived from the stone after more than a week, if it had been ten years…

But who was to blame? Was it her? The only mermaid she ever remembered meeting was Verena, but she was the only thing in the world that was cursed with the Eyes. What else could have caused this? There were other things that could petrify people, but for ten years? That kind of magic was rare. Still, she refused to believe it was her.

But… but Emony was constantly signaling her to be quiet.

Why, Emony? Do you think it was me?

"My queen, how do you like the palace?" the king asked delightedly. "Oh, I know it's gotten a little grimy since you left – I've only just been back for a month or so myself, so I hope you'll forgive me. But now that you're back, fixing it will become our top priority!"

"Aulduyen, you know she likes the algae," Verena said. "That was always your pet peeve."

"Is that so? In that case, it will remain as is. What do you think, Imarah? Ha, I am a fool! I know you cannot really move just yet, but I cannot stop imagining that you are! All these years, I've been picturing your face in the abyss, looking for a way to come back and retrieve you… and now you're finally here! We've just got to fix up this one little snag. Don't worry, it will be quick. I've amassed quite a large amount of magical power; I only need to find out how to use it properly. And I've got an expert that can show me! Lamia? What was it… ah, yes, Tiphaine? Yours is a name worth remembering. Oh, do not fear, finish chewing first. I'd just like to ask you – how quickly do you think we could get to work on the depetrification process? I imagine you must know something, since you possess a curse that could cause something like this yourself. I can see a string of magic connecting you to… Oh, never mind. How quickly do you think our queen might recover?"

She found herself quickly growing nervous, not knowing what to say. "R-ravenwood bark is what I've always used," she said. "It's worked every time on Emony, and on everyone else… It works instantly, but... not after they've been gone for very long."

"I see… Perhaps the problem was quantity? I'll cut down the whole forest if I have to."

"That… could work? I'm sorry I can't be of much help. I'll try to figure something out."

"We'll do our best to find more solutions," Emony said, swimming over to her quickly with a swing of her golden tail and grasping her hand. "We have a friend, a witch, I'm sure she will be able to tell us something. We just need to go to the surface and ask her."

"Really? That's excellent! Thank you, Emony. Please do so as soon as possible – I'd rather not discomfort Imarah for any length of time – but you may finish eating, of course. You've earned a reward. Wouldn't you agree, Imarah? Speaking of earning things – I believe you've expressed discomfort at your new siren nature. Of course, I do not understand in the least – mermaids are the most graceful of creatures – but if you wish to become a werewolf again, I can give you that gift whenever you wish. I can see the magic tying your soul to your altered form, it should be easy to remove. Of course, we will have to do that on land, lest you lose your ability to breath underwater."

"Thank you, my king, for the offer. I'm… very grateful."

"You've earned a reward! Actually, I feel like it will do nothing at all to repay the debt I owe you. If there is anything else at all that you may desire, you will have it. I'm sure my queen would want me to make this promise as well."

"Thank you."

With a final nod, the king hastily turned around again and ran back towards the statue of his queen, taking her hand with his own and speaking to her again.

Verena swam over to him and Tiphaine, a smile clear on her own lips, too.

"I'm so happy you've managed to return my sister to us. I knew I could count on you, Tiphaine. And you, too, Emony. You've done an excellent job."

"We're just glad to help," she responded.

"You've helped far more than you know. I was getting impossibly worried about Aulduyen. You saw what he was like only yesterday, Tiphaine. He was talking about invading the south, to scour the whole world with the puppets. But now... Look at him. He's so happy... I only feel regret that so many people died already. The horde of corpses was completely unnecessary, all we needed was you two. Tiphaine, are you looking forward to being able to take off the veil? I'll be sure to convince Aulduyen to help you with that tomorrow."

"Do you... do you think I might really be able to? I've been so afraid to get my hopes up. Emony? You might be able to see me without turning to stone!"

She was shaking her hand, so excited. Emony couldn't bring herself to tell her. She smiled, giving her a moment of happiness.

If only it were possible, she thought.

"I'm sure we'll be able to help you," Verena continued. "Aulduyen says the curse is more deeply rooted in you than in Emony, Tiphaine, after all, it is the Eyes, but I'm sure he'll be able to do it. You helped return his queen to him. He'll do anything for you. I – Oh, I'm sorry. Please excuse me, Emony, I can see you'd like to say something to Tiphaine as well. In private, I suppose? Well, you'll know where to find me. Have a great time."

The mermaid swam away, apparently after reading the anxiousness Emony was trying to hide from her face. Tiphaine was still so excited, sitting beside her.

"Can you imagine, Emony? We might finally be free of this. I'll be able to see the world without these crystals covering my eyes, and you'll be able to see me for real… So why are you so worried? Your heart is beating so crazy I think it might stop. What's wrong?"

"I can't say," Emony said.

"We're back to that again? Well, you… um… you said you were going to kidnap me?"

Emony nodded, nervously waving back at the king. He was pointing at her, still speaking happily to his queen.

"We need to leave, Tiphaine," she said, not moving her gaze from him. "We need to get far away from here, before things turn ugly."

"Why would things turn ugly, Emony? We just gave the king what he wanted, look how happy he is. Won't things get better now? Don't you think the king could free Imarah?"

"No. We need to get to Lenah."

"But… our curses, too… Don't you want to be free of them? I've been waiting for ten years. And you desperately want to be a werewolf again, I know it."

"Trust me, there are things far more important. Just ask the king over there. No, don't. Stay away from him. I'll tell him we're leaving. We're off to go get Lenah, and she'll help him find a way to free the queen. Then we can come back and get you cured of the Eyes, okay?"

"Why are you lying to me, Emony?" she asked, a small trembling in her voice. "Was it really me?"

She spared her a glance, her expression full of worry, and leaned in closer to her. "Please just trust me, Tiphaine."

Her cute little face harbored so much fear... Emony was never afraid. She was right. It was her.

"I trust you. But we'll come back, right?" Tiphaine asked, her hope sinking in her throat.

"We'll come back," Emony said again, her heart skipping a beat with every word.

Chapter 11

1

Emony

"Where were you two?" shouted Lenah as soon as they broke the water's surface next to the shore. "I was worried I wouldn't see you again!"

"We got held up. The queen is back," Emony said, pulling herself out of the water with her thin arms.

Lenah swirled her hand through the air and all the water lifted itself off of Emony, returning legs and male features. At the same time, another set of clothes materialized around him. Casting the magic hurt her, he saw. There was too much darkness in the air.

"I know," she rasped. "Aylard's on his way to meet up with the humans. Their camp is empty. They've evacuated the villagers, they're all on their way to Terrena."

Tiphaine nodded beside him. "That happened a few days ago. I told them not to go, but they did anyway. The magic you used to control the knight commander must have weakened, Emony."

"Damn it, I thought it was supposed to be permanent. That king is still affected, ten years later!"

"That's only because he wants to be," Tiphaine replied. "He wants to be under her spell. So, what now? You haven't told me where we're going."

Lenah closed her eyes for a moment before pointing towards the nearby hills. "That way. I can't teleport us out of here, the black magic is too thick. We have to follow the humans on foot.”

“It’s that bad? Lenah, if the knight commander broke free, he will know what we did to him. There’s no way to know what he’ll do if he finds us. At this point, even the humans are a threat to us!”

“Then we just have to hide from them too.”

“What about Aylard? You said he’s with them,” said Tiphaine.

“He’ll want to appease the king, to keep him from killing the humans.”

“Why would he kill the humans?” she demanded. “They’ve returned Imarah to him!”

“Just trust us,” Lenah said, grabbing her hand with a tight smile. “Please, just for a little while.”

Just as they were about to get going, a head bobbed out of the lake. A voice called out to them from the water – it was Verena.

“Hey, Tiphaine! You two left in such a hurry! Emony, over here! And is that you, Lenah?”

“Sorry, we have to go!” he called back quickly, keeping Tiphaine from turning around. “The villagers left and we’ve got to catch up to them! We’ll be back soon!”

“Are you sure? What’s the rush? Don’t you want Aulduyen to cure you two first? Come on, you don’t have to solve everything today! Relax! We can break your curses tomorrow!”

“It will have to wait!” he shouted, before pulling Tiphaine’s hand and dragging her towards the forest.

“Okay…” Verena’s voice faded behind them.

They walked throughout the night, right up to the point of exhaustion, when they finally reached a place where the strength of the black magic was faint enough for Lenah to teleport them to her shack in Hewlett's range. There, they slept while the sun made its way across the sky, and while they were doing so, Lenah invaded Emony's mind, making them share a dream.

In that infinite expanse of whiteness, while she watched his memory of the king and queen's feast, Emony just sat on the nothingness, wondering if one of the times he'd most dreaded had finally come.

"You know, we can't outrun him forever," Lenah said, finishing with the memory. "If he manages to choke even more of the ley lines with his black magic, teleportation might become impossible throughout the whole continent."

He shook his head. "He hasn't done so yet."

"No, but it's only a matter of time. I can tell, from this… he can see the strings of magic. Only the strongest beings in the world can do that, he's practically a divine. And he saw the one connecting Tiphaine to Imarah. He didn't understand yet what it was, but he will. And he'll come for her."

Sitting on the floor, Emony just kept gazing into the nothingness. "If you're going to tell me to give up, save your breath."

"You know that I want to help you. I've been your friend for these couple of years, haven't I? Look… I'm sorry, Emony. I really am. I made my peace with Tiphaine having petrified half the countryside. I was going to lock her up like every other bearer of the Eyes, to minimize the damage, but when I saw what you sacrificed, so she could live a normal life… I wanted to give it to you two. I really did. But now… The king will kill everyone in his way. They won't be petrified. They won't come back after a couple of decades. They'll be dead."

"I know."

"And he will find her. All he needs to do is follow the magic that's binding Imarah."

"I know."

"So... considering all that... I'm sorry, Emony. I don't know how much longer I can help you. I love you both, but I've sworn to protect people. Everyone... not just those I care about most."

He nodded quietly, letting a couple of tears leave his eyes.

"Please don't tell her. Just let me give her a few more happy moments, before the end. She's had so few."

Two soft arms embraced his shoulders as Lenah sat down next to him.

"She's had you, Emony. She couldn't have asked for anything more."

"Ha... I wanted to kill her when I first met her, did you just forget? After what she did to my parents, I'd been following the trail of statues all across Evaria in search of her."

"I know. But you didn't do it. You couldn't. So that she could live, so that you wouldn't hate her, you instead killed—"

"It doesn't matter. Or are you saying I made a mistake? Should I have killed her back then instead, while she lay with her mom and dad? She would have asked me to, if I'd told her it would bring them back."

"No, you didn't make a mistake, Emony," Lenah whispered.

"But you want me to kill her now, anyway, only a few years later? Because some dead person wants to bring his wife back to life?! Why, why should he get what he wants?"

"Forget the king, you should consider Tiphaine's wishes in this. You know her, Emony. She wouldn't want people to die for her. I think… Given the choice… Maybe she would want it to be you. Not some cruel king… But her friend."

He buried his head into his knees. "But that's not what *I* want! Damn everyone else, damn what she wants, *I* want her to live! Can't you see, Lenah? It's just her! She's the only one that matters!"

He could feel his friend's embrace tightening around his waist, droplets falling onto his shoulder from where Lenah laid her head. "Then tell her that. Give her those happy moments. You're running out of time."

"Yeah… Yeah, I will. Please… Let me out of this dream, Lenah. I've… got something to do. After this is done, you'll have to mess with my mind again. Do a better job next time, will you? I don't want to remember this."

"Yeah… If you ask me for that again tomorrow, I'll do it right. Look, Emony, I've only got one terrible idea left, but I'll tell you about it later. Go, now. I'm going to talk with Tiphaine for a minute, but I'll give her to you right after. Get something nice ready for her."

Emony awoke from her sleep to find herself a mermaid, the tears from her dream wet on her real face, while Tiphaine's tail was wrapped tightly around her. Careful not to make any noise, she wiped her face dry and regained legs before getting up, taking Tiphaine's hand and gently removing her silver ring.

She stirred, slowly, sleep still heavy on her mind. He crept around her quietly and stepped over Lenah's sleeping form. He noticed a few blue sparks crackle out of her hand while she slept, quickly being absorbed by Tiphaine. Likely the magic of them sharing a dream.

"Forgive me, Lenah," he whispered, before placing the silver ring into her half-open mouth.

In an instant, the witch was awake, struggling madly against him, grabbing at his hands, trying to remove him from her, but he held her mouth shut. He pushed her head up and down as fast as he could, forcing her to swallow the silver. The way she looked at him, her eyes wild with fear, it nearly broke him, but grim determination forced him forward.

Tiphaine awoke suddenly, their shared dream being broken, and stared at him for a mere instant before pouncing on him and pinning him to the floor.

"What are you doing, Emony?!" she cried. "What did you do to her? Stop it! Whatever you did, stop it, please! She's in pain!"

"I can't! She'll survive, Tiphaine! It's just going to hurt for a while!"

The witch was still struggling madly on the floor beside him, gasping for air with raspy breaths, the silver having made its way down her throat. Struggling for breath, she curled up into a ball, clutching her stomach in pain.

"Emony, was that silver? Why?! Why did you do that?" demanded Tiphaine, on top of him.

"I didn't want to do it," he shouted, pushing her away, feeling new tears well up in his eyes. He leaned into the vibration streaming down his face again, regaining his siren form.

"But you'll forget that I did," Emony said. She couldn't describe how much he hated herself for singing to her.

"Emony, no—"

"You're going to forget what you just saw. You'll remember that she went ahead of us, to Terrena, to warn King Raynardt that the men of the lake are coming. You'll remember that we'll see her again soon. You'll remember that… that you should spend what time you have left doing whatever it is you want in this world."

"Emony—" Tiphaine struggled to speak.

"Please! Just… Live a little longer, Tiphaine. Enjoy the time we have left."

She let the magic leave her tongue, as she lay pinned underneath her. Tiphaine breathed heavily for a few moments, unmoving, before shaking her head and then staring at her, apparently confused.

"Emony?" she asked.

"Yes?"

"How did we end up in this position?"

"Ha… I don't know. You must have had an interesting dream, Tiphaine," Emony said, wiping the tears from her face and regaining her original form again.

"Oh. Let's… um… Let's get moving, then. The sun hasn't set yet, and I want to get on the road for some reason… Unless you're half-naked because you want something different."

Emony smiled thinly, trying to make sure no more tears left his eyes. "Whatever you want," he said. "Let's do whatever we would do if the world were ending tomorrow."

2

"Well, I remember I said that, but I hope you know what you're doing, Tiphaine. I really don't think they'll be too happy to see us again," he said, eyeing the long convoy of humans traveling along the road to Terrena.

The soldiers were in the front and the back, forming a shield to protect the villagers as they shepherded their meager belongings on their carts and horse-drawn carriages. Old people and children rode with the luggage while the adults walked on the dusty dirt and stone, hunched over in exhaustion. They must have been walking for a long time.

"I'm sure at least one of them will be," Tiphaine said, slithering over beside him atop a little hill. "Lenah said Aylard went to join them again."

"Yes. But his commander probably wants us dead."

"He's called Yperian. You should try to remember at least a few people's names."

"Why bother? None of them have yours."

Tiphaine cringed at him nervously for a moment before turning back to look at the humans. He wondered what was going on inside her head, with the magic he had forced into it and the lies he had told her before that. But he said nothing as they slowly made their way down the hill towards the road and the humans.

"Allies returning! Hold your fire!" shouted a human wielding a bow upon seeing and recognizing them, before the command was repeated a couple more times along the line of the convoy. The man glanced nervously at Tiphaine's golden mask before pointing out the commander's location in the center of the convoy.

As they made their way alongside it to reach him, Aylard ran out of the crowd to meet them. He was wearing steel-plate armor, a sword at his waist and helmet in hand. He stopped in front of them with a troubled expression.

"Tiphaine, Emony, it's good to see you again. You managed to escape the king of the lake, then? And you managed to get here faster than we did. Does that mean Lenah is okay, too?"

"Yes. But we didn't make it in time to destroy the statue."

"No, we missed it. The knights had already brought it to the lake by the time we saw it from atop the hill. The shore was teeming with those monsters. I saw the king, though. He stepped out of the lake, lifted the stone mermaid like it was a feather. The undead saluted them like…"

"Like they were royalty? They are."

"Yes, I guess. But anyway, he looked happy. Stupidly happy, even though she was stone. I thought maybe the war could end now. He's got what he wanted."

Emony shook his head. "Not quite. It's not over yet, it's good that everyone left Coldbarrow. But I don't know if you should all go to Terrena. The king, the living king, he said he's amassing an army there, right? It's where me and Tiphaine are going, but the king of the lake will definitely attack."

Aylard's eyes widened in shock. "Are you sure? It had better be a big army, then. The number of corpses I saw on the beach…"

They had no hope of winning, Emony knew. He just hoped they would buy them some time. There was one other witch that could help him.

"Aylard, can I ask you for something?" Tiphaine asked.

"Hm? Sure, what is it?"

"Actually, it's Emma that's asking." she added with a wink at Emony. "She needs you to do something for her."

"Anything. Does she need help?"

"Yes, but it's... something private. Emony mustn't hear. Come here, let me whisper it to you."

Emony shot her a glare, but quickly decided to let her make up nonsense about him. The snakes on her head continued hissing in his direction, taunting him.

"Can you do that?" she finished. "I'm sure she'd really appreciate it."

"Of course," Aylard said. "I guess I have to go get that... thing... that I'll need."

With a brief farewell, he ran off back towards the crowd of humans, quickly getting lost in it.

"What was that about?" Emony asked.

"I told him Emma needs him to deliver her a bra," Tiphaine replied. He could tell she was smirking under her mask. "She really likes wearing those, and they help keep her safe from the king's wrath... But really, you know, I think she wants to confess to him. Would you agree?"

Emony shook his head. "Divines, Tiphaine, you're so annoying. You of all people should know who it is she has a thing for."

"Oh? Should I?" she asked, slithering just ahead of him and swinging her head from side to side in front of his face.

"Shut up."

"No, really. Should I? Who is it? I feel dumb."

"It's me, of course. Emma's been head over heels for me for weeks," he said. "So, what next? It's going to get dark soon."

"I want to meet Yperian again, but afterward, can we camp outside, just the two of us? It's been a while."

"Sure."

A little while later, the knight commander walked out of the crowd of people to meet them with four other soldiers, the convoy not stopping for a moment to let him have a chat with them. The man had a hard expression on his face, and the other humans flanked him with their weapons ready, clearly seeing them as enemies.

"We mean you no harm," Tiphaine called out while there was still some distance between them. "We only want to talk this time."

"You said something similar in the past," Yperian responded. "And your companion controlled my mind. I'd never have guessed what he was. But why should we talk to you now? Why should we believe anything you might have to say?"

"We don't mean to ask anything of you, we only want to help. To tell you the truth, and warn you."

"Help us? Tell us the truth? Nonsense. You've had a chance to cooperate with us."

Emony shared a short look with Tiphaine, then stepped forward, putting himself between them and her. The humans' stances changed. They all pointed their blades at him in unison.

"The men of the lake are going to come this way soon," he said. "You've done well to come this far, but now, what you should do is get as far away from Terrena as you can."

"This is the capital, siren. I've received word from the king, the true king, that all the armies in the Evaria are on their way. And I know the threat they face. I know that even with that, our victory is far from assured, but if not Terrena, then where should we go? Would you have us run, rather than fight? The end of the world isn't far enough."

"True. But you don't have to run forever. Only for a day or two. The king of the lake has enough soldiers already. He might pick up more on the way to Terrena, but if you avoid his path, you should be fine."

"Ha! Am I supposed to believe that? I'd sooner think you want to lure us into a bad position, so he can pick us off more easily."

"I am not on the side of the undead! There's nobody I want dead more than that king! Listen, I plan to try to kill him, but chances are, I'm going to die, and so is everyone else that stays here! If I were a good person, I wouldn't be telling you this, I would grow a tail right now and force you to leave!"

"But you are far from a good person," the human growled.

"Exactly. Which is why I'll tell you of a far more foolish option. Get only the civilians to leave. Tell the soldiers to ready as much silver as they can, and get ready for war."

3

Aulduyen

"Why does my queen not awaken?" Aulduyen asked himself, perplexed, staring into the unmoving stone eyes of the siren he'd loved through life and death.

"I can see the magic in the ravenwood bark, but it does not absorb the curse as it should. And if I attempt to use my magic to destroy it, her life starts slipping away. The evil is not merely wrapped around her, it has ensnared even her heart.

The lady Verena entered the hall, seeing him and swimming closer. He had the water close the doors behind her.

"Any luck?" she asked hopefully.

"Nothing. The curse refuses to be untangled."

"You've cut down half the forest surrounding the village! Surely it must have weakened at least a little."

"It has not," he exclaimed. "As the lamia feared, the ravenwood does not work."

He was even more troubled than she had appeared to be during their feast. She must have known what a difficult task it would be, to remove the curse while preserving Imarah's life. Even his mass of black magic seemed poorly suited to helping her. He could see the curse's strings laced across her stone body, but as soon as he touched one, it split itself in two and bound her again. He could sense the strings that lay inside her too, they were far from only on the surface. The curse that kept her petrified had made a home in his queen. It didn't seem like even time would weaken it.

Still… a single loose string of magic separated itself from her body, coming straight out of her heart, and leading somewhere out of the lake.

He had seen it on the night they had celebrated her return, too. It had led to the lamia, Tiphaine. He hadn't thought anything of it, he was too rejoiced to see his queen again. Perhaps the curse linked itself to her because she possessed a similar one? But she had had no idea how to reverse the spell. She would have told him if she knew.

"What do you know of curses, Verena?" he asked, sighing. "How can lesser ones be undone?"

The mermaid swam closer to him and laid a hand on her sister's cheek. "It depends on the curse. There are two ways. Most can be undone by a witch simply waving her hand and casting stronger magic to rip it apart.

"That does not seem to be an option in this case. The curse is strong, and it has made a home in her heart. But do not worry, Imarah. It is no issue. This will not deter us. What is the other option, Verena?"

"If the first is to break the curse, the other is to undo it. Curses are like knots linking their sources and their hosts. If you can untie it at the source, you can pull it out of the host."

"To 'untie it at the source'. By that, you mean killing the one who cast it, correct? Before I died, all the peasants I'd met in Evaria used to speak of that as a solution."

"That is the usual way," Verena said. "And by far the easiest."

But it would mean Aulduyen would have to find the source, somewhere upon the world's surface. More people would die, and Imarah would have to bear witness to it, as he couldn't bear to let her leave his side. But she wouldn't like that.

"What do you think, Imarah?" he asked her. "Come now, give me a sign. Any kind at all, any kind you can. I know you're there; I can feel the life inside you, past all this stone and the strings of magic. I know you can hear me."

The queen remained silent; her beautiful stone body unmoving, but for the tide.

"If you do not, my queen, then I will have to choose," he sighed sadly.

He stood up straight, looking towards Verena. "How may I sever the knot? Assume the curse is not a lesser one."

"So, the safest option is to destroy the source of the curse," Aulduyen said.

Verena nodded. "I think so, yes. It's certainly the least complicated, it leaves little room for error. There are less destructive methods.

Theoretically, the knot can be undone without harming the source, but that is far more dangerous. Is… is the source a person, do you think?"

A realization crept into Aulduyen's mind while he thought, staring vacantly into the banquet hall. While he looked towards where the two had sat.

"It may be," he said.

"One of the humans' sorcerers?"

Slowly, he shook his head.

Glancing back towards his petrified queen, understanding slowly settled into his mind. An old memory from his past life revealed itself to him. Aulduyen turned to Verena. There was no doubt that she had considered it, she was well-versed in magical theory. But her mind seemed to refuse to believe it. The two had left so quickly after finishing their meals, they hadn't even stayed long enough for him to repay them for their help… There was no doubt left in his mind.

"Lady Verena… Shortly before I met you, I was travelling across Evaria, surveying my kingdom—"

"I know. I've already heard this story a thousand times," she said, a brief smile on her lips. "You stopped six times before reaching Coldbarrow. And here, on your seventh stop, you met Imarah."

"But on the very first, in the desert down south of Terrena, I met a tribe of lamias. I don't remember if I told you that part, I never found it important. I shook their hands. I looked in their eyes. And, afraid as I was, I did not turn into stone."

So suddenly, the smile was gone from Verena's face.

"Well, of course you didn't. But what are you saying?" she asked.

"Some of their kind truly are forced to bear a terrible curse, they told me, but it is exceedingly rare, despite the stories we humans told ourselves. It is a curse inherited by a single unfortunate lamia in the entirety of the world, passed on to it by the death of the last one who had it."

"You're describing the Eyes, but what are you saying?" Verena asked again, more forcefully than the last time. "That it was Tiphaine? Is that it? You're… guessing, merely guessing, that it was her of all people that cursed Imarah? There are hundreds of other things that can turn people to stone! There are djinns and spirits, not to mention simple witches! You could do it, if you tried! It wasn't Tiphaine – she wouldn't!"

"Turning someone to stone is one thing, but forcing them to remain one for years is another, Verena, you know this. Please, look at Imarah. She hasn't aged a day. This wasn't recent."

"You're wrong!" Verena said, shaking her head.

"It pains me to say this, but during our feast, I could see the string of magic binding her and the snake together. I'm not angry, Verena. I'm not saying she cursed my queen on purpose. Only that she did."

"No. You're wrong. Tiphaine wouldn't do that. And she couldn't, even if she wanted to, she was still a child back then. She said she inherited the Eyes when she was… when she was…"

Aulduyen walked over to Verena, who was desperately struggling in her mind to deny the obvious truth.

"It happened ten years ago, didn't it?" he asked quietly, laying a hand on her shoulder.

She was trembling as though freezing cold, so afraid of accepting it. But he could see, through her fear, that she knew.

"But that doesn't mean... You still don't know for sure!"

"I'm sorry, Verena. I don't know her as you do, but I know she is your friend. I owe her much myself for returning my queen to me," he said.

"Aul... Aulduyen. Don't do it. Please don't. We... We can wait. Even if its true... The curse will break after she dies, no matter how that happens. You're undead, and I've... I've still got at least another century. We'll see her again, just a little later! Aulduyen, we can wait!"

"I cannot condemn Imarah to suffer for a century in stone. I'm sorry, Verena. It's truly a shame.

"Aulduyen, don't," Verena begged in desperation, tugging on his hand.

He brushed a cold hand against her shoulder, looking towards the floor for a moment.

"I will not make you a part of this, Verena. Remember these words, if you ever come to suffer from guilt. There was nothing that you could have done. Puppets, be gentle with her."

The corpses he'd quietly commanded as he spoke suddenly leaped onto the siren from all sides, grabbing her arms, stomach and tail and trapping her between their limbs. She stared at him in dismay and struggled fiercely to break free, as he knew she would. The water began swirling around her in a whirlpool as she unleashed a pulse of magic, trying to throw the corpses off herself.

"Aulduyen, stop!" she screamed with magic, trying desperately to bewitch him. The blackness surrounding him kept the song from touching his mind.

"Please, don't do this!" she shrieked.

With a flick of his wrist, he commanded the darkness into her mind, sending her to blissful sleep.

Once she'd awaken, it would all be over, and her sister, the queen, would console her. But until then…

"Make the dungeon beautiful, then close her in it," he ordered his puppets. Though he couldn't see how she might leave the lake, he would take no chances. It was only natural and honorable that she would attempt to save her friend. He wouldn't hold it against her.

He walked through the water to the throne again, gently picking up his queen.

"I'm sorry… But we will reunite, my queen. After just a little more ugliness, we will meet again."

Chapter 12

1

Emony

"Tiphaine? Are you cold?"

The lamia's tail was curled up twice around the small, gently crackling campfire they had made atop the grassy hill about an hour prior, but he could still see that she looked uncomfortable. The human part of her body was trembling slightly, and he had goosebumps all over her arms. Her long scaly tail, which he was leaning on, shifted on the ground.

She shook her head. Her mask was fastened to it slightly poorly. "No, I'm not cold, Emony. The fire is nice. And later, I'm sure you'll be warm, too," she said.

He glanced away from the glowing embers towards her and gave her a little smile. "Are you planning on strangling me while we sleep again tonight?"

"No, but it's going to happen anyway. It always does."

For a moment, he wondered if she might only value him for his body heat, but he dismissed the thought in an instant.

"You can take your mask off," he said. "I won't look."

At that, she stirred slightly, throwing another couple of sticks into the small flames herself. "It's been a while… Are you sure? Do you have any ravenwood, just in case?"

He nodded. A minute later, he could hear her removing the straps, her hair-vipers hissing.

"Ah, it's been forever since I've taken it off. The air feels so nice…"

"I'm glad," he replied. He continued gazing into the flames.

"Emony?" she asked.

"Hm?"

"My eyes are closed. Look at me."

He turned and gazed towards her, seeing her face again for the first time in far too long. He couldn't help but smile weakly and notice a vibration trickle down the skin below one of his eyes. He wiped away the tear before he'd be forced to transform.

"How do I look?" she asked after a while, her eyes still held tightly shut.

"Dirty and ugly."

"I'm serious!" she laughed.

"You also smell. When's the last time you bathed?"

She tried to blindly hit him a couple of times, but she was too far away and she didn't get close to reaching him. The vipers on her head hissed, drowsily complaining.

"You're beautiful," he said.

"Really? Am I pretty enough to die for?"

"Yes."

"I'm glad… If you really think so. I've been a little worried, since... Never mind. Hm… You know, Lenah's going to see this memory in your head later."

He gave Tiphaine a tight smile that she couldn't see. "She might, yeah."

"And she'll tease you again if you waste this opportunity."

"What opportunity?" he asked, noticing the slight tremble on her face.

Tiphaine moved herself closer towards him. "This one. The one to kiss me, before I die."

His eyes widened. She knew. She knew... but how much? Everything? In a panic, Emony tried thinking about what to do. He didn't know anything. What could he—

"Emony?" she asked. "Please do it." Her voice had suddenly changed. She was pleading with him.

"I... I don't know—"

"I don't want to die without knowing what it's like. I've been waiting for so long."

"Tiphaine... You're not yourself right now. I did something to your head. I can't. I'll do it in the morning, okay?"

"You're lying again. I always know when you are, Emony, and I already know what you did. I don't care. Please, just do me this one kindness. I know I'm annoying, but I'll never ask for anything else."

There were tears streaming out of her closed eyes, streaming down her cheeks.

"You'll be rid of me soon enough," she said. "So maybe just this once?"

"Tiphaine..."

He couldn't stop himself any longer.

What felt like centuries later, they finally parted lips. Tiphaine fell silent. She'd stopped shaking a while ago, opting instead to remove her tail from around the fire and wrap it around him instead.

"It's your turn to close your eyes," she said quietly, a while later. "It's been so long since I've seen you clearly."

"The crystals aren't clear enough?"

"Be quiet. No. Just… keep your eyes closed and stay with me tonight. You're so warm, and… I do feel cold."

In the distance, thunder and lightning boomed across the cloudy sky.

2

Lenah

She awoke from her suffering in a pool of vomit, seeing Aylard's worried face staring at her.

Her stomach churned and swayed, making her feel like she was going to throw up again, while her bowels rebelled against her and her head felt like it had tiny ants crawling inside of it.

Her eyes flitted open and closed in the sunlight shining through the shack, her nose trying to keep away the horrid smell. In her mind, she began chanting magic.

"You're awake!" exclaimed Aylard. "I got the ring out, you'll be alright! I'm sorry, I guess it was my turn to drug you. But Lenah, by the divines, how is this supposed to be a love potion?"

Because if someone sees you after you drink it and stays, you'll know for sure that it's true love.

Sparks of magic sizzled along her insides as she chanted, clearing her head before making their way down her body all the way to her toes. She'd gotten far better at healing magic than she'd earlier let on.

She sat up quickly before shaking in disgust one more time and running out of the shack. There, in the field, she began coughing up muck into the ground.

Aylard came running after her. She heard the startled neighing of a horse.

"Are you okay? Dammit, not so fast, witch, you're as pale as a ghost! Here, I brought some bread. Oh, divines… Was that from the silver or the love potion?"

"The love potion," she gasped, after hurling.

She took the bread from his hand before gulping it down in one go. She was so light, she felt like she was empty. Her stomach was. Of course it was the love potion, what else? That amazing invention of hers could even help a girl lose weight. Silver only hurt and killed the magic.

"Stand back," she mumbled, taking more bread from Aylard's hands and stuffing it in her mouth. Aylard did so, and she sent another surge of magic along her body.

Suddenly, with a flash of blue, the disgustingness clinging to her flew off in all directions, showering the surrounding grass and coloring it brown. She pinched her nose, still unable to endure the smell, and made her robes fly off too just in case before conjuring new ones.

She skipped gingerly past the mess on her tippy toes and made her way to Aylard, who was looking stunned in front of the hut and his horse. Still pinching her nose, she motioned to him.

"Come here. Smell me," she ordered him.

"What? No!"

"Come on! Please! I don't want to do it first! This was your doing, wasn't it?"

"Yes, but I had no choice! I had to get the silver out of you!"

"Well, I'm very grateful," she said, grabbing the air with her free hand and altering gravity for him so that he flew towards her, before turning it back. "Now smell me."

"Are you aware of how evil you are?" he muttered, making another disgusted face before he took a whiff. The next moment, his expression turned to surprise.

"You… You smell good," he said.

"Oh, thank the divines," she sighed, unpinching her nose. "And you, Aylard. Hurray for magic. Oh… I am going to kill that mutt!"

"He did this to you? Emony?"

"He did this to me while I slept, that damned dog! I was in the middle of something! Urgh! Thank the divines I protected Tiphaine in time! I just know that he must have tried singing to her!"

"He tried to mess with her mind somehow, she told me. I thought only you could do that. But she's the one that sent me to you and told me what to do."

"Really? Good girl… I'll definitely have to return the favor."

That was when she noticed how dark the magic in the air was. A creeping blackness was steadily getting stronger all around, invisible to most living beings, but felt, regardless, by all of them.

Not bothering to finish her thought, she looked, stunned, at the dark horizon. "Ready the horse, Aylard. He's coming."

"Emony? No, is it them? The men of the lake? I knew something was wrong, I've been feeling it in my bones for hours! What the… Is this… snow? So close to Terrena?!"

"The men of the lake cannot go on dry land. Snow is water – they're coming. Do you know where the kingdom's army is gathered? Good. Then let's move!"

"What are we going to do?!" Aylard screamed merely minutes later, running his horse so fast it'd break its bones if not for her stream of magic.

Chasing them from almost every direction, thousands of gurgling corpses threw themselves towards them across the snow, their limbs clawing the ground and falling off while they stormed the white fields.

"Just keep going! Look ahead! I'll slow them down!"

Lenah breathed in magic from the air, disgusted by the taste of darkness, and hurled a blue ball of fire behind them, in the path of the corpses.

"Hahaha, take that, monsters!"

"Lenah?! What's going on, what was that light?!"

"Dark-ish magic! But if you want me executed for my crimes, you'll have to get me to Terrena! They're still coming!"

"Then do it again!"

She focused her mind and breathed in more magic, letting it fill up her lungs and unleashing it at the corpses again. The corpses running in front were blown apart by the fire, while the ones following made their way around the searing heat, following the snow, still charging madly towards them. The snowstorm was getting stronger and stronger up ahead. The king of the lake must have already made it into the city.

"I can see the walls! Lenah, Terrena is right there, but they've already reached it! What the – Another earthquake?! What is going on?!"

The ground shook under the horse's feet, nearly throwing Lenah off it, but she grabbed onto Aylard for a moment and stabilized herself.

"Where is the army?! We need to get to Tiphaine!" she shouted.

"They're – they're right ahead! What the – duck, they're shooting at us! Lenah! They can't see us through this blizzard! They're already fighting!

What is that noise?! Divines, the city wall has been destroyed up ahead! It must be the king! He's here!"

"What?! We can't be too late! Go faster!"

"What do you mean?! Horses can't go any faster! Where do I go?!"

"Left! Go left! Get us away from the fight!"

"That's impossible!" he shouted.

"Damn it all!" she cried suddenly.

"What is it?! Did the archers hit you?!"

"No! Just keep riding! I can feel Tiphaine! We're running out of time! We're not close enough! Aylard, do you trust me? I need you, right now, if we're going to give those two that small chance!"

"Lenah, something's happening! I can feel something is wrong! Something is really wrong!"

"Do you trust me, Aylard?! Do you agree to this?! Tell me now! This will only work if you do!"

"Yes! I do! Why?! Divines, it's getting stronger! Lenah! Is that… wait, is that you?! I feel like… I'm dying! What are you doing, Lenah?! What is that?!"

The earth trembled once more. More of the walls of Terrena roared and collapsed up ahead. Her eyes shifted from blue to black as the sparks of dark magic hissed through the air all around them.

"Black magic," she hissed.

3

Emony

"You said we were going to fight!" Tiphaine screamed, kicking and screaming as he dragged her forward. "You promised me and the knight commander!"

"Well, I lied, damn it!" Emony shouted back. "That was just a backup plan! The first one was always running!"

His whole body was vibrating, demanding change, the snow finding its way onto his face and hands and melting into water. He couldn't afford to stop moving for a second, he'd lose his concentration instantly. He was resisting it with all his might.

"Tiphaine, the whole kingdom is fighting him! If they can't beat him, then we won't make a difference! Come on, let's go! We have to get south! To the desert!"

"We had a plan! We can still go through with it!"

"It's not worth the risk!"

"Yes, it is! Urgh! This is my life it's all about, Emony, it's my choice! You'll have to sing if you want to take it from me! Go on, do it again! See if it'll work this time!"

"So it really didn't, back then?! I thought you were kidding!"

"Lenah protected me! She told me everything! And Emony, we have a plan!"

Emony clenched his teeth, struggling even harder to resist the change, trying desperately to move forward with Tiphaine resisting him. A carriage was waiting for them at the gate, the horses blinded so they wouldn't fear her. But Emony had the strength of a human, he could barely move her at all.

"You should have told me!" he shouted.

"That's my line! Emony, stop trying to leave me in the dark all the time! It's my choice! Nobody else has to die!"

"You damned, stupid snake! This is precisely why I leave you in the dark! I'm making the decisions this time! You're going to live!"

"Just you try it! I'll plug my ears! I won't hear a thing!"

"Now isn't the time, Tiphaine! Please, just go! Listen to me! We can still get out of here!"

"No! Too many people have already been hurt! Emony, even if we fail, as soon as I'm gone, all of this will end! And thousands more people will come back, you know how many people I've turned to stone over the years!"

"I don't care! They can stay stones! You're coming with me!"

Suddenly, an earthquake shook the city, the trembling ground knocking him off his feet into the snow. Instantly far more wet, he abruptly lost his fight with the transformation and found himself a mermaid again.

"Damn it, damn it!" Emony shrieked, her suddenly high-pitched voice breaking hundreds of windows in the surrounding houses. "Tiphaine, please!"

Only a mile behind them, scores of corpses were already falling from the top of the city walls onto the streets and charging toward them in a deranged and broken horde.

"Tiphaine, go! Leave me and go!" she begged. Finally, she tried to lace her voice with magic again, to force her to comply. She had no other options. She had to make it to the carriage, to the witch.

But Emony couldn't speak a word. She couldn't move her tongue or her mouth. Tiphaine was shaking her head at her, her mask lying on the ground beside her.

Ever so slowly, wasting so much precious time, Tiphaine lowered herself toward Emony, her soft green eyes exposed to his stone ones.

"I'm taking my choice back, Emony," she said quietly. "I wanted to kiss you one more time for real before I left, but… I just want you to know, I really cherished every moment I've ever spent with you."

Please run, Emony thought, unable to move a muscle. The mass of corpses was so close. They were almost upon them. The dark sky was swirling so close to the ground. The king was coming.

As she could only watch, horrified, Tiphaine didn't try at all to get away. She just wrapped herself around Emony one more time, embracing her tightly in the snowstorm and laying a long kiss on her stone lips.

And then, the king was there.

In the distance, the castle walls were blown apart in an instant, massive stones flying through the sky in all directions and showering the snow-covered city with resounding crashes as they demolished roads and houses. The dead finally made it, they crawled up towards them and stopped a little distance away, surrounding them. There were enough of them to fill the entirety of Terrena. And then slowly, ever so slowly, holding his queen in his arms, the king of the lake approached.

The world became quiet as they came closer. The snow stopped, the clouds making their way upwards to reveal a clear blue sky. The dead became as still and silent as the grave. The only sound Emony could hear was Tiphaine's heart beating against her stone chest.

The king strode toward them, stopping just in front of his legions of corpses.

Tiphaine's eyes moved for just a moment from his own to glance at the king before, giving up, she laid them upon Emony again.

"You don't turn to stone?" Tiphaine asked.

"No curse could overpower my love," the king said.

"I see… Then I guess this is it, Emony," Tiphaine said, a sad smile across her face. "This is where we part. It's a shame you won't be the one to do it, but… I guess that really would be asking too much. I'm glad you're here with me, at least. How many people get to die beside their friends?"

Emony wanted to shake her head. To scream. To do anything at all, but the stone trapping her was far too strong.

"Tiphaine," the king breathed, laying his queen on a throne built of corpses. "Yours is a name I will remember."

"I want you to help him, before you do it," she interrupted him with a shaky voice. "You promised you would help him. Keep your word. Do it."

The king slowly nodded, understanding on his face, and lifted a hand towards Emony. Suddenly, Emony could feel an overwhelming dark magic pulsating all throughout her petrified body and changing her to the very core. Her veins and heart shrunk and expanded over and over again. If she weren't a statue, she would have been screaming in agony.

"It is done," the king said. "The spell has been lifted. Once she… he is freed from the stone and removed from all water, he will be a werewolf again."

"Thank you," Tiphaine said, glancing sadly at Emony again. Emony desperately tried to scream at her to run, but still, no sound rang out of her mouth.

"Have you said your goodbyes?" the king asked Tiphaine.

"I tried. I couldn't think of anything good enough."

"I understand. I was the same way myself. Then… Are you ready?"

She looked one more time towards Emony while the king unsheathed his sword. The look on Tiphaine's face… It was just like that night on the cliff, when they first met. When she was trying to convince herself to jump.

Emony had to get out of the stone. *Now.* There was no more time. She struggled wildly against the magic.

That was when the second earthquake shook the ground.

"Friends of yours?" the king asked, gazing towards the collapsed city wall. A string of black magic seemed to pulse across Tiphaine's skin for the briefest of moments.

"Do not fear. They will not be harmed. They will be given whatever in this world that they desire. Thank you for returning my queen to me… Tiphaine."

Tiphaine looked over into Emony's eyes and gave her one final smile, which she kept on her beautiful lips even as they were stained with blood. Then, paralyzed in agony behind the stone, Emony saw the sword leave her chest, and the king gently lay her to the ground.

Instantly going mad, Emony moved her eyes as soon as she could, to look more directly at Tiphaine. Then even her head. But it was difficult. So difficult.

She heard terrible coughing somewhere. The king's blade clattered to the ground as he ran towards his queen.

"Aulduyen," said a raspy woman's voice. "Aulduyen, you've awakened me."

Emony struggled, trying to move her arms, but found herself unable to do so. She didn't understand. Ravenwood always cured her instantly. Unless this was different, something was wrong. She could only move her head, maybe the smallest bit of her neck. But none of that really mattered.

Tiphaine…

"Aulduyen, what have you done?" he heard the queen ask as he gazed at Tiphaine's dead body. "All these dead…?"

"My queen!" the king exclaimed. "You're back! You're finally back. I've struggled for ten years…"

Emony slammed her head to the side, trying to move herself. She had to get to Tiphaine. She was right there, lying on the ground with her chest open, her blood staining the snow.

She gasped at the horrible sight, tears streaking down her eyes without restraint, sobs freely escaping her lips.

Only near a minute later, when she was already sick with grief, looking for ways to perish, herself, did a realization break through her sorrow.

I still sound like a girl.

She was still a mermaid. It was impossible, the curse should have been broken, but it was undeniable. She could feel the king's magic wrapped around her; he'd said it was done. But no… He said it would be once he was freed from the stone and dry. And she wasn't yet, not dry nor truly free of Tiphaine's curse. *But why not? Unless…*

She barely dared to look up towards Tiphaine again. If she was wrong, her false hope would strangle her. But she did. And through her tears, she saw it. That little spark of black magic dancing on her open and bleeding chest. It rose and fell as Tiphaine took a silent breath.

"My queen! I have climbed out of the bottomless abyss to return to you, that you may reign at my side once more! My love… We can be together again!"

Emony, fighting through the agony it took to do so, turned back towards the king and queen. She couldn't afford to reveal to them in any way what was happening.

"Aulduyen, no… Our lives ended *ten years ago*. I was at peace in the stone. Why could you not find the same in your death? Why continue our tragic tale?"

"For you, my queen! Only for you!"

Imarah, tightly embraced by the king, silently turned her horrified gaze towards Emony before slowly returning it to her husband.

"But why does your body not return to flesh?" the king suddenly asked, taking a step back. "Your perfect body… I can see the magic is still snaring you, it has merely loosened its grip. Do you require time to break free? What is going on?"

"Aulduyen, look at me. No, no! Don't turn towards her! Look at me! Look only at me! Please, come back. Just embrace me one more time. Aulduyen… I'm sorry. I'm so, so sorry that I did this to you. I didn't want any of this. I don't want it now. All of this death, just to continue our sad story…"

"My queen, please, I do not understand—"

As the two held each other one more time, she spoke again, this time with her gaze pointed at

Emony. "Death will untie any curse. Kill the caster, break the spell."

"Yes," the king murmured into her neck. "You're right, of course. I'm sorry. But the death I had to seek… It was not easily found. But now that you're here, it can all be over. Our lives will not be tragedies anymore! We can live in harmony!"

"Aulduyen, please. Every story is the same, if only in a single way. They all end. Aulduyen, please come with me. Reunite with me there, if you really love me. Join me at the end." The queen looked towards Emony once more, a single tear running down her cheek. She nodded.

"Die," Emony gasped, as the queen closed her eyes.

Darkness erupted all around the king, shielding his ears from the words.

Only a moment later, however, he began breathing hard. Suddenly, he began screaming.

"No! No! No! Imarah! Imarah, don't leave me again!"

Suddenly, only a moment later, he grabbed his head with his hands, struggling to stand upright. "Imarah! I cannot hear your song anymore! Imarah! Where did you go?! Please, I need you!"

Emony heard quick footsteps approaching from out of her field of vision. Suddenly, she was lifted off the ground. The human knight commander, Yperian, was standing over her, shoving something into her mouth. Her rigid stone limbs instantly turned to flesh and she was able to move around freely again.

"My love! My love! Why did you leave me?! Why do you continue to run from me?!"

"The lady Lenah sends her regards," Yperian hissed, standing over Emony. "She and

Aylard are keeping the snake alive, but it won't last. You need to leave!"

"My love! Why?!"

"I can't move, I need to get dry! Help get me off this snow!"

"We don't have time! Just get dry and get her out of here!"

"No. Do not," the king suddenly said darkly, turning towards them. The world reverberated with the sound of his voice.

Emony hadn't noticed that the king had stopped wailing, but then, in an instant, the silence was deafening.

"My queen is gone," he said, tears streaming down his face.

He was crying freely onto her chest, cradling her in his arms as he stood facing them, his sorrow so clear it brought down a heavy torrent of rain. Sorrowfully, he gently laid the queen down on the wet ground and walked past her.

"Your friend's strength is fading. She will be lost soon," he said, walking over to Tiphaine.

Emony turned quickly towards her. The pool of blood around her had soaked through the snow, and it was still growing. Hers must have been all gone by then, there was so much of it. It was someone else's that was spilling out of her heart now. Black magic or no, she needed help.

Emony looked around desperately for a bandage, before ripping off her tunic and pushing herself on the ground towards her, her heavy tail slowing her down.

"My love is gone… but I will see her again," the king said. "I will chase her all the way to the realm of the divines. As she wished, we will reunite in death," He crouched by Tiphaine while Emony was still desperately trying to pull herself towards her.

"And yours… Yours will join you in life."

A torrent of black magic suddenly flattened Emony to the ground, crashing from the king's heart into Tiphaine's. Darkness instantly covered everything in sight, streaked with a crimson red, cascading into Tiphaine and lifting her off the ground. An earthquake rumbled all around, by far the strongest one yet. The road they were on suddenly split itself apart around them and began falling into a black, bottomless abyss.

Epilogue

Emony walked along the ruined stone roads of the city, the knight commander beside him and Tiphaine, leaning her exhausted head on his shoulder. Thousands upon thousands of corpses lay on the ground at their sides, unmoving and untouched by the raging magic behind them.

They slowly made their way to where the king had collapsed the city wall with his fist and climbed slowly through the rubble, exiting the city. There, a crowd of humans awaited, and with them, Lenah and Aylard.

While the knight commander, Yperian, took his leave to find his men, the two came running towards them.

"Divines, I'm so happy to see you two again!" Lenah shouted. "I was so worried I couldn't hold the spell, Aylard began dying so quickly all of a sudden! But then it all stopped and he recovered on his own, before I had even done anything – I've never seen anything like it! Did you really do it? Did you beat the king? Oh, divines… But Tiphaine, are you really okay? Are you really here right now, I'm not just seeing things?"

"I'm here. I'm alive," Tiphaine said quietly, throwing a hand off of Emony's shoulder to reach for her. He quickly changed his stance to stabilize her.

"I was pretty worried there myself, for a moment," Aylard said. "Lenah explained nothing, and then the next moment, I felt like I'd been stabbed through the heart. I thought for certain I was going to die."

"You were, Aylard," Emony said. For the first time in a long time, he felt truly happy that he had met a human. "I couldn't thank you enough… You saved Tiphaine's life. I owe you… the world."

"Hey, don't sweat it, doggy. Just introduce me to Emma again, will you, and I'll consider it worth it."

Tiphaine chuckled weakly on his shoulder. His lips stretched into a smile.

"The lord commander didn't tell you?" he asked.

"Tell me what?"

Within seconds, in the middle of so much rubble and death, he and the two girls burst out laughing. The happy sound spread across the snowy plains.

"Hey, Tiphaine, did you forget your veil back there?" Lenah asked, freeing her blue hair from the grip of Tiphaine's vipers.

Still with her face buried in his shoulder, Tiphaine shook her head. "I still have it. I just want to feel the air on my face right now. Because I'm alive, and… because I can. That, and… Emony?"

"You want to show them?" he asked.

Behind him, she nodded.

"There are a lot of innocent people in front of us, Tiphaine. Try not to get them all, will you?"

She hit his shoulder lightly and lifted her head from it. "I have something to show you. Verena was right all along. The king's black magic… it was stronger than the Eyes."

While Lenah's hands shot up to her mouth, Tiphaine opened her eyes, and not a single person looking at them turned to stone.

They were all at a loss for words. Luckily, those weren't necessary. They simply stepped into a large embrace.

Days later, they were enjoying a casual stroll across Coldbarrow, the village where it had all begun. The villagers were moving back into their homes, the knight commander and his soldiers helping to repair the damage caused by the storms and all the fighting. People looked upon them nervously, still somewhat afraid to talk to them, but most of their fear had subsided with the news that they had helped defeat the evil king and the men of the lake.

They had freed Verena from her prison in the sunken palace and laid the king and queen to rest there, in the throne room, despite the protests of the other king, Raynardt. The bottomless abyss that lay in the lake was still there, tainting the waters with black magic, but Lenah was doing her best to find a way to deal with it.

Life was ever so slowly returning to normal.

And the best part? A full moon was coming.

"Are you looking forward to howling at the moon again?" asked Tiphaine, smiling brightly at him, holding his hand as they made their way across the village. "I've almost forgotten what you used to look like. And it's been a while since I've gotten to pet you."

"Tonight, you can pet me all you want. I just want to know that you're beside me, alive."

"Then I'll never leave."

"Aw, is this how it's going to be, you too? Is this what happens when you upgrade your relationship to one where you can actually bear to look at one another?"

"Zip it, Lenah."

"Oh, you don't want to be so rude to me, doggy. I know all your secrets. I even know what you're thinking right now."

"I think she does, too," he replied, glancing at Tiphaine's eyes and losing himself in them momentarily. He really would have to make up for lost time. He planned to stare at them at every opportunity.

"Urgh. Young love. Gross, am I right, Aylard? Hey, now that you've seen them both, who do you think is prettier, Tiphaine or Emma?"

"Are we really going to talk about her again?" Emony asked, provoking a small chuckle from Tiphaine. "I am so glad she's gone."

"But Emony! You promised Aylard you would help them meet up again!" Tiphaine said.

"Yes, actually, I've been meaning to ask – where does she live? Is she back in that river, by Terrena?" inquired Aylard. "Or is she still in that bathhouse? How did she manage to get out of there, anyway?"

"She's closer than you think," Lenah said.

"No, no she's not. She's impossibly far away. Sorry, Aylard, she's gone forever."

"What?!"

"I bet Lenah could make that potion again," whispered Tiphaine, leaning closer to him as they walked. She seemed to have a very mischievous expression on her face. "We could make her come back."

His eyes narrowed at her. He knew that expression. "What are you plotting?" he asked.

"Just this," Lenah laughed.

"What—"

He was interrupted by a torrent of water smashing into his face out of nowhere and knocking him to the ground. Startled, as he heard Lenah and Tiphaine laughing by his side, he started to feel that familiar, terrible vibrating sensation.

"No," he said, shaking his head. "No, no, no, this should be over! This can't be happening!"

"I'm afraid it is. Don't you have somewhere to go, Emony? Come on, go and get your friend," said Lenah.

"What's going on? Why did you do that?" asked Aylard, confused.

"Because they're jerks!" Emony shouted, running off past them in the direction of the lake, before the change could force itself on him.

"Huh? Where is he going? That was mean, Lenah, but… Is he really that afraid of water…? Really? After everything else?"

"Didn't Tiphaine tell you? His mom dropped him into a puddle when he was little. That's how he became an orphan."

"That nonsensical story again? Whatever. I have some quick errands to run. I'll buy a towel. I'll be right back."

"See you."

Emony spied on their parting, watching with only her head breaking the lake's surface as Tiphaine and Lenah made their way towards the shore.

With a few kicks of the golden tail she hated so much and her mind thoroughly poisoned, she swam over towards them, watching them chuckle together as if they had already known that this would happen.

"I demand answers," she growled at them, lacing magic into her once again adorable voice. Those damned blue sparks flew off of the witch and plucked the magic out of the words. "Why am I still half mermaid?!"

"That's a funny story," Lenah laughed, crouching down on the wet pebbles in front of her.

Tiphaine dipped the end of her tail into the water and laid down next to her.

"I thought something strange was going on with your magic, so I hung out with Tiphaine in her dreams last night. We watched a couple of memories to figure out what, exactly. What we found was pretty funny."

"Explain. Now."

"Well," said Tiphaine, chuckling, "you already know that, before the king tried to kill me, he cast a countercurse on you to undo the effects of the mermaid spell. But apparently, it couldn't take full effect until the stronger curse – my petrification, was gone from your body, and water stopped feeding the other. That's why he said you would be cured once you were freed from the stone and removed from all water."

"Yes, I remember him saying that. What of it?!"

"Well… He died before you got dry, so..."

Emony's face fell. He was rapidly becoming very irritated. "You're joking."

"His countercurse died with him, Emony," Lenah said.

"Please tell me you're lying."

Tiphaine shook her head, having a hard time trying to hide her smile.

"You're lying! Do not tell me that I'm stuck like this!"

"Well, since you're back, Emma, we might as well bring Aylard over here, right?"

"What? No! Don't! Stop waving, Lenah! Tiphaine! Why would you do that?!"

"Because he wants to see you, and you owe it to him to see him, and… Oh, look! He's already here! Incoming!"

"Tiphaine!" Emony hissed. "Damn it! Lenah! Hide me! Urgh, why is nobody on my side?!"

Blue sparks crackled through the air again. Frowning, Emony wondered if she should dive into the water to escape. They probably couldn't stop her from getting away if she really tried. But then she noticed something else. It was Tiphaine, her tail was wrapped tightly all around her, even under the water. Smiling, she tightened her grip even further.

Aylard ran over to the three of them, a surprised expression on his face.

"I thought you'd gone after Emony, that you were talking to him," he said.

"Well, we found Emma instead," Tiphaine replied. "Come on, be nice to him, Emma, he saved my life."

"Urgh, well I saved his before that, so maybe we're even. Actually, I'm ahead. Considering what you're doing to me right now, Tiphaine, your life is rapidly losing value to me."

"You know, you talk a lot like Emony," said Aylard, coming closer to the shore. "It's good to see you again, though. You're a lot prettier than he is."

Tiphaine tightened her body's grip around Emony's waist and tail again. "I can explain that. So, the thing is, when Emony fell into that puddle when he was little, Emma was actually already living in it. That's how the two of them met. They've known each other forever."

"You're going to continue that fairytale?" asked Emony.

"Yup. Unless you'd rather we tell him the truth?" she asked.

"No, that's alright. Keep going."

"Why do you guys insist on lying to me at every turn?" Aylard asked. "I think I've proven myself trustworthy by now – or is it just because I'm the only human here? Damned monsters. By the way, how did you get here, Emma? This lake isn't connected to any rivers."

"Stop asking questions. It's just magic. Now, if you'll excuse me, I'm going to kidnap the idiot that thinks she's keeping me here."

"What?" asked Tiphaine.

"Have fun, you two!" said Lenah.

With a few pushes of her golden tail, Emony quickly pushed herself off the shore, dragging along Tiphaine, who was still wrapped up around her.

After surging through the beautiful, life-filled waters for a while, they stopped right under the surface in the middle of the lake.

"You're better at swimming than you used to be," Tiphaine remarked, tightening her tail around hers and staring at her with her beautiful green eyes. "Far better than the average doggy. So, why did you bring me here? Is this what a kidnapping looks like? What are you going to do to me?"

"How would you like to make some memories for Lenah to enjoy later?"

"Haha! What a great opportunity! I'd love to – but we can do that after we're done. No, let's try to keep this one between us."

It was a beautiful day.